THE STRENGTH OF JASIREY

also by Bonnie Arnot

The Devoted of Jasirey

The Husbands of Jasirey

the Strength of Jasirey

Bonnie Arnot

Book Three
the Destiny of Jasirey
series

Haley's

Athol, Massachusetts

Haley's
488 South Main Street
Athol, MA 01331
marcia2gagliardi@gmail.com • 978.249.9400

Copy edited with editorial consultation by Phillis Scott.

Cover by Elizabeth Lindgren.

International Standard Book Number: 978-1-956055-45-0
Library of Congress Number: pending

for my mom,
who often visits my mind with good memories

Knowing is not enough. We must apply.
Wishing is not enough. We must do.
—Johann Wolfgang Von Goethe

To be what we are and to become what we are capable of becoming is the only end of life.
—Robert Louis Stevenson

Contents

Preparing for Destiny

Mtombe jolted out of a sound sleep to inconsolable wails impossible to place as male or female. He crept to the bedroom door and inched it open. Jiggling a screaming bundle of squirming arms and legs, Fael paced the hall.

"Sorry to wake you," Fael said. He shushed the bundle in low tones edged with pleading. "Jasirey wished to nurse our little ones this morning so refused medication last night. Her pain slows down the process, and Jaimie is impatient. Lee and Ian help with Sunny and Safia."

Fael, Ian, and Lee were Jasirey's husbands along with Liu, so Mtombe assumed the other names belonged to three of Jasirey's five-month-old quadruplets.

Living with Jasirey in a compound built in the Pioneer Valley of western Massachusetts, all the men belonged to the Devoted, a multicultural underground society that had recently found and served Shannon, who passed a grueling test to become Jasirey—a woman destined to bring stability to their precarious world.

Mtombe had trained among the Devoted Protectors, men and women who comprised Jasirey's security. The men also served as candidates from whom she might choose her husbands and/or fathers of the multiracial children she would bear to continue her work. Mtombe started to close his bedroom door but stopped as a whimper sounded from Fael's shirt pocket.

Fael huffed out a sigh. "Colin is waking up. Lend a hand." He pushed the annoyed infant he carried into Mtombe's stiff arms, cooed into the monitor he took out of his pocket, and sprinted down the hall toward the nursery.

As surprised as Mtombe, the child blinked and debated whether to cry or to explore. Curiosity won. Afraid a wrong move might set off fresh wails, Mtombe attempted a smile and watched the baby's eyes in fascination. They morphed from hazel to green according to the child's mood.

Ian stepped out of the bedroom with Sunny to call in Fael and, after a stressful morning, got a welcome laugh from the look of panic mixed with intrigue on Mtombe's face. Ian beckoned him into the bedroom.

Mtombe cautiously glided down the hall so as not to drop nor bruise the bouncing youngster. Ian deftly hoisted Jaimie from Mtombe while handing him a black-haired baby. Mtombe wondered if Jasirey's husbands conspired to make him look inept.

Jasirey watched Mtombe enter the bedroom, laughed hoarsely, and stopped. "Ow. Mean, Ian," she said in staccato bursts, all her traumatized throat allowed. "Sorry, Mtombe."

Jaimie launched toward her mother with a squeal of delight, but Ian had a firm grip on the rambunctious child.

Mtombe stood stock still. Sunlight coursed onto the huge bed and exposed every welt, bruise, and swelling not covered by her sundress that the human trafficker Marcus had inflicted on Jasirey. It was her first full day home from the hospital after Mtombe and several other Protectors rescued her.

Marcus had slashed at Jasirey with a riding whip and used it as a noose to cut off her airflow. At one point, he lost his self-control and used his fists.

Ian held the baby to Jasirey's breast. Jaimie's foot got away from him and kicked her.

She hissed in a sharp breath, and Ian's voice gritted out, "Sorry, baby."

"I am guessing most of the morning has gone this way," Mtombe said. He knew Jasirey balked at weaning the babies despite needing to if she were to heal properly. A tiny hand patted his troubled face. He glanced down at the baby he held and into eyes as black as his own but merrier. The baby smiled beatifically. He resembled Liu. While unsure about Jaimie, Mtombe suspected the one he held was a boy.

"His name's Sun Li," Jasirey said. "We call him Sunny."

An apt name for the little fellow, Mtombe thought. Sunny smiled, a smile much like his mother's. Mtombe clutched the child a bit closer. "And that one?" His chin pointed at Jaimie. "Boy or girl?"

"Girl. Jaimie Lee," Ian said, "and all stubborn will like her mama."

While nuzzling her daughter's head, Jasirey stuck her tongue out at him.

Fael carried in Colin. After Jasirey painfully completed her part of the feeding, Ian carried Jaime to the bedroom's sitting area for a supplemental bottle the baby held by herself. Mtombe sat and folded Sunny into a sitting position on his lap.

Three magnificent sculptures adorned the fireplace mantel: a pond and surrounding fauna found on the island of the Devoted and carved in wood by Lee; the spirit animals in metal of Jasirey's four husbands—Ian's eagle, Lee's grizzly bear, Liu's ferret, and Fael's viper—placed about a fallen log; and also in metal and sculpted by Fael, the flower garden with its miniature waterfall, stone-rimmed fishpond, and swing from the compound of the unorthodox family. Jasirey had legally married Ian in America but had married Ian, Lee, Liu, and Fael on the island of the Devoted.

Ian gestured to Sunny as he began squirming in Mtombe's embrace. "Hold him under the arms. They like to stand and bounce."

Mtombe did as bid. Crowing or laughing nonstop, Sunny bounced. Mtombe's eyes narrowed in sudden suspicion. "This will not make him vomit, will it?"

His huge hands nearly covering the baby, Lee turned from changing a diaper. "Sunny ate first, so has had time to digest a bit. He's good."

Good or not, the little fellow certainly enjoyed himself. Lee sat beside Mtombe who peered at Safia, soon dancing on Lee's lap. The beautiful child possessed the same mesmerizing gold eyes as Fael.

The tiny girl noticed Mtombe watching and stopped a moment to stare at the newcomer. She gave him the same smile as her brother, grabbed hold of Lee's dreadlocks, and played with one of the colorful baubles he habitually attached for the children.

"What is that little one's name?"

"Safia Souzan."

"A lovely name. It suits her."

Liu, a healer, entered. He held a pain-medicated drink for Jasirey, and Fael joined the men to give Colin his bottle. Jaimie burped lustily and looked amazed by the loud sound. Colin pushed the bottle away to study Mtombe.

Mtombe cocked his head. "Colleen, was it?"

Lee snorted. "Considering he's a dead ringer for Ian, it's better Colin's a boy, Colin Everett."

Mtombe quite agreed. He watched the dynamics of the men caring for the youngsters and realized their equal affection for all the children.

"You shall drink it." Liu's tone drew everyone's attention. "For you to heal properly, the weaning must progress more rapidly. Skip the next feeding and express the afternoon milk. The pain medication shall be out of your system by bedtime."

Jasirey glared but drained the glass.

Liu's tone gentled. "Come, precious one. Use the bathroom before sleep overtakes you."

Lee held out a massive arm for Sunny. "Why don't you help Liu and say goodbye. Jasirey will go under for several hours."

Mtombe had joined the family on Ian's plane after Jasirey's release from the hospital in Boston. Marcus had captured her not only, as her husbands believed, in revenge for their missions as a Devoted team to aid people facing disasters that sometimes led to the team's interference in Marcus's human trafficking operation but, as Mtombe believed, also because her strength of mind challenged the trafficker. Thanks to Mtombe's intervention, she had suffered no permanent damage. Having assured himself of her welfare, he planned on leaving that morning.

"Swing her legs over the edge," Liu said and pivoted Jasirey's upper body.

Grasping her knees, Mtombe guided her legs to the floor. Pain marred her lovely face. "Would not a bedpan be easier?" he asked.

Jasirey glowered. "Not an invalid."

"Try getting up on your own."

"Leave anytime."

"Stop being stubborn. You will heal faster."

"He coach you?" She pointed an accusatory finger at Liu.

"Your condition is obvious, except perhaps to you." Her smile warmed his heart.

"Lucky can't smack you."

"That smile hits quite hard enough," he whispered in her ear and kissed her cheek. "Be well. I like your babies." Her smile again rewarded him. The warmth spread lower.

Shadows clouded eyes the color of blue spruce trees. She kissed him lightly on the mouth. "Thank you, Mtombe, for everything."

He kissed her other cheek and nodded at the men.

Jasirey watched him leave.

After Jasirey had made it through the Imperiatu, the test to find Jasirey, she then had a vision, a prophecy, about her future children, husbands, and another important relationship, her wild boar. Knowing Mtombe's destiny lay outside the Devoted, she had excused him from his vows as a Protector during the husband ceremony in the Imperiatu. He had left the island, looked for a job, and unaware the boat was Marcus's merchantman, had signed on with the first mate as a crewman.

When he put his life on the line to stop Marcus from killing her, Jasirey knew he fulfilled the prophecy. She said nothing to anyone, however, because she also knew Mtombe had not yet found his destined path.

⁂

Kharia was waiting for Jasirey's return from the hospital before taking her husband's ashes home to the island of the Devoted. Knowing her lady's injuries prevented a prolonged talk, she hugged her and said, "Even working on the compound did not fulfill Robin as fully as did his direct service to you. Blame yourself for his death and you dishonor his memory."

Jasirey, named Shannon at birth, had two teenage boys from her first marriage to one man. That marriage ended in divorce before she learned of the Devoted.

Kharia and Robin also had two sons the same ages as Jasirey's. They came to America to help Jasirey's new family. Robin, a builder, worked on the compound walls and outer buildings. Kharia prepared meals for the people who served the family—security, groundskeepers, and housekeepers. They lived in the dormitory, basically an apartment building. Outside the compound walls, Kharia's family shared a duplex with a schoolteacher from the island of the Devoted who homeschooled Jasirey's and Kharia's sons.

The need for building had slowed after the babies' birth. Robin also had experience as a mission driver and drove the family on a visit to Jasirey's parents. He had been murdered by mercenaries sent by Marcus to abduct Jasirey.

Warmth literally and unexpectedly eased Kharia's sorrow, and knowing the source of the warmth, she pulled back. "No, lady. Grief must be endured before one can move forward. I know of your gifts, your ability to lessen people's burdens. Please respect our period of mourning."

"Kharia, sorry. Didn't intend to interfere."

"Then you may wish to consult the Imperiat on training to control your gifts."

Though Jasirey realized her friend hadn't meant her comment as a condemnation, it still stung her conscience.

Kharia managed a watery smile. "The Imperiat is sending a young couple to prepare meals for the people in my absence. They shall arrive soon." She kissed Jasirey's cheeks. "Kirani, Bazir, and I shall return. I love you."

Jasirey sat alone in her craft room for some time and finally let fall the tears for Robin she had yet to shed. A bit in awe of her, he had often flushed and stammered in her presence. To others, he spoke eloquently of Jasirey's mission and the fine qualities he attributed to her, qualities Jasirey was not sure she possessed. Her sobs strengthened as she realized she no longer had the opportunity to watch his awe diminish and his comfort around her grow.

That afternoon, the stepfathers—Jasirey's four husbands—spoke to Jasirey's older sons, Michael and Christopher, about Robin in their mother's stead. They told the teens it was because of her throat injuries, but truthfully, they hoped that by assuming the task they would lessen her burden of grief.

They went to the training building in case the need rose to whack something, say a punching bag.

"It's not Mom's fault." Michael's flaring eyes dared anyone to disagree.

"It is not," Fael said, his golden eyes radiating calm assurance. "After sufficient time has eased the pain, your mother shall accept that."

"Do you think Kirani and Bazir blame her?"

"Kirani doesn't," Christopher said. "His father told him their family was blessed to serve Mom. He wants to go to college for computer coding to help the babies when they're older."

"Those five new guys," Michael said, "Nikolai and that bunch, look strong. We're safe here, right?"

The Imperiat, one of three ruling bodies of the Devoted, had jurisdiction over Jasirey's protection and missions pertaining directly to her and hence, over the Protectors. When Marcus had captured Jasirey, the Imperiat had sent Nikolai and his team—Sajan, Andwar, Chen, and Favian—to join Kimika, head of the family's security.

Lee hugged Michael. "Protectors learn in training that only the arrogant assume they are immune from danger. The wise do not. I can tell you we've done everything possible to protect the compound."

❧ ❧ ❧

After several days, Jasirey's voice normalized sufficiently to telephone her mother, an inexplicable desire to her husbands.

"Whatever her mental problems," Jasirey said, "my mom's the first one I want to call whenever something especially good or bad happens." Jasirey's imp surfaced. "She loves me. She just sometimes forgets that in the heat of battle."

"Battle?" Lee said as though she'd uttered a four-letter word.

"You've heard her. She has decided opinions."

Lee scowled. *That was one way of putting it.*

Anne picked up Jasirey's call and, always glad to hear from her eldest, asked, "How are my handsome grandsons?" The family had left abruptly after a party at her brother James's. Anne never got a satisfactory answer as to why.

"Studying hard." Jasirey bit back an update on the babies. Her parents would never accept or at least keep quiet about her marriage to four men and multiracial grandchildren.

"Are you okay?" Anne had bouts of on-point sensitivity.

"Friend of mine," Jasirey said. "Her husband died."

"You mean Lizzie? That was a while ago."

"No, another friend. She has sons Christopher and Michael's ages."

"Oh, poor little boys. I'm sorry to hear that. Cancer?"

"An accident."

"Why are people always in such a hurry? I swear drivers get worse and worse."

It relieved Jasirey that her mother concocted a story for herself.

Anne had a bone to pick. Her younger sister told her things her daughter hadn't bothered to tell her own mother. "Marion said the parents of her daughter-in-law recognized your bracelet, and you said it was a historical heirloom. You never mentioned that to me."

Jasirey heard the ping of her mother's bullshit radar and deflected. "I haven't kept up with my cousin. I'd never met his wife or their kids."

"Children are awfully dark. The wife's from India. It's not like there aren't plenty of our girls looking for husbands. Cute kids, but people should stick to their own kind."

Jasirey restrained a sigh, changed the subject to Anne's health, and listened patiently to a point-by-point account of the eccentricities of Anne's colon.

❧ ❧ ❧

From Boston, Jasirey's obstetrician Jesse and his wife, Lill, visited the compound. The families had become close friends.

With the warm, engaging smile that had first drawn them to her, Jasirey greeted the couple. She led Lill into the living room while Jesse went in search of her husbands.

Lill studied Jasirey's fading injuries. "What in the world happened to you?"

Jasirey placed an arm around Lill's trim waist. "A man who had a vendetta against my husbands tried to use me to take revenge."

"Like Eric?"

"The same man Eric intended to give me to." She studied Lill's frown. "You still have nightmares." Eric, one of Marcus's henchmen, had dragged the women away from a family outing and taken Jasirey while leaving Lill unconscious in a filthy alley.

"I wouldn't call them . . . I think maybe your insights are more than just intuition."

"So they tell me. Now that I'm weaning the babies, they'll probably expect me to start training to develop the gifts they believe I have."

Lill bristled and glared at her husband as he rejoined them in the living room.

Jesse immediately went on the defensive. "What?"

"Sorry. I'm not mad at you. But training—is that what you meant about them pushing her too hard?"

Jesse's second "What?" carried a totally different tone.

Jasirey smothered a laugh and turned an accusing eye on him. "Caughtcha—discussing patients—shame." She took pity as his cheeks bloomed bright red. "We're talking about the abilities the Devoted see in me and the training they're planning."

Anger blanched Jesse's face. "God, couldn't they at least wait for you to heal?"

Jasirey hugged him. She thought of him more as a friend than her doctor. "My welfare is always their first priority."

Jesse sniffed. "I hope so." He turned to Lill. "You, shoo. I have things to discuss with my patient not meant for indiscreet ears."

"She's my friend, too, but I'll go—for now." She grinned at Jasirey. "In bed, he's putty in my hands. He has no idea the strength of character it takes to refrain from taking advantage."

Jesse swatted at his retreating wife's posterior and then rooted in his bag for a list he handed to Jasirey. "I don't handle pediatrics beyond the first few months. Any of these local doctors can deal with immunizations and things Liu isn't comfortable caring for alone. Pick one, and I'll send over the babies' medical records to date."

"Send us the records," Jasirey said. "We may change them for security purposes."

Expectations and enemies—Jesse didn't know which to fear more but patted her shoulder and went to round up his wife to play nurse and examine the babies for the last time before referring Jasirey to a pediatrician for them.

He played with the children as part of the exam. Each had distinct personality traits. A pretty child, Jaimie loved to latch on to adult fingers, pull herself up on sturdy legs, and chortle proudly. Colin enjoyed exploring people's faces and had a special affinity for nostrils. Though greatly resembling Ian, he had inherited one or two traits from his mother, especially the smile that made him unique and arresting.

Jesse was fascinated by Safia's gold eyes and sweetness. He believed she understood people's moods and swore she sometimes strove to ease the less positive ones. Safia possessed her mother's inner light. Not that he would admit to any bias, but she had perhaps wormed a little deeper into his heart.

Lill played peekaboo with Sun Li, who delighted in interacting and had inherited his mother's knack for dispensing joy and peacefulness. Like Liu's, his eyes usually sparkled in merriment. Lill adored him, an endearing bundle of fun, not that she ever claimed any preference.

❦ ❦ ❦

A week after Jasirey had weaned the babies, a car stopped before the arched, gated entrance of the compound. Called master—as were both men and women—for prowess in a particular skill or trait such as wisdom, Master Kai, head of the Imperiat, lowered his backseat window to study the sculpted spirit animals of Jasirey's husbands on the archway above the gate. *How like their lady to celebrate others before herself,* he thought.

The gate swung open, and the driver continued down the long tree-lined drive to the stately three-story stone house.

Jasirey surprised everyone when she declared herself ready to begin the training she hoped would illuminate her gifts and hone her ability to control them.

Master Kai joined the family in their living room. Jasirey jumped up and gave him an enthusiastic hug. Energy unlike any he had ever experienced poured through his veins.

He beamed at her. "You have been practicing."

Jasirey laughed and gestured to one of two burgundy-plaid sofas. She sat beside him and talked about the welfare of people they both knew on the island and at her home.

"And now, dear one, tell me how you fare," Master Kai said.

Knowing she might be treading on tradition, Jasirey hesitated a moment, then squaring her shoulders, said, "When visiting my parents and at a party given by my uncle before everything with Marcus, I met a cousin's wife and her parents visiting from India. They recognized my bracelet."

"Fael took them aside," Lee said, "and explained our family's need for discretion. They knew of the Devoted through the wife's brother, a farmer on the island."

"They understood our concerns," Fael said, "and agreed not to say anything about us."

"Sweet people," Jasirey said. "But if one person recognizes me, it's a safe bet there are others who will as well. I'm concerned about wearing the bracelet in public."

Her husbands understood she proposed the removal of the bracelet, a wide gold band etched with interweaving lines and welded together on her wrist when she underwent the Imperiatu. Five gold chains attached along the band ended at a ring Jasirey wore on her middle finger. Delicately wrought, the names of her children formed a web among the gold chains. The ring had an oval opal surrounded by small diamonds, amethysts, emeralds, and sapphires that enhanced the colors of the opal.

The husbands saw the bracelet as a symbol of Jasirey identifying her as an integral member of the Devoted community, and hence, the problem. The Devoted had maintained an underground society for centuries that allowed them to work behind the scenes to help people or countries in distress with an efficiency most bureaucratic governments could not manage.

The odds of being recognized expanded as Jasirey interacted with people outside the Devoted to fulfill her destiny and exposed her to other enemies of her men and of the Devoted as a whole. Introducing her as Shannon—her original name—when in non-Devoted company helped but not enough to keep her safe.

"Recognize me by the bracelet," Jasirey succinctly summarized, "and then recognize my children or people of the Devoted by association. You can't count on everyone's discretion. I won't jeopardize my kids or people's safety."

It irked Lee that Jasirey had not included her safety on her list.

"There must be a solution other than breaking the band," he said.

"It only requires the addition of a clasp, so I can take it off when warranted."

Ian saw their wife's body tense. As team commander of the three younger husbands, he signaled Lee, Liu, and Fael to cease further arguments. He found Jasirey's request sensible and believed Master Kai would as well.

Lee and Fael headed security for their wife and for missions pertaining to her. They called in Kimika, head of their home security and his squad leaders Yusef and Mirai, who had recently arrived from the island.

Yusef had a plain square face and squat shape that he allowed outsiders to believe indicated the opposite of his agile mind and trained body.

Slender and petite, Mirai wore her waist-length jet hair in a thick braid she could weaponize with a fierce cunning her opponents seldom expected.

Lee recounted Jasirey's concerns to the three security people.

Mirai believed her lady's request valid. "The day has passed," she said, "when Jasirey can travel unnoticed in public. The ability to remove the bracelet is a reasonable precaution."

Kimika seconded Mirai.

"The etching on the band has significance," Master Kai said. "Fael, contact the Imperiat. They shall be able to instruct you on the proper procedure for cutting the band."

Jasirey moved on to their home security. "We have cameras on the compound walls. I'd like others installed around the entrances of the house and inside the hallways."

"It shall be done," Kimika said. He, Mirai, and Yusef clasped their right fingers over their left in the Devoted's traditional yin-yang symbol of respect for Jasirey and bowed as they left the family to the rest of their evening.

"Precious one," Liu said, "experiences this past year have left you anxious for our family's safety. How might we reassure you?"

Jasirey loosely draped her arms around her drawn-up knees. "What more can be done besides the changes you're already implementing?"

"You have insights different from ours," Fael said. "Tell us what troubles you."

Cagey, she thought. "Danger's coming, my loves. I saw it in the Imperiatu during my vision quest before the husband ceremony—colors that felt threatening and then bled together into a lifeless gray. I don't know what they mean yet." Jasirey turned to Master Kai. "Didn't the council tell them about that part of the prophecy?"

The council elected its members from the Elders and Imperiat and managed Devoted businesses throughout the world as well as missions unrelated to Jasirey to aid countries in crisis. The Elders governed the island.

"Truly, the Imperiat fully understood only the prophecy of your second pregnancy and that it would be fathered by others, most likely, your Protectors."

Jasirey tamped down the spike of anxiety Master Kai's words raised. Her vision had prophesied the difficult symptoms of her first pregnancy of quadruplets but an easier second pregnancy of quintuplets. Yet, the vision hadn't shown the stillbirth of a fifth child the first time. What else might be hidden heightened her unease.

What We Must Learn

"I don't believe death is the end of our existence," Jasirey said. "My vision—more a feeling than visual—felt cold, soulless, and a definite end to life." She ruffled her pixyish hair.

"During the prophesy in the Imperiatu, I saw reds, oranges, and yellows in ugly bumps and swells that melted together into a muddy sludge. I've continued to see them in dreams." Jasirey's mouth opened on a soft "Oh." Her thoughts drifted back.

"I saw them in reality," she continued, "before I even knew about the Devoted. Ian, you remember the glass blower's shop we went to after we met in Vermont. I saw ceramic plates with the same colors in their display window. I shuddered in revulsion and didn't really understand why."

"A premonition, I suspect," Master Kai said. "In the present, has your sense of danger intensified or become more imminent?"

Jasirey took a deep breath. "I wish I had an answer for you."

He patted her hand. "Fael, where are you in your training with our lady?"

"We have continued self-defense lessons begun on the island primarily to reintroduce exercise after the babies' birth. She has made great strides. A wordless communication has also sprung up between us, and her ability to perceive another's thoughts has grown markedly with her training."

"Perhaps a good place to begin my training with her," Master Kai said.

Jasirey looked down at her bracelet. They had gotten sidetracked. "Tell me about the etching on the band and the beading at the waist on the dresses the Devoted make for me."

"You have guessed the significance of the beads' colors, yes?"

"The top band of blue beads would be the sky, I suppose, and rain from it flows down to the bottom green band—the earth—to form lakes and rivers. I'm not sure about the purple band in the middle."

"That signifies a protective force for nature's interdependent systems—you. No matter our political or religious differences, the planet houses us all and must be kept inviolate from bickering factions, greed, and shortsightedness."

Startling the men, Jasirey popped up from the sofa. "The putrid yellows and oranges I saw in the Imperiatu during my vision—barren wasteland or maybe desertification. No blues or greens. Dead. That's the danger to the world."

She plopped back down. "How the hell am I supposed to prevent that?"

Master Kai wondered the same thing but couldn't help smiling at the outrage on their lady's face. "Our historical records suggest Jasirey's children bring about the necessary changes or evolution in humanity's thinking and practices. Your gifts, however, surpass what lore we possess on other Jasireys. We believe you are destined for a more direct role in nurturing the seeds of change or reform you shall sow."

"What about the etching on the bracelet?"

"The connections and crossings of all systems of nature."

Jasirey stared into space until Master Kai took her hand in his.

"Tell us your thoughts," he said.

Guilt suffused Jasirey's face. "Saying I may have a more direct role reminded me of the mental bridge I form to make people feel things. I realized when kidnapped by Eric that I can also make them do things. God doesn't take away free will. Who am I to decide what others should do?"

"Thus, you shall step up your training to learn to prevent unintentional use of your gifts and, while doing so, consider why you would be given your gifts if not to use them. We shall meet tomorrow morning in your training building. I have asked Nikolai and his team—Chen, Andwar, Favian, and Sajan—to assist you."

The young Protectors had been sent to America to help rescue Jasirey from Marcus. Master Kai found Jasirey's nickname for the young men—The Five—entertaining. He nodded cheerfully to the husbands.

"I am for bed," he said. "No doubt, you have much to discuss with your wife."

Jasirey fumed. "I'd like to tell Kai what I think of him asking The Five to help train me."

The Protectors had introduced themselves to Jasirey during her tour of the Devoted security facility hidden within a dormant volcano on her last visit to the island of the Devoted where most of the people lived. The young men intended to make an unforgettable impression ahead of the other Protectors for the day she decided on fathers for her next pregnancy—a serious breach of protocol.

She and her husbands sat in their bedroom sitting area to discuss the training. The men hadn't known much about the colors and design of her ring and bracelet. As they had personally experienced her ability to project feelings of well-being, only the disclosure that she recognized her gift and sometimes consciously used it surprised them.

"Protectors are chosen," Fael said, "when their vision quests show a strong emotional resolve to aid Jasirey. Master Kai has reasons for choosing these men."

"Don't get it, do you?"

"Get what, beloved?"

"Five guys of different races and cultures. Ring a bell?"

"Son of a bitch," Ian said.

Lee's dimples popped into view. "The impudent ones from the security center."

"Yes." Jasirey had protected their identities from her husbands' wrath at the time but saw no reason to continue. They'd agreed to place themselves in her husbands' path.

Liu's dark eyes sparkled as he tipped her flushed face to kiss her. "With that gleam in your eyes," he said, "you shall once again have their tails tucked between their legs."

"I suppose Lee and Fael filled you in about my saying that." The two husbands had been escorting her on the security center tour until The Five conspired to have them drawn away on other business.

"Precious one, people in the building witnessed the young men's ambush. Did you think the tale of our lady slapping back five upstarts would not spread to the entire island?"

Jasirey tried to be annoyed but wound up laughing. Except for maybe Ian, her men accepted the idea of the five Protectors as possible fathers for the next pregnancy. She hadn't yet accepted another batch of kids, let alone more lovers—especially like The Five, who were closer in age to her teenage sons than to her.

"They want Jasirey," she said with a sour purse of her lips, "not me."

Lee shook her gently. "You. They know no one else is equipped to be Jasirey."

"We are secure in your love for us," Fael said. "Be Jasirey—in whatever manner seems right to you."

Jasirey sighed. She didn't understand why her life had to be so complicated. She loved her family the way it was.

"Your power over us," Liu said, "is not a sad thing. We rejoice in it."

Jasirey slowly stood. "Power—you think I exert some kind of power over you?"

Lee cradled her face. "Do you know any power greater than love?"

***

Early the next morning, Jasirey checked in on the nursery and found seventeen-year-old Christopher and fifteen-year-old Michael making their brothers and sisters squeal by blowing air bubbles on their bellies. They played on a floor mat since the teens refused to pick them up. Squirming babies made them nervous.

Christopher had tight curls he'd let grow into long spirals fashionable for the rock band he had formed with Kirani and two friends from town. Loving the quadruplets' maniacal laughter, he allowed them to grab hold of his hair while howling in pretend pain (or for real if he lost focus and a dimpled fist got a good grip). Occasionally, he had to plead for adult assistance.

Christopher had recently acquired his license, worked a part-time job at the compound cleaning the barn where five milk cows resided, and thereby contributed to paying for a secondhand fuel-efficient car and the astronomical cost of insurance for teenage drivers.

As a young man with a car and hormones, he had also been required to sit down with his mother and stepfathers to discuss security and rules for driving with friends and going on dates. Security personnel would shadow his every step outside the compound.

"They'll be discreet," Jasirey said with empathy, "but you may feel awkward if your friends notice. Sorry about that. I bet sometimes you wish your life could be different."

Christopher's eyes widened. "Like how?"

Jasirey shrugged. "Maybe less complicated?"

"Nah. I'm used to it. I love everyone here." He hugged his mother.

"My baby," she murmured.

Christopher grinned and rubbed his hands together. "Not anymore. I've got wheels."

❦ ❦ ❦

After helping the babies' nannies, married couple Satoko and Mashita, to serve breakfast of small pieces of soft foods and sippy cups of formula to her little ones, Jasirey walked to the two-room training building. The first room received natural light from an exterior wall of large windows. The side walls contained shelves for exercise equipment. Machines that targeted different muscle groups lined the interior wall. The second room had been set up as an infirmary where Liu treated the people, the name the Devoted called themselves.

Master Kai and The Five waited for her. Immediately apparent to Jasirey despite the buzzing of nerves in her own brain, Nikolai struggled to hide his jangling feelings. She zeroed in on him, and though he remained calm, she literally felt him stiffen from head to toe.

Master Kai saw the pair's tension and decided it would be an excellent starting place. "What do you sense?" he asked Jasirey.

"The same as you," she said, unable to soften the edge to her voice.

Master Kai raised a brow as Chen, Andwar, Favian, and Sajan winced.

Jasirey sighed. "I said I would train. I'm uncomfortable doing it at the expense of another's feelings."

Master Kai said nothing. The other men started to fidget.

"Fine." Jasirey's fists went to her hips. "We're all uncomfortable."

She glared at the gaping younger men. Their expressions hardened, and she couldn't help a lopsided smile. "I've seen that look on my husbands' faces. They'll commiserate with you over how impossible I can be."

The Five smiled—foolishly in Jasirey's uncharitable opinion. She drew a deep breath. "Okay. Nikolai, do you want to share the feelings that have you so balled up?"

"No, dear one," Master Kai said. "Recognizing that he has misgivings—she is correct in this?" he asked Nikolai, whose face reddened.

When Nikolai nodded, Master Kai turned back to Jasirey. "As the training progresses, concentrate on determining the cause of the problem without speaking to him."

"I must return to the island for several weeks," Master Kai said to everyone. "Today, I shall impart instructions on how to proceed until my return. Fael has been teaching our lady self-defense techniques.

"Gentlemen, I wish you to assume that task, to devise exercises three days a week requiring Jasirey to anticipate offensive moves and to build a repertoire of logical counter moves. On the weekdays between, assist her in the vegetable garden she plans.

"Dear one, instruct them nonverbally. You may at first rely on body language, even if obvious. Your goal is to use nothing more than your eyes. The challenge to all of you shall be to offset frustration with patience. Nikolai, end the training for the day if our lady becomes fatigued."

Because it sounded like a game of charades rather than trying to control someone, Jasirey allowed a little impishness into her smile. "They'll likely be the fatigued ones after I yell at them several times for plucking out my vegetables instead of weeds."

She put a hand on Master Kai's arm. "Kai, my friend Lizzie is coming to visit this weekend. Can we start after that?"

Master Kai bowed to hide the happiness that washed over him whenever Jasirey—the only person who did so—called him Kai. "As you wish."

❦ ❦ ❦

The young couple Kharia told Jasirey to expect had arrived with Master Kai and settled in on the third floor. Born on the island and of Indian descent, Dharum had floundered in choosing a course of training. His parents sent him to university in the States where he met Isa, an African American similar in skin tone to himself. Dharum fell in love during her constant teasing about his Caucasian hair as she ran her fingers through the dark, straight strands. She indoctrinated him into the rules of hair weaves and extensions with a stern warning never to run his fingers through her hair.

Since the meeting that morning with Master Kai and The Five took less time than Jasirey had planned, she asked Isa and Mirai to accompany her shopping. She needed a present for her parents' anniversary but knew better than to try to find one thing that appealed to both. She bought some Louis L'Amour books she hoped her father hadn't already read. In a consignment shop for local craftspeople, she found an enameled pin of geometric designs—not something her mother would normally pick, but in the blues and roses her mother favored in her clothes. The pin complemented the silk-screened scarf Jasirey also chose.

A bit starstruck, Isa remained quiet.

Jasirey wanted her to be comfortable in her new home. "Isa, you've been a member of the Devoted longer than I have," she said. "I wonder if your life has changed as drastically."

"Hardly." Her eyes widened. "I mean, you're Jasirey."

"Has it been cleared for you to tell your family and friends?"

"No, ma'am, too many of them." Isa realized her lady meant to forge a connection between the two of them and loved her for it. "Our circumstances aren't the same. You have to hide whole parts of your life. I just hide who I work for. That I can share it with Dharum is enough for me." Her luminous smile indicated she and Dharum were still in the honeymoon phase.

"Were you born on the island, Mirai?" Jasirey asked.

"Yes, and my parents before me," Mirai responded. "My mother is a talented seamstress and designer of children's clothing. She sells her designs in Europe. My father recruited people for the Devoted before they married and afterward chose to work at the security center. I have a brother, a boat mechanic."

"I thought the training to become one of the Devoted was intense," Isa said. "I don't think I'd have survived security training."

Mirai smiled. "It's not for everyone. Your dedication is tested by stringent training and questioned threefold for physical and emotional preparedness. Male or female, the requirements apply equally."

On the return to their car, Jasirey discreetly drew Mirai aside. "I sense something weighing on you," she said as Mirai blinked away her surprise. "I won't intrude," she assured the younger woman. "Just know you can talk to me should you wish to."

Tempted to confide in Jasirey with her powerful motherly aura, Mirai fortunately had steadfast friends and family always there for her. She believed their lady carried too many burdens already and did not need the extra weight of Mirai's memories.

"Thank you, lady." Mirai smiled warmly. "I shall remember your offer."

⁂

After family prayers that night, Jasirey watched her husbands prepare for bed. She marveled at how strongly their desire and need for her fueled hers for them. She delighted in their every touch from whisper-light to pulsing roughness so controlled and powerfully exciting when she could strip that control away. The one question—whom to pounce on first?

Lee sat on the bed. Taking him by surprise, she managed to flatten him onto the mattress, straddle his hips, and devour his mouth. His large hands reflexively caught her and normally would have gentled over her curves, but her demanding mouth a clear clue to her mood, he grabbed her shapely bottom to grind his pelvis against hers.

Usually distracted by multiple assaults on her senses, Jasirey seldom knew how she came to be naked. That night, before joining her men in the bedroom, she had decided she wanted something different, to give her men a gift. Lee's face showed surprise and then concern when she pulled back. Her imp surfaced as she gestured to the men to sit on the bed. She placed a CD with a sexy beat into their audio system.

Her husbands had never seen her dance solo. Gleaming eyes watched her swaying hips and graceful, come-hither arm motions.

Jasirey faced away and peered over her shoulder while unbuttoning her blouse. She slowly pushed it down one shoulder, then the other. Her bra straps followed. One arm glided back to release the hooks. Her slacks and underwear shimmied down her heart shaped bottom. Jasirey turned and undulated in a belly dance. Mesmerized, her men saw the image she projected—no pouching stomach or stretch marks. She danced around her husbands and briefly brushed against each one until their heightened breathing reached the desired peak.

"Love me," was all she needed to say.

Ian lifted her onto his lap and lay back on the bed. With a twist of his body, he ranged over her. Jasirey's legs automatically cinched around his hips. Eyes on each other, they joined one slow inch at a time. Two strokes, a mighty shudder, and Ian collapsed.

Lee bodily moved him to the side and settled in at Jasirey's breast. "Little one."

She pulled at his dreadlocks. "Now, teddy bear."

Seating himself in her body with one slide, Lee lasted one thrust longer than Ian. Even knowing the men acted deliberately so as not to overtax her body, Jasirey mewled in protest, launched at Fael, straddled him, and nibbled on his mouth before lifting her face to Liu. She slowly ran the tip of her tongue over her lips.

Fael remained still within her and suckled one breast, then the other when Liu's fingers slid into their wife's hair as he stepped closer to her mouth.

Jasirey licked and laved and swirled her tongue until Liu started thrusting. She relaxed her mouth on his forward sway and clamped down around him as he slowly pulled back.

Liu's voice grated through a clenched jaw. "Harder," he said.

Jasirey grabbed his lean hips and held him until he detonated. He landed on the floor, legs crossed, head hanging.

Jasirey turned aggressive eyes on Fael and squeezed around him. Behind her, Lee fondled her cheeks. She froze when Lee pressed coolly wet, small, and hard anal beads part way inside her. The remaining string protruded from her bottom and swayed against her sex. They hadn't done much anal play since she developed hemorrhoids during the babies' gestation.

Ian and Liu used their mouths and hands to drive their wife to surrender to passion. Lee kneaded her cheeks, pushed the beads deeper, and looped a finger through the outer ring. Jasirey's pleasure coiled tight, then sprung into bliss as Lee slowly drew out one bead at a time.

Shattered, drained, and sticky, they all basked in the relaxed glow of cherishing, the warmth of cuddling, and the quiet words of love.

⁂

Close friend to Jasirey for more than twenty years, Lizzie found it impossible to call Jasirey anything but her original name, Shannon, and difficult to accept her marriage to four men. Thanks to Ian, Lizzie managed a business from home as a legal consultant. Online computer records greatly reduced the need to go out to a library and wrestle with heavy legal tomes, a boon to her ailing body suffering from rheumatoid arthritis and debilitating neuropathy. With her growing clientele—she felt sure Ian had also helped there—she could even afford an assistant to do research when needed.

Jasirey supervised the babies, who had reached six months, trying to feed themselves lunch in the kitchen when Lizzie made a loudly grand entrance. Her friend spent the next half hour dabbing tiny noses covered with green or orange pap and trying to sneak the little ones chocolate when Jasirey had her back turned.

Colin worked to deliver softly cooked green beans to his mouth, missed, and flung a handful in Safia's face. She reciprocated with well-steamed carrots to his hair.

Lizzie wiped her laughter tears. "Haven't you heard of spoon feeding?"

Jasirey grinned. "What fun's that? They learn more this way."

Satoko and Mashita put the babies down for their nap so the two friends could use the indoor pool. Sun rays speared through the glass walls into the water. Lizzie braved the pool with only one wistful glance at the hot tub.

"Seriously, Shannon, those babies are the most beautiful I've ever seen, and it's not their looks so much as how they look, if you know what I mean."

"It's their reactions and smiles," Jasirey said, "their joy and delight."

"Exactly. They make you feel like the best thing to come along since sliced bread."

"And they don't even know what that is yet."

"Ha, ha. I love the little twerps, but I'm too old to drum up this much energy every day."

"I have really good help," Jasirey said.

"Satoko and Mashita are jewels, though I sincerely doubt those kids lack attention from their mother."

"Or their fathers."

Lizzie hoisted herself onto a flotation chair. "Well, they have plenty of those. They really don't show favorites?"

"They really don't have favorites. As far as they're concerned, our babies belong to each of them equally. It was kind of cool to watch them deliberately interact with each child and see the bond forming—more quickly than I thought, too."

"I suppose it's no different than if the kids had been adopted." Lips pursed, Lizzie regarded her friend. "Shannon, do you ever get out?"

"We were at the island for several weeks and in South Carolina visiting my parents."

"I mean here at home."

"Haven't had the time or the inclination, especially while I was nursing. You know I'm the kind of shopper who grabs what she wants and gets out. I have the pool, puttering in the greenhouse, and the kitchen garden I'm going to plant. I'm happy."

Lizzie believed her. Still, she talked to the men before leaving. "Shannon seems chained to the house. Her whole world revolves around being a wife and mother. Women this age are usually facing an empty nest and can get involved in outside, personal pursuits."

Lizzie's observations reminded the husbands of Jasirey's wider mission, something they had put aside since the pregnancy and birth. She reveled in being a mother, and their sex life had never been better. With the children the family's priority, the men had given little consideration to Jasirey's interaction in the world but should probably do so soon, possibly in correlation to her training.

They agreed to consult Master Kai on his return.

The Five

Jasirey had embraced training with Fael, even the grueling strength exercises, though she debated the usefulness of whipping heavy ropes up-and-down. She loved the self-defense classes and lasered in on tactics: go for the soft spots—throat, solar plexus, groin—and more technically, leverage the attacker's weight and momentum to her advantage.

Her ability to predict an attack improved with her young but seasoned team of Protectors. Her creative responses impressed them. Nikolai wound up on the floor several times and asked Fael if she'd learned more from her husband's lessons than she let on, a mistake Nikolai rued for several days.

On one hand, the cold shoulder from Jasirey stung. On the other, Nikolai decided it distracted her from the assignment to figure out what bothered him. He didn't know she had already solved that puzzle.

Twice a week in the mornings or late afternoons, the team helped Jasirey plant seedlings or seeds and mulch her beloved garden. She took Master Kai's order to stay silent way too literally, in the opinion of The Five. They exploited her natural benign nosiness and sincere interest in others to break down her reticence toward them.

The most comically inept at gardening, Sajan wriggled more than the worms it didn't take a sixth sense to realize weren't his favorite things. One glare from Jasirey taught him that killing them displeased her.

One day, he dug up an earthworm as big as a baby snake. Shuddering, he removed it from the spot where Jasirey wished a tomato plant to go and let it slither into a pile of compost. She turned away from him as he glanced up, but he clearly felt approval and, he was certain, affection. He logged only the silent communication of approval.

Sajan had grown up in Salem, a large city in the state of Tamil Nadu on the southern tip of India, and had a large extended family, too many to trust with privileged information. They had not been informed of his membership in the Devoted.

"On my last visit home," he said, "my parents sent me out to buy rice, a chore usually given to one of my sisters." Aware of Jasirey's dislike for pigeonholing women, he smiled. "They hoped I would see the merchant's daughter and give consent to arrange a marriage."

Sajan guessed correctly that different concerns darkened their lady's eyes. "I have no desire to be married right now," he said. "When I do, I prefer to choose from the people. My parents have numerous children to uphold tradition. I am content."

Jasirey recognized the effort it cost Sajan to conceal his strong attraction to her, his infatuation. She stayed aloof but nevertheless failed to discourage his feelings.

An African American, Andwar had been brought to the island at the age of three by his parents. It was home, though he'd often visited grandparents in Illinois, gone to college in Chicago, and felt completely American as well. A younger sister and brother attended college at Andwar's alma mater. His mother and father had returned to the States to care for elderly parents.

He grinned wickedly. "They all encourage me to be married to my job."

Jasirey laughed, but her twinge of guilt didn't escape him.

"There's nowhere I'd rather be. My decision," Andwar said.

Andwar possessed adequate gardening skills, and Jasirey trusted him with her children. Not much older than her eldest, he often accompanied Christopher on his outings. Both Michael and Christopher appreciated him as a partner for video games and sparring, though with his superior training and adult build, he'd taken to allowing them the advantage of two-on-one.

One day before her training, Jasirey observed Andwar giving a lesson to her sons in the training center.

Showing off, Andwar encouraged the teens to come at him together. He praised their passable job of blocking him, stopped abruptly, and dismissed them.

Andwar felt Jasirey's disapproval and approached her quietly. She met his eyes. Andwar gasped at the mental flash she projected to him of three attackers surrounding Christopher.

He immediately understood his mistake and added the encounter to his log, writing,

> I trained Christopher and Michael in self-defense and allowed them to attack me two-on-one. Jasirey observed and, though she said nothing, clearly disapproved. She projected a fleeting mental image that made me realize they cannot always rely on being together. Each must learn the best defense possible for himself.

In her own journal, Jasirey wrote,

> I had reservations about one of Andwar's methods for training my sons in self-defense. We didn't speak, but I think he understood my concerns.

❦ ❦ ❦

An older, childless couple from the island adopted Chen or, technically, kidnapped him. He considered it being rescued.

A mission by the Devoted to an impoverished nation included surveillance of an orphanage where two-year-old Chen languished, the disgraced child of an unmarried mother who died in childbirth. He had no chance for a future.

Much to the displeasure of the Elders and council, the couple smuggled him out. They unapologetically faced censure—removal from the roster of mission duty and confinement to non-classified work.

The couple and Chen contentedly settled into family life. No one made Chen feel different from or less than the other island children. His vision quest reinforced his belief that he had landed exactly where he was meant to be and led to him joining the Protectors.

Chen's soulful eyes glowed with wisdom beyond his age. Jasirey admired his candor and the ease he displayed in his own skin. He accepted that his gangling height and large hands made handling the babies' tiny limbs awkward and that he preferred to provide security for the older children or, even better, lend a hand with the animals or crops. Though the best hand at gardening, he didn't know everything.

On one gardening day when he had finished setting tomato plants into the soil, Jasirey held up four-inch-high circles of plastic cut from the soda bottles she allowed her sons when they had guests.

Jasirey's impishness, which Chen found utterly adorable, surfaced as she handed the rings to him. His dislike of wearing work gloves left his hands grimed with soil and green plant juice and made the temptation to touch his lady easier to resist.

Jasirey narrowed her eyes and glanced at the rings dangling from his fingers. She sensed Chen fighting attraction and closed her eyes to help him concentrate. Didn't help. She sighed, took one of the rings and placed it two inches into the soil around a tomato plant to keep cutworms from destroying the tender seedling. She pretended not to notice Chen's flushed face as he finished the chore.

Nikolai reminded Jasirey of a rawboned Slavic Gary Cooper. His Ukrainian father and Georgian mother met on the island. Both skilled in computer work, one handled the hardware while the other handled software, both endeavors too sedentary for Nikolai, their only child. Not particularly talkative, he nevertheless had the most forward demeanor. His crystalline blue eyes often met Jasirey's in frank invitation. Yet he didn't offend nor even annoy her—much, probably because he hid under his cockiness a true eagerness to please.

Jasirey often pointed at him, her sign to replant something erroneously pulled as a weed, until she finally declared he sucked at gardening. When Nikolai agreed with winsome good humor, she fought the compulsion to push back the waving hair always in his eyes.

Jasirey made short work of divining his secret. Nikolai adored her babies and longed to pull baby duty but was terrified of hurting them through his inexperience. She astonished him by giving him a book on childcare. Her smile assured him she'd keep his secret safe from the others. Neither wrote of the exchange in their logs.

Favian, an erudite man with a questing mind, possessed an off-color sense of humor and a biting wit just shy of meanness. With three children, all boys, his parents were recruited from Colombia. Favian was an *oops* baby born a decade later on the island and the only one of the brothers to become a Protector. When a beautiful toddler, he hero-worshipped his older brothers, who spoiled him and carried him wherever he wished to go. Favian's first step occurred well into his second year.

Favian's sense of entitlement had been fostered at every turn, so his ego suffered an enormous blow when the Imperiat twice refused him as a Protector of Jasirey. Even after his vision quest strongly pointed to the Protectors, the Imperiat required Favian to undergo personalized training to disabuse him of his inaccurate assessment of his worth and abilities, an excruciatingly humbling process and the best thing anyone ever did for him. He wanted the self-sacrificing life of one devoted to Jasirey. Favian learned realistic expectations and responsibilities. His wry wit was left unchanged.

Jasirey appreciated that about him. She thought the one vice he hadn't ever cultivated, despite his classically handsome features, was vanity. He had no qualms about getting dirt under his fingernails or breaking a sweat working in the garden. It tickled her, though, when he drew the line at changing dirty diapers. She suspected he might be petrified by her rambunctious brood.

Favian most enjoyed lively debates with Jasirey and encouraged the others to chime in.

"For navigating life's curves," Favian said one day after being chastised for his overzealous thinning of a carrot patch, "I keep in mind the Serenity Prayer. Acceptance, courage, and wisdom—mottoes to live by."

"I found a different take." Jasirey's lips twitched as the young men perked up. "It recommends accepting people you can't change, having the courage to change those you can, and realizing the only person you can truly change is yourself."

Andwar's dark eyes glinted. "Except for our most precious lady. You have a gift for changing hearts and minds."

"But ability without wisdom—" Chen said, "like driving a car without brakes, is it not?"

Sajan assumed a scholarly expression. "Or a garden without worms."

"Or," Favian said, "a man without a good woman behind him."

Hands on hips, Jasirey said, "How about the man stands behind the woman?"

"Excellent idea." Nikolai took a lunging step and gently grasped Jasirey's elbows to keep her in place. The others queued behind him. He purred in her ear. "What will you do with us?"

Jasirey broke his hold and pushed. All five toppled like dominoes in a satisfactory heap.

It took her a while to admit that the young men devised such exchanges as foreplay.

❦ ❦ ❦

Since the previous year's Christmas shopping when Jasirey was too close to term with her quadruplets for outings, she had gotten used to shopping online, but some things she preferred to see in person. She decided to visit a garden center for fruit trees, flowers, and vegetables they might add to the farm. She also wanted to pick up a kiddie pool for her little ones.

Kimika assigned Nikolai, Chen, Sajan, Andwar, Favian, and Yusef to accompany her. The designated driver, Yusef bowed and aimed a jovial good morning at Jasirey.

She left the conversation to the young men—a tactical error, she quickly realized. As she'd become more familiar with them, they too had come to understand her. They hoped to discuss her ambivalence toward them and her destiny, neither topic something Jasirey considered their business, at least concerning her private feelings.

Sajan gently chided. "Anything affecting your well-being is a Protector's business."

Jasirey's stiff reserve bent. "You can't help. It's my responsibility to decide whether to have more children or lovers." She repressed an involuntary shudder.

Beside her, Nikolai felt the tremor. "There is more. What else concerns you? Something about the training?" She shook her head, but as the one man in the van unperturbed by the willful temper she occasionally let loose, he persisted. "What, Jasirey?"

"I have no problem talking about my feelings." Her lips twitched at their scoffing noises. "Everyone chooses what they want others to know. I don't even mind our nonverbal communication except for the idea that I might be able to sway people to do things they haven't chosen for themselves. It's too much like bullying."

"Or persuading someone to do the right thing," Chen said.

"Only we're not talking about persuading, are we? It's an intrusion, a violation."

"You would not violate a mind, as you term it, without great provocation," Sajan said.

"I don't want to do it at all. Could you?"

"Without hesitation to save an innocent," Yusef said.

Jasirey's shoulders tightened. "Easy to say when you won't be put to the test."

Favian winked at the others. "Our lady has become disenchanted with us, perhaps her love waning—not as blind as it was before she came to know us."

Jasirey snorted a laugh that snuck up on her.

Sajan expertly fielded the ball Favian tossed. "Whether she's blind or seeing, once Jasirey gives her love, it is surely unconditional."

Jasirey wanted to resist the anticipatory gleam in the young men's eyes. "I'm not a proponent of unconditional love other than for your children."

That shocked all the men. Unconditional love formed the bedrock of their veneration and vocation to care for and serve her.

Jasirey realized she had truly shaken them and relented on her stance not to explain herself. "Bring children into the world," she said, "raise them, and you owe them love and support no matter what." She raised a finger to halt the arguments brewing in Sajan's eyes.

"I'm not saying condone or enable inappropriate behavior," she continued. "That's contrary to love, which should strive for what's in the child's best interest, not what's easy or expedient for the parent. Child rearing is plain old-fashioned hard work. Sometimes you get so tired that shortcuts become tempting. What does it hurt to give in to a temper tantrum one time?"

"Once, twice, maybe more, and no harm done," Favian said. "Give in consistently, and you produce an arrogant, selfish adult who believes he is entitled to whatever he wishes despite exerting no effort to obtain it for himself."

Favian had told Jasirey of his excessively privileged childhood. "Granted," she said, "a mistake on your parents' part, but they gave you a proper foundation. Otherwise, you'd never have acknowledged the problem and worked so hard to remedy it. You turned out fine."

To cover his friend's emotional reaction to praise from Jasirey, Sajan forged ahead. "Your husbands, do you not love them unconditionally, precious one?"

Jasirey winced. Liu called her that as an endearment. The people often used it as a title. She feared that, even if unconsciously, Sajan meant it as an endearment. "Spouses and friends are people you allow into your life to fulfill relationship needs, sort of a contract," she said. "If you've made your needs and expectations clear and they're continually or deliberately not met, you may decide to end the relationship and move on. I divorced my first husband."

Andwar defended her. "After many years of working at the marriage."

"My husbands explained to me that the Imperiat gives my Protectors background information on me that might be pertinent to my security and more personal details to the males who might be candidates to father my children. I don't like it, but I've come to accept it. So, pertinent details about my first marriage—I didn't stay so much out of duty or noble reasons as from financial dependence."

More experienced than the others, Nikolai saw that the failure festered in Jasirey and needed lancing. "May I ask what caused the divorce?"

Jasirey drew in a breath. "Roger was affectionate, said he loved me but turned away from anything requiring work—learning and remembering what I wanted and needed, figuring out and being clear on what he wanted.

"Love, friendship, even humanitarian love—charity, kindness, tolerance—shouldn't be simply feelings. No matter how sincerely meant in the moment, words mean little if the day-to-day choices and actions to back them up are missing. For me, the true test of love is what you do about your feelings, especially when the relationship hits the inevitable potholes."

Fascinated by the uncharacteristic fountain of private thoughts from their lady, the men remained quietly attentive.

"Roger had problems we attributed to fixable, exterior things—a stressful job, lack of experience. Before our marriage, he lived with his parents, never on his own. I didn't recognize his problems went deeper until after the wedding. Some problems he was born with—attention deficit disorder.

"Maybe his insecurities stemmed from his inability to focus or learn new information as easily as his schoolmates or coworkers, but he compensated with lies, fantasies of how he wanted others to see him. They became so real to him. He believed them himself.

"In those first years, I think he told me one true thing. He said, 'This is the way I am, this is the way I've always been and the way I'll always be.'"

Jasirey shook her head. "Too bad I didn't believe him sooner. I said the vow to unconditionally accept him in sickness and in health, for better or for worse, to stay in a dead-end relationship with a man only capable of superficial love.

"After years of soul-searching, I decided the terms of the marriage contract had been unfulfilled from his end, leaving me free to pursue my own happiness."

"What do you mean by superficial love?" Nikolai asked.

Jasirey sensed giving in to her temper would only reinforce the steely determination in Nikolai's bright blue eyes, so despite her unwillingness, she continued.

"Jesus mentioned one condition for divorce, infidelity, and the apostle Paul said you're no longer bound to a spouse who refuses to live with you. Both said that, when marrying another after divorce for any other reason, you commit adultery with him or her. Neither condition for divorce applied in my case. I chose it anyway."

Her imp surfaced. "I'm already grievously straying, and you think I should add to the offense?"

Chen did not join in the others' snickering. "What about divorce in cases of abuse or where one spouse has an addiction and refuses treatment?"

Jasirey nodded. "Good points. Your spouse can leave you emotionally without ever going out the door."

Aware that Jasirey had skillfully skirted his question, Nikolai smiled—a hunter's smile, quarry in his sights. "And how did your first husband break the marriage contract?"

Jasirey frowned but said, "I guess there's no reason to hide what's done and over. Roger and I weren't sexually compatible. Showing arousal skills to him didn't work, advice was never remembered, books never read. Ninety-nine percent of the time, I initiated sex. He had little interest. My frustration became a physical torture just as painful as the loneliness."

Her gaze focused outside her car window. "Looking back, I suspect he unconsciously withheld sex to punish me for making him feel inadequate. I couldn't fake arousal."

Her rueful smile disarmed the bridling men.

"Our failure in the bedroom caused him a great deal of pain, too," she told them. "The main difference, though, involved that he found comfort in being affectionate. He didn't recognize the lack of a deeper intimacy between us, couldn't understand my pain over that lack."

"Trust that our love as your Protectors will never be superficial." Andwar's declaration shimmered with adoration.

Devotion shone from Chen. "For our lady has unparalleled grace, love, and wisdom."

Favian's brown eyes glinted. "Regardless of not recognizing her own skills."

"It is unreasonable to expect perfection," Nikolai said, "even from our precious lady."

Jasirey wished for reassuring arms to hold her but refused to turn to her Protectors and encourage their hopes.

Andwar gently placed his hand atop hers. She slipped her fingers out from under his. He sighed but accepted her choice.

Not as accommodating, Nikolai drew Jasirey against his side, kissed her forehead and stiffening neck while holding her loosely, waiting for her to relax. She pushed away again, and assuming she still needed to talk, Nikolai let her go. "No matter the risk," he said, "whether to our bodies or our hearts, we will remain at your side."

"That's the problem. At what personal cost to you, my Protectors?"

Sajan leaned forward. "Nothing comes before our mandate to safeguard you and your children. Any personal relationship would be secondary to that goal. Believe me."

Jasirey breathed deeply and tried to shake off the gloom she shouldn't project onto her Protectors. They were so young. "I'm truly grateful for your devotion. Don't be offended that I'd rather change the subject for now."

"Always as you wish," Favian said. The men only ever sought her peace of mind.

"Thanks, guys. Yusef, I've heard the others' stories. How'd you become one of the people?"

"I was born on the island of the Devoted, as were my parents. My paternal great grandparents and my mother's great grandparents originated from Egypt. Thinking of it as a father who had given them life, they kept a proud cultural tie to the country and loved the island as a nurturing mother. We visited Egypt often in my childhood. I disliked it at first. Compared to the tropical colors of the island, the country seemed dull, arid, and crowded."

"Water supply is something I worry about," Jasirey said. "Egypt has one of the driest climates in the world as well as a surging population that places a strain on the Nile, a strain that, I've read, could disrupt the country's economy, agriculture, and industry. And rising sea levels may turn millions of Egyptians into environmental refugees."

For the benefit of the others, Yusef said, "As most of Egypt's land is desert, cities concentrate along the Nile River, its delta, and the Suez Canal. To lose any fertile land from the sea's encroachment is potentially disastrous."

"Something like sixty-five percent of the world's population lives on a seacoast and faces similar problems," Jasirey said. She smiled at Yusef. "But we were talking about you. I assume your family is Muslim?"

"No. Coptic Christian, the largest sect of Christians in the Middle East, though we do not advertise this fact on our visits. The country had been Christian for centuries before the Islamic conquests of the seventh century. Today's Christians face discrimination—even violence—and have minimal representation in Egypt's government and problems getting official documents such as identity papers or permits to build or repair churches."

"Do you have siblings?"

"Older twin sisters. The Egyptian culture especially shocked their island sensibilities. They at first hated wearing the hijab, but since most women wore them, they soon felt strange without it.

"My favorite thing about visiting was the food," Yusef continued. Meat is expensive, so fish is common, and the country relies on many wonderful vegetarian dishes. I also never tire of the parks and museums. Egypt has one of the longest histories of any country."

"Are you a citizen of Egypt?"

"To keep the island off the world's radar, we who travel must have citizenship in a recognized country. Ours is rooted in family history. In the beginning, as members of the Devoted, though from dismay rather than regret, it disturbed me to realize how far from the Egyptian culture we had strayed."

Yusef threw Jasirey a provocative smile in the rearview mirror. "My vision quest led me to the Protectors and security. I am content in all my roles."

She fought panic as his smile sent a warm rush tingling through her. *No, no, no, no, no—I've too many in my life already. Please don't do this to me.*

❧ ❧ ❧

Planting finished, the garden needed only routine maintenance, so Jasirey spent an afternoon with Ian in the playroom watching Colin, who was not interested in a nap. Ian told her of a meeting he needed to attend in New York City to discuss the possibility of negotiations between his corporation and China.

"The political climate in China has shifted," Jasirey said. "I've read that foreign business is less welcome and more obstacles set up in favor of state businesses. It's hard to find internet browsers not controlled by the government. But you must have dealt with Chinese business people before."

"Actually, we have a team specializing in Chinese relationships, but the company we're dealing with now insists on a face-to-face meeting with me."

"Chinese business customs and ethics are different from ours. Are you talking to the company's negotiation team or the CEO?"

"Does it matter?"

"To them, yes. If the CEO, he—most likely a man—would probably consider it an insult to be asked to deal with underlings, people inferior to his status. If the negotiations take place in China, you should enter the meeting room before the rest of your team. Chinese tradition calls for the leader to enter first."

"If we both decide to negotiate, I'm not sure where the first round of meetings will take place. I don't expect them to last more than a day or two."

Jasirey shook her head. "If they're in China, don't count on that. Business may not even be discussed on the first day. Speeches will be given—you'll be expected to give at least a perfunctory speech celebrating opening negotiations. Then general conversation will set the mood of cooperation and good will. Even subsequent days will start with chit chat to create a comfortable atmosphere."

Jasirey raised an eyebrow at him. "I've never seen you drink much. In China, alcohol may be served throughout the meeting, and how a man handles that is used to judge his strengths and weaknesses."

Ian's fingers skimmed over his shaven head. "Maybe there'll be a plant nearby where I can dump it."

Jasirey laughed. "As long as no one sees you. Such rude manners—hinting the alcohol's quality is inferior—could cause your host to lose face and you to potentially lose any chance of doing business with him."

"Thank you, love. I appreciate that brilliant brain of yours. I'll be interested to see what cultural information our strategy team brings up."

He pulled her into a hug and rested his chin on her hair. "On a personal note, I also have a formal dinner dance to attend while in New York—an anniversary celebration of one arm of the corporation for department heads and other business colleagues, including spouses or dates. Be my date?"

"As in just you and me?" Jasirey wrapped her arms about his waist and moved her lips along his jaw. He cupped her bottom.

"Can't you guys do that in your room?" said a disgusted Michael.

Ian's eyes crinkled as he moved his hands up a bit but kept his wife close.

Colin held out demanding arms to his brother. "See? He thinks it's gross, too."

Michael picked up the baby. "Hello, kid. Want to ride the pony?" He carefully lowered Colin into the safety seat of one of the wooden rocking horses made by the people and moved it slowly. Colin bounced and pulled on the horse's wool mane.

Jasirey watched in surprise. "How long have you been doing that, Michael?"

"What, the horse? They all love them."

"No. I mean, yes, I know they do. When did you start picking them up?"

"I don't know. Since they got big enough to get a good hold on 'em, I guess. Giddy up, horsey."

Colin squealed and grinned, an identical grin to his older brother's.

A Corporate Wife

Ian and Jasirey arrived in New York two days before the party along with Yusef, Chen, and Favian as security. Leaving the bracelet behind, Jasirey rubbed at her naked hand the entire plane ride. They checked into the Waldorf Astoria on Park Avenue where the party was to be held. Jasirey managed to restrain her gawking until she entered her and Ian's en suite bath with its marble tub.

"I thought about the Presidential Suite," Ian said, "Georgian furniture that mirrors the White House's, JFK's actual rocking chair, but three bedrooms seemed a bit much."

"You think?" Jasirey saw no point in bothering the staff to unpack her one suitcase and garment bag. She hung up her gown for the party and laid her casual dinner dress on the bed.

Ian suggested a walk before dinner. Jasirey suspected others besides Yusef, Chen, and Favian followed but saw no sign of them. She liked the feeling of being alone with Ian.

He steered Jasirey inside Tiffany's on Fifth Avenue. "I thought you might appreciate a replacement when you don't want to wear your bracelet."

Inside the jewelry store, case after case of diamonds glittered, mostly from wedding and engagement rings. Jasirey unconsciously hid her hands in the pockets of her spring slacks. "I like the bracelet I have. I don't need diamonds."

Ian suppressed a grin at his nonmaterialistic wife. "No, I suppose not."

A woman in a conservative suit and pearls approached. Ian politely waved away her assistance. "I know the floor," he said and ushered Jasirey into an elevator. When the doors opened, Ian headed for a gentleman in a formal suit and tie whom he had previously asked to set up a surprise for Jasirey. As usual, for her safety, he introduced Jasirey as Shannon to people outside the Devoted. "Bertrand, my wife, Shannon."

Bertrand watched her smile fade to a you've-got-to-be-kidding frown as he fawned over her and warm when, a little shamefaced, he gave her a genuine smile. He laid a jewel case on the counter. Inside lay a delicate platinum bracelet and matching ring with thumbnail-sized amethyst surrounded by small diamonds and opals that made the deep purple scintillate.

"Tell yourself you're accepting it for my sake," Ian whispered, "so I don't have to suffer watching you rub your hand raw."

"Smart ass," she whispered and, not caring who watched, kissed him.

Bertrand boxed the jewelry with the added flourish of a purple bow.

Ian and Jasirey went to Chinatown for dinner and sampled dishes with names they couldn't pronounce. Jasirey feared she might wet herself from laughing so hard after Ian bit into a hot pepper, turned beet red, and had tears streaming down his face. He thought her lack of sympathy woefully unwifely and threatened to make her pay for continuing to burst into fits of giggles on the taxi drive back to the hotel.

In their suite, Ian quickly disrobed his wife and laid her on the bed. He lifted a bucket of ice chips surrounding a bottle of champagne he had ordered delivered to their room.

Jasirey made a break for it. He dragged her back from the edge of the mattress, but knowing she was a wily opponent, he pinned her beneath him and restrained both arms over her head with one long-fingered hand shackling her wrists.

"Have mercy."

He gave her a lazy, predatory smile. "Not on your life." Placing a piece of ice between his lips, he ran it up and down her throat. Tiny melting rivulets sent prickles over her skin. Ian and the ice slithered down a slow, torturous trail to her breasts. Growling, he replaced ice for the umpteenth time. "You're too damned hot-blooded."

A giggle lodged in Jasirey's throat as he sucked her nipple into his warm mouth and up against the ice.

Ian had to release her hands to open the champagne. He let the bubbles fizz down her torso. She squealed as cold sharp wetness hit her skin. Ian began a slurping journey down her body to the juncture of her parted thighs. His frostbitten tongue instantly warmed deep inside her scorching heat.

Jasirey shivered at the bite of the ice and again at the burgeoning pleasure of his slow slide in and out, the light massage of her clitoris. Panting, she gripped the sheets.

Ian kept his weight on his elbows, laced her smaller fingers with his, and smoothly entered her welcoming body. Jasirey's legs draped over his hips as he set a rhythm of long, slow strokes he kept up despite her whimpering and pleading for him to go faster. They crested with a consuming ferocity even more unexpected for the lazy pace. Ian sank onto his wife's damp body. Neither felt the least inclined to move.

When Jasirey's brain registered the location of her arms still above her head though Ian's hand had fallen away from her hands, she caressed the long line of his back.

He shifted his weight to the side and rested his head on her breast where the steady beat of her heart lulled him to sleep.

⁂

The next day, Ian Skyped Jasirey from his personal computer during an afternoon break from his preliminary online meeting with the Chinese corporation. Jasirey sat with her feet up after hours of touring the American Museum of Natural History. She spent most of the time in the Asian Hall of Mammals, as she was less familiar with the animals there than other continents.

Learning about the Sumatran rhinoceros both fascinated and saddened her. Critically endangered, the animal—once common in India, many of the east Asian islands, and China—lived in Sumatra and Borneo. Much smaller than its African cousins though still a solitary animal, it marked the ground with its feet and bent saplings into patterns to communicate with others of its species.

Jasirey put down her tea as she noticed lines of strain around Ian's mouth.

The lines relaxed, and he touched the corner of his mouth in wonder. "I literally felt your touch. Training?"

Jasirey's cheeks tinted a soft rose. "I don't think so. Ingrained, maybe."

Ian's eyes traveled softly over her face. "Along with your love for me."

Another man's deep dulcet voice sounded from Ian's laptop. Warning bells clanged, and her breath felt barricaded in her throat. She wanted—needed—to see the man's face, his eyes.

"We're back online," Ian whispered. "I'll see you in a few hours." He ended the call.

Not sure what had just happened, Jasirey scrubbed cold hands over her face, got her breathing under control, and called in Yusef.

One glance, and he went directly to his lady. "What's wrong?"

"I don't honestly know—a weird reaction to a voice." She waved away his bubbling questions. "Ian called, and I heard a man speaking from his laptop. I couldn't see his face, but the voice sent me into a flashback of the Imperiatu, the dead colors I saw during my vision quest."

She shuddered and let Yusef draw her into his arms for a minute, then stepped away. "I'm okay. Do you have any information on the people wanting to do business with Ian?"

"I do not, but I can find out."

"Just the name of the corporation and the CEO, please. I can look them up myself."

* * *

Jasirey spent most of the day in her suite with two novels she'd bought months ago but hadn't had a chance to read. Along with popcorn and a few chocolates, she was in heaven.

Ian returned late and found his wife dancing and singing to a Linda Ronstadt greatest-hits album. Rising lust edged out the stress of the day. He knew Jasirey could sing. She had impressed his business associates at his corporate headquarters in Boston at the party held to introduce her and celebrate their marriage. But even after the unforgettable night of her strip tease, he had no idea she could dance like that—uninhibited and sexy.

He fitted his front to her back, ran his fingers up to her breasts, and palmed their glorious weight in his hands.

Jasirey relaxed into him and settled her bottom over his straining zipper. "Now that's what I call room service. Remind me to be very generous with the tip."

Ian's voice purred. "I have another tip in mind."

"So do I."

Ian's breath caught as Jasirey turned and slowly lowered herself down his body.

The couple decided on a candlelit dinner in their suite sitting room.

"How did your meeting go?" Jasirey asked.

"It took a year to get a face-to-face conference with a negotiation team from this Chinese corporation that could actually make decisions. Now, we're talking to the CEO, Sheng Qian, and it's like starting all over. We spent most of the day on points already acceded to and me fencing Sheng Qian's subtle maneuvers to get me to continue negotiations in Beijing."

"In his territory, he has the advantage—psychological as well as physical."

Ian rested his elbows on the table, his chin on linked fingers. "Exactly."

"Was it his voice I heard at lunchtime on your laptop?"

Ian recognized the question wasn't idle and cocked a brow at her.

Jasirey reached out to link her hand with his. "I had a weird reaction, a sense of danger. Is your business with him American corporate or Devoted related?"

"They're often intertwined." For a better barometer of Jasirey's state of mind, Ian's fingers feathered over the pulse point on her wrist. One of the first things Fael had taught her in their training sessions was how to control her facial expressions.

"Do your negotiations include environmental concerns?"

"More with working conditions, I'd say, for manufacturing goods aimed at high-end consumption. Of course, his corporation includes businesses not involved in our negotiations, and I haven't researched them."

"High-end as in maybe the supply of the chips everyone worries about?"

Ian kissed the tip of her nose. "Can't discuss that, I'm afraid."

Since the corporate party would go late, the couple slept until ten-thirty the next morning, made love in the shower, and ate a leisurely brunch.

Butterflies began fluttering in Jasirey's stomach. Large groups of unfamiliar people unsettled her. The pressure to make a good impression for Ian's sake intensified her anxiety, and owing to security concerns, his business associates knew nothing of the babies' birth, which left her at a disadvantage.

"Ian, all these people, what do I tell them? Everett already worked for you when we married. You don't need two house managers."

"Pardon?"

"I'm busy with the babies, but I can't say that. Did they ever ask what I do?"

"Yes, now that you mention it. I believe I told them you homeschool the boys."

"Okay. I'll stick to that."

Ian's long arms surrounded her. "We can tell them you're a singer if you prefer something more glamorous. It isn't a lie."

"Uh, no thanks. They might ask me to sing."

"I enjoy listening to you sing." He believed her voice could have led to a career.

Jasirey snuggled closer. "I'm happy as I am, my Ian."

Her sincerity touched and troubled him. He wondered if perhaps on Lizzie's visit she had brought something even more vital to their attention than her belief that Jasirey should have more outside interests. Jasirey had an untold and untested wealth of gifts to share outside the family.

For the party, Ian wore a dark gray suit with a pewter shirt and coordinating tie. Jasirey's eyes sparked with appreciation. She wore her ivory silk dress that he had given her for Christmas. It had printed lilacs over one shoulder and the opposite hip. He draped a necklace about her neck that matched the new bracelet and ring but left to her the task of weaving the accompanying drop earrings through her pierced ears. That completed, Jasirey tucked her pixyish hair behind small ears to showcase the earrings.

Ian's frank appraisal made her blush. "Baby, even the women won't be able to take their eyes off you."

"Don't say that. I've already got butterflies."

"I can't imagine why. Is it part of being introverted?"

"I suppose, but come on. People are expecting your wife to measure up to you. It could be embarrassing. And don't you dare get mad at me." She glowered at the annoyance he didn't bother to hide. "It's easier for extroverts. You draw energy from interacting with others. Introverts expend a lot of energy to be sociable. The more people, the more strenuous."

That was something concrete Ian understood. "What makes it easier?"

"Stay with me when you can and be patient with my neediness?"

"I won't leave your side."

"Silly, I'm not that bad. Once comfortable with a few people, I'll be fine. It's business. You have to play host and dance with wives or female corporate leaders, I'm sure."

"True, I'm afraid." He took her hand. "You'll have a wonderful time, love. I know several people you'll enjoy meeting."

"Then I feel better. Thanks for being so sweet, my Ian."

"I love you, my beautiful girl." He forgave her the sweet remark—that time.

* * *

Charlotte, Ian's administrative assistant and a member of the Devoted, met the couple in a large hall leading to the venue before the crowd arrived. She hugged their lady. "It's been a while," she said. "How are those beautiful babies?"

Jasirey beamed. "Growing and thriving. You're welcome to visit anytime."

Ian expected manners to prevent his associates from descending on his wife during dinner, but to be safe, charged Charlotte with running interference. Set for ten people, each round table stood far enough apart from its neighbor to allow a moderate voice level.

A waiter offered Jasirey her preferred iced tea and— another member of the Devoted—inclined his head in a modified bow. Employing their own people lessened security concerns.

Three other couples, Charlotte, and a single man sat at their table and ranged from middle age up. They came from different branches of Ian's corporation in various cities. Most still had children at home. Conversation flowed easily through the multi-course dinner.

"I ought to make the rounds," Ian whispered to Jasirey during dessert. "I'll introduce you before the dancing starts. You're all right for now?"

"Go ahead. I'm fine." He kissed her lightly, ran his knuckles down her cheek, and set more than a few hearts fluttering.

Asked how she met Ian, Jasirey gave a vague, romantic answer about the two of them rescuing each other from a stale life and soon had the group recounting their life stories. Blue-green eyes sparkling in the candlelight assured them that she found them fascinating.

Ian observed the table on his return. Jasirey reminded him of a benevolent queen or celebrity holding court. The men vied for her attention. She skillfully juggled them without neglecting the women. He caught Charlotte's wink.

"Excuse us, please," Ian said as he pulled out Jasirey's chair and linked hands to escort her about the room.

As he introduced her to seemingly hundreds, she remembered only a few names. A gorgeous redhead, six feet in her considerable heels, approached them on the arm of an equally gorgeous man. They both wore black and white, though Jasirey doubted they were a couple.

Ian introduced Rachel as a vice-president of something or other. Jasirey correctly guessed that the woman chose her designer black-and-white dress—too severe for her coloring—as a power statement. Reginald was CEO of the British arm of Ian's corporation.

"Finally, we meet Ian's wife," Rachel said. "We wondered at his not introducing you to the wider corporation." Her tone implied she understood why he wouldn't want to.

Jasirey could never understand why otherwise intelligent people failed to see how such juvenile behavior highlighted their own insecurities. She knew when first meeting her that most people saw an average woman—height five feet, four inches; neither fat nor thin, though with a larger than average bosom; prematurely silver-white hair cut short to wave in abandon around her face; pleasant features with a mouth perhaps more lush than average and full, perfectly proportioned lips.

When she smiled, eyes the color of blue spruce trees seemed to expand and command everyone's attention. When she zeroed in on an individual or small group as if she found them eminently worthy of attention, they experienced a peaceful feeling of well-being. What people found extraordinary about Jasirey stemmed from the force of her personality.

Even Jasirey's husbands had yet to fully comprehend the intentional power their wife employed to put people at ease and dispose them to trust her, an ingrained trait. She balked against exploiting that power for personal gain despite her training to use her gifts to raise the odds of meeting her destiny.

Rachel took possession of Ian's arm. "We must greet Owen."

"Shannon?" Ian again checked on her welfare.

Jasirey beamed at him. "Reginald and I will get acquainted."

Reginald regarded her with interest. She exhibited no distress at her husband being dragged away by the unmarried femme fatale. Extraordinarily secure or lack of interest?

Jasirey assessed him equally and liked the look of him, something more than his handsome face. His gentle wariness beckoned to her. "Do your friends call you Reggie?"

"Not if I have a say in the matter."

"It's softer, nicer than Reginald. It suits you."

Her open face lent Reginald no clue as to the motive behind such a personal statement. She grinned and linked her arm through his—not flirtatious, but rather companionable and nevertheless powerfully sensual. An unusual peacefulness suffused his being.

"I think we'll be close friends," she said. "I promise to call you Reginald, though I may think of you as Reggie." Her warmth beguiled him.

The orchestra started, and Ian and Rachel circled the floor. Reginald expected the arm in his to tense. Ian's wife remained relaxed.

"They dance well together," she said. "I suspect, with Ian's and my height difference, we look off balance. It's still fun." Her gaze turned shy. "Do you enjoy dancing, Reginald?"

He swung her gracefully out onto the floor. Not as tall as Ian, he easily leaned in to whisper, "Call me Reggie."

She gave him a scintillating smile that made his breath catch. After the dance, Reginald lost track of her as nearly every man in the place queued up to claim her as a partner.

With Rachel still attached to his arm, Ian soon found Reginald. "Did you lose my wife?" he asked good-naturedly.

"She has become the belle of the ball."

Ian disengaged Rachel's arm. "Excuse me. I'd like to get in one dance with her." He stepped into the crowd.

Snide, but Reginald couldn't resist. "He seems quite attached to his wife."

Rachel spared him a cool glance. "Soft and sweet is always attractive to a powerful man until it gets saccharin and boring."

Reginald understood why Ian's wife had no worries. He did not bother to say he thought Jasirey the most warmly engaging woman he had ever met. *A corporate diva*, Reginald thought, *Rachel is incapable of perceiving Shannon's appeal.*

Rachel could not discern Jasirey's appeal in part because Jasirey decided she could do little to soften Rachel's strong prejudices so chose not to reach out to the woman.

Enchanted by Jasirey's dazzling smile and Ian's outright adoration, the crowd backed away to watch the couple. The music ended, and numerous people waylaid them for a word as the pair wound their way back to Rachel and Reginald.

Jasirey glowed, and Reginald gallantly declared, "My dear, tomorrow you shall be the talk of our corporate world."

Ian nuzzled her hair. "My thoughts exactly, love."

"Do you have a pet name for Ian, Shannon?" Rachel asked in a bored tone.

"Ian, just plain Ian." It was a private reference to their first intimate encounter.

Rachel smothered a smirk and missed the searing bolt of heat between husband and wife. Reginald felt singed and thought Rachel unlikely to advance beyond vice-president.

"We ought to circulate a little more before leaving," Ian said.

Jasirey offered her hand to Reginald. "Are you free to have lunch with us tomorrow?"

Seeing Ian's approving nod, he said, "I'd love to."

❦ ❦ ❦

On the way back to the hotel, Ian cuddled his wife in the back of a roomy sedan driven by Yusef. "You made any number of conquests tonight. Did you have a good time?"

"I met a lot of nice people. I really like Reggie—Reginald," she said at Ian's cocked eyebrow. "He gave me permission to call him Reggie. It suits him."

"Does it?" Ian would never have considered the nickname appropriate. "Nothing will get done at work next week, everyone too busy gossiping about my stunning wife."

"And buzzing about the jewels you draped her in and what she had to do to get them."

Ian choked on a laugh. "I think you're confusing wife with mistress.

I believe wives receive them as part of the marital package. Much more respectable."

"Oh, good," Jasirey purred. "I'd hate to have a reputation—bedding a bunch of guys, all kinds of children with different fathers."

"Spanking," he said, a sensual threat. He pressed his lips to her kissable mouth and sank in comfortably. Gazing into her loving eyes, he tapped the end of a cute nose. "You're tired, baby."

"A little." She nibbled on his ear. "Do you want to know your nick-name, something more than just Ian with the handsome, smart ass?"

"Do I have one?"

"Oh, yes—my heart, my safe place, my first love, my Ian."

"All of that?" he murmured huskily.

In their room, they made love with more sweetness than heat. Sleep restored their energy for a laughingly rambunctious bout of shower sex before a light breakfast. Ian had made an early lunch reservation at a casual restaurant.

Reginald arrived early and enjoyed watching the couple holding hands as they walked in. He kissed Jasirey's cheeks and marveled that a woman with silver-white hair and a face that moved naturally in soft lines appropriate for her age nevertheless looked so radiantly vital.

She asked about the work he did for Ian and about his small estate in the English countryside. "Most of my ancestry is English," Jasirey said. "I've dreamed of visiting England, Scotland, and Ireland."

That was news to Ian.

"Then you should," Reginald said. "You're welcome at the estate."

"Thank you. That's sweet. Do you have a spouse, Reggie? Kids?"

"No children. I had a partner for seven years. He decided to move on to greener pastures. That was five years ago."

"I'll bet he regrets it," she said, "and if not, you deserve better." She had a gift for making him feel lighter in heart.

"I suppose that's a polite way of saying be more selective in future," he replied.

Jasirey regarded him kindly. "Did you choose him for more than his pretty face?"

"In hindsight, perhaps not."

"So, you learned. You'll find the right one when you figure out what you really need." She smiled lovingly at Ian, leaving no doubt she had found her right one.

Spellbound by Jasirey's insight and fearlessness, Ian mostly listened. Few people dared to ask the intimate questions she asked on such short acquaintance. Yet, none of the people he'd heard her talking to at the party seemed put out with her. Quite the contrary, her deep, sincere interest flattered and imparted warmth and caring. She belonged out in the world.

The meal ended long before the conversation, and the time came to part. "Uh, Reggie, do you mind having kids around?" Jasirey asked.

"I've not had much experience. I have a nephew and a niece I see briefly at holidays."

"It's just that if we visited, I'd want to bring my children."

"If they are anything like their mother, they would be most welcome."

Jasirey's smile blazed, and she kissed Reginald's reddening cheeks as they left.

On the plane back home, Ian asked, "Are you seriously considering descending on poor Reginald with our entire family in tow?" He immediately wished he'd rephrased when her face fell.

"It would be a security nightmare, wouldn't it?"

"That's not what I meant. You barely know Reginald. Do you really want to spend that much time with him?"

"I like him," she said as if that settled the matter, and Ian supposed that for her it did.

A Complicated Life

School finished for the summer. Michael joined Christopher at working in the newly finished barn inside the walls of the western Massachusetts compound. The barn housed eight dairy cows and a rescued, gentle old mare in need of pasture to roam. The boys loved the horse almost as much as they did Nick, their massive, half-grown Saint Bernard puppy.

Jasirey's Himalayan Persian cat, Dusty, often joined watchful adult caregivers in the playroom connected to the nursery adjacent to Jasirey and her husbands' master bedroom to practice dashing through an obstacle course of babies while evading chubby grasping fingers. The cat especially enjoyed the greater challenge of babies beginning to stand up and walk while holding onto furniture.

Master Kai returned to the compound as promised. He found Jasirey, her back to him, gazing at the fountain in the flower garden awash in the many colors of zinnias, lilies, pansies, petunias, and in shaded areas, decorative foliage plants.

"Do not face me, dear one," he said before she turned.

Jasirey sensed his happiness to see her and focused on infusing him with her love.

A gentle hand settled on her shoulder. She turned, and Master Kai hugged her warmly. "Well done, dearest one."

The Imperiat had read reports from Nikolai's team and considered them as proof that Jasirey had the power to sway minds. Master Kai had just received personal proof of her ability to positively alter one's emotional state. She continued to balk at adding negative emotions to her arsenal.

"Dearest one, you should know that Mtombe accompanied me here and Kharia, her sons, and her daughter Zubeena have returned from their time on the island. Zubeena vacillates between studying nursing at university or healing on the island. Liu has agreed to apprentice her with him for the present until she decides. Also, Kirani has finished his high school studies and wishes to go to your Massachusetts Institute of Technology."

"Does it offer more than the island provides?"

"Considering the events of the last year—your bracelet being recognized, Marcus knowing where to find you—we believe outside training shall benefit us through Kirani and others. We have underestimated the impact of social media on information sharing. He also wishes to continue to live here to be near his family and would commute to MIT when necessary but mainly live here and complete much of his work online."

"That will make Christopher happy. He would miss Kirani if he lived elsewhere. Going back and forth will make him more visible, though. Anyone associated with us or more specifically, me, is a potential pawn, a preferred target for Marcus and his like."

Master Kai studied Jasirey for a moment. "I see I have made a grave error in assuming that Nikolai and his team's usurpation of your tour of the security center when you last visited the island did not interfere in your receipt of the information we wished to convey. I do not believe it sufficient to simply tell you of our endeavors to keep your family and friends safe. I shall confer with the council on how to remedy that."

"All right," Jasirey said. "I'll be happy to see Mtombe, but I assume he hasn't come just to visit."

"He wishes to speak to Ian regarding a human relief agency in Africa for young men forcibly conscripted into armies and eventually released with no homes or families to return to." Master Kai's expression sobered. "I also wished to speak to you alone to guide you in approaching Kharia and her children."

Jasirey drew herself up tight. "You mean so I don't overwhelm them with my feelings."

"Your concern for their welfare would override any other impulse. My concern rests on the possibility of constraint to the point of unnaturalness. The goal of your training is for you to gain trust in your instincts, not to muzzle them."

❦ ❦ ❦

Jasirey tapped one of her four husbands, Fael, for information on Islamic mourning traditions.

"Islamic tradition is fairly straightforward," he said. "The widow observes a period of four months and ten days when she shall not remarry, which rules out pregnancy and, therefore, inheritance issues. She must also show discreet behavior out of respect for the departed."

"Straightforward and efficient," Jasirey said, "but not really useful for how to approach Kharia emotionally."

"Do not worry, loved one. You shall know what to do."

Jasirey gathered flowers from the garden for Kharia and walked to the duplex outside the compound where the family lived.

The women hugged for a long moment. "I've missed you," Jasirey said.

Kharia's teenage boys Kirani and Bazir had never been embarrassed when Jasirey hugged them, which gave a feeling of warmth and belonging. Except at that moment—nothing. Surprised disappointment flashed in their eyes and caused a painful twinge in Jasirey's heart.

"Forgive me," she said. "Training has confused me a bit." She took their hands and smiled with her love for them.

The teenagers beamed back at her.

Kharia's older daughter Zubeena returned Jasirey's hug without a hint of shyness, and Jasirey made room for another in her heart.

❦ ❦ ❦

Mtombe, staying at the main house, joined Jasirey's family for dinner. Tired from the long journey, Master Kai, also staying there, retired early to his room with a dinner tray.

Mtombe had been slightly acquainted with Kharia's family when they all lived on the island, and he greeted them before turning to Jasirey to kiss her cheeks.

"You've found your calling," Jasirey said. "Purpose and contentment shine all around you."

"Yes, lady. Confusing, however. It seems wrong to feel good in the face of the suffering I have witnessed."

"Finding your path is a big deal, something to celebrate. I'm happy for you," Jasirey told him.

Her sincerity lightened a burden Mtombe had not been aware he carried—guilt for leaving her service despite the vows he'd taken as a Protector to always put her first.

Everyone sat in the dining room, and Jasirey asked Mtombe to tell them about his work. "So many displaced people," she said, "It must be difficult for them to maintain hope."

"Yes, the young people especially," Mtombe said, "their lives upended, the years when they would have learned a trade or some other means of a livelihood gone. Though it sounds unrelated, I have come to consult you, Ian. I am told your company studies geological satellites that track the temperature of land. Healthy plants give off water, like sweating, as I understand it, and cool the land. Unhealthy plants and areas of insufficient water show on the satellite pictures as hot spots."

Kirani fairly bounced in his seat. "These are the areas of study I want to pursue. Computers compile information from satellites and make predictions from known data. Too much water retention can predict mosquito populations and possible malaria outbreaks." At his mother's incredulous stare, he said, "I read about it in an environmental magazine."

Mtombe smiled at the young man. "Perhaps we shall work together one day. The program shall be especially important in areas where poor phone service, bad roads, or unstable authority structures—the very places where many of the young men we help will reside—make information on crop and animal failure difficult to track. Isolated spots of famine are easier to turn around before they become widespread and harder to halt."

"They can even track water holes for nomadic tribes," Kirani said, "and give daily water level reports to them, maybe on satellite phones if cell phones don't work."

Ian smiled at the boy and said to Mtombe, "Seems you two ought to consult with the corporation's environmental team. I'll set it up."

The two excited young men thanked him.

Sitting next to Kharia, Jasirey squeezed her hand, the women united in their shared love for Kirani. To Mtombe she said, "I assume this kind of information could lessen the number of environmental refugees, but what about those fleeing from war or political persecution?"

He nodded. "I think my work shall center on children torn from their homes and forced to become soldiers, many before they reached puberty." He glanced at the teenagers.

Jasirey understood his concern, whispered with Kharia, then gave Mtombe their permission to speak freely.

"I met a man in his late twenties," he said, "whose village had been overrun by a militant group when he was a boy. They lined the males up on one side and the females on the other, then asked one boy if he wished to join the rebels. He wished to go home, and they shot him. Another boy's mother was asked to become a bush wife—a woman who cleans, cooks, and provides sex for the soldiers. They killed her when she pushed one of the soldiers away."

Mtombe's eyes glinted. "The remaining boys, of course, agreed to be conscripted. They were plied with drugs and sent into targeted villages to draw fire so the seasoned soldiers could pinpoint the location of any resistance. Just children, those boys walked in guns blazing and left with no idea of how many they wounded or killed, provided they themselves survived."

Lee leaned toward Mtombe. "Consider contacting Amador. She has returned to the island but was a recruiter in central Africa for ten years. She made many contacts. Who knows? Some might have information on the boys or men you hope to help."

"Thank you. I shall contact her," Mtombe said.

"Can you tell us a bit more about the man you met?" Jasirey asked.

"He suffers from nightmares and impulsive behavior. He had been accepted to the US as a political refugee, but few countries, not even the States when refugees first started arriving, allocated sufficient resources to work with those suffering from the emotional wounds of war and displacement.

"He and other boys and men I have talked to fear psychological therapy, the stain of being crazy—their words—that would contaminate their families and their futures. This one man, an addict after his experience and with no knowledge of US laws or cultures, committed a few minor crimes and was deported." Dark sorrow filled Mtombe's eyes.

"I read something about these child soldiers," Jasirey said. "They miss crucial stages of their psychological development. The article suggested that instead of encouraging them to get psychiatric help, they should be told they need to learn skills for coping with the abnormal situations they were forced to endure."

Mtombe lit up at her caring. "I hope to provide the transitional skills they need to rejoin the world, but finding a home for them is hampered by the current political climate, everyone afraid of terrorists invading their countries, of poor vetting processes. Many have no birth certificates or even knowledge of their age, no proof of relationships to family who may already live in a country where they seek asylum. A fifteen-year-old with a beard may be suspected of lying to pass as a minor."

"A difficult task," Fael said, "but I cannot imagine more important or rewarding work."

Mtombe's hand unfurled toward Jasirey. "We have the hope that our lady's work will in coming generations lessen the need for mine."

❧ ❧ ❧

Ian took seriously what Mtombe said about Jasirey, and that night asked for Lee, Liu, and Fael's input on what her world mission ought to entail and how they might be instrumental in encouraging her to branch out.

"She has shown no interest in outside pursuits," Fael said. "I doubt she desires to split her energies much from us and the children."

"I don't mean activities for her entertainment," Ian said. "I witnessed Jasirey's impact at the corporate party—her presence, her effect on others."

Lee thought out loud. "As in she can set the stage for the children."

"She has changed our world immeasurably," Liu said. "So much more might be accomplished with her boundless love."

Fael rose to pace. "What more can be expected of her? She does not have boundless energy or strength despite that stubbornness of hers. If she feels responsible for another's welfare—and when does our wife not?—she will pursue it until all possible aid is rendered."

"Mm, that's a point." Ian massaged his neck. "So how do we prompt her toward her destiny while preventing it from becoming overwhelming?"

The next morning, they invited Master Kai to weigh in at the training building.

"You and the children shall always be her first priority," he said. "We must also consider her physical health. That cannot be threatened. Prophecy predicts more children. Allowing her to become overwhelmed by outside concerns is contrary to that goal. I recommend a slow, uncomplicated introduction with no long-term commitments."

The husbands glanced at one another.

The old master smiled. "Begin with a social setting our lady can comfortably handle physically and emotionally, perhaps a visit to the man she connected to at your party, Ian."

"We might manage that with minimal security problems," Fael said.

"Master, Europe has different attitudes from the States," Liu said. "Do you consider it prudent to dispense with our cover story?"

"Legal marriage there is also between two people. Introduce Ian as Jasirey's husband and leave the rest to speculation, often far more interesting than the tamer truth, yes?" Master Kai's eyes twinkled. "The various stories your curious family engenders shall be sufficient to entertain and distract in the short term."

Ian called Reginald, who suggested a visit in September during his vacation when he'd be free to entertain them properly.

"Reginald," Ian said diplomatically, "we have a large contingent of people—family, friends, and security. It's probably more convenient to rent a house nearby. You'd be aware of anything suitable."

"Nonsense," Reginald said. "This house has sat empty for far too long. There are plenty of guestrooms and a separate carriage house, if you prefer, for your security. It will please my staff to have a more stimulating task than caring for one old bachelor."

"A small estate, didn't you say?"

"Size is a relative term here. I sold a good portion of the land once belonging to the property. The manor has ample space."

Ian decided to be blunt. "Reginald, we'd be bringing four babies nearly ten months old."

Reginald hesitated for only a beat. "My housekeeper will be thrilled to air out the nursery. She has long despaired at its neglect." He looked forward to what promised to be an interesting visit.

"That's very kind of you. Jasirey will be excited to see you."

"I beg your pardon?"

"A nickname for Shannon. We don't use it outside the family."

Reginald understood the implication perfectly. Though flattered to be included in their inner circle, he was curious why they hid it from outsiders and even more perplexed when Ian stated that, with Reginald's permission, safety precautions required him to send a team beforehand to secure the estate. Reginald graciously consented and agreed to speak again when Ian finalized plans on his end.

Christopher and Michael asked their mother if Kirani and Bazir could go to England with the family. Jasirey promised to ask Kharia.

"Such a fine opportunity for them," Kharia said when Jasirey asked her. "They should experience the world to better fulfill their dreams of serving your children."

Ian invited Jesse and Lill. Since Jasirey no longer needed medical care beyond routine checkups that Jesse handled and, since he didn't handle pediatrics, the families had gotten together less often. Jesse and Lill loved the idea.

Jasirey also asked Lizzie, but her doctor didn't recommend such extensive traveling. Jasirey suggested to Everett that he come along and visit his sons. She hoped to meet them. After adding the security people, no room remained on the plane for Satoko and Mashita.

Jasirey broke the news. "I thought you might want to visit your brothers, sisters, and friends in Japan. You haven't seen them since you moved to the island."

"A gentle hint," Mashita said, "that it is time to face going home. We have been discussing this, the good it would do us to see the healing of the devastation wrought by the tsunami." Feeling the loss of family and friends years before, Mashita knew that without their lady having provided a purpose and healing for them, they could not have faced going home.

Satoko hugged Jasirey. "You have somehow shouldered some of our burden, supported and encouraged us. I bless the day you came into our lives."

❦ ❦ ❦

Jasirey helped slice strawberries for Everett to make into a pie. "Are you comfortable with the guys' plan to introduce the families?"

Everett smiled. Ian had presented the idea as fait accompli—an old-fashioned, weekend-long party at Reginald's estate, to which Everett's family was invited. "I expect the pomp and circumstance to overwhelm my sons and daughters-in-law and stop them from wondering overlong how all the pieces of this family fit together."

Jasirey lightly perched her chin on his shoulder. "I want them to be comfortable with us, so they'll come visit you here next year."

"Not to worry. They shall adore you if for no other reason than their old man does."

She laughed and kissed his cheek. "I adore you, too." She checked the kitchen clock. "Ooh, I'll be late." Kai and The Five waited for her at the training building.

For their next assignment, Master Kai ordered Nikolai, Chen, Andwar, Sajan, and Favian to step up the difficulty of Jasirey's training in the weeks left before her vacation. She had progressed faster than expected.

"This morning," he said, "I wish to see our lady's defensive capability."

Unnaturally quiet, the Protectors stood, hands folded, while waiting for Jasirey to initiate the exercise. It made her nervous and then pissed. She hated being the aggressor. "Just start."

One by one, the men mounted no-holds-barred attacks. Unable to keep anything else in mind, Jasirey fell into the familiar dance—block, anticipate, countermove. They kept it up, giving her no room to breathe. She grew tired of reacting. *Watch for openings. Push back.*

Andwar landed on his backside with no understanding of how he got there. Jasirey had never attacked them before. His gaze flitted from her set face to Master Kai. She wasn't playing.

Master Kai signaled to continue two-on-one.

Nikolai sent Jasirey sprawling and hoped she would stay down.

Chen put out his hand to help her up. She planted her feet in his gut and sent him flying over her head.

Favian dropped to pin her to the floor, but she anticipated, and he landed on the mat.

Sajan moved forward warily and stopped short with his hands clawing at his clothing. The crawling-worm sensation ended abruptly. Sajan goggled at Jasirey.

The heat The Five had barely registered as emanating from her dropped in a rush along with her color.

"I'm sorry, Sajan," Jasirey said.

The young men instinctively stepped toward their agitated lady.

She stepped back and turned toward Kai. "This isn't working. I need—" She speared two fingers into her temple.

Andwar pulled her into his arms. "Stop." Her every muscle resisted him. "Lady, you're pissing me off."

Surprise trembled through her, and he cupped her face. "Why are you so hard on yourself? We all train bodily and mentally, but your gifts are new and untested. None of us knows precisely how to guide you. We're learning together, and it is an honor." He kissed her forehead and released her.

Chen kissed her hand. "It was a good move."

Sajan gave a smile tinged with embarrassment. "You had the advantage, disarmed me completely but did not follow through, which must come as naturally as the countermove."

Jasirey wanted to argue but recognized the wisdom. "I hate having to even think about doing this stuff. It's taking me a while to accept it. I appreciate your patience."

A positive step forward, Master Kai thought.

Jasirey invited Mtombe to help put the babies to bed the evening before he was scheduled to leave. He learned to change diapers, hold a bottle, read stories to sleepy young ones, and lay them in their cribs. He'd never have believed such homely chores could be so stirring. Jasirey's gentle touches, loving expressions, and soft vocal intonations—motherly love—made Mtombe's breath catch. Though pleased to help, he puzzled over being asked.

"I have reasons," she answered the question she saw in his mind. She smiled at his mute shock and led him to the sitting room in her bedroom.

Mtombe was not sure her husbands would consider his presence there appropriate.

"You feel that you are on or at least approaching your destined path," Jasirey said as she handed him a mug of tea. "Where do you stand in your role as a Protector of Jasirey?"

Mtombe gulped his tea. "Pardon?"

For a moment, his lady looked sad. The urge to hold her made him set down his mug.

"You heard my prophesy. The Imperiat believe the second pregnancy will not be fathered by my husbands."

To combat hyperventilating, Mtombe struggled to remember his training. "Are . . . are you asking me . . . ?" He cleared his throat. "What are you saying?"

Jasirey laughed. She couldn't help it. He looked so flustered. "Poor man. You look exactly like I felt when presented with the destiny of Jasirey."

A strange way to phrase it, he thought. "I believed you supported my leaving the Devoted. Have you changed your mind?"

"I supported you leaving the island, Mtombe, to find a future you couldn't find there, not the Devoted."

"Forgive me, lady. I still do not follow."

"How could you? No one could follow my absurd, completely weird life."

Mtombe's pique vanished. "It is an unusually complicated life, yet you seem successful at it. Is that merely a façade?"

A peaceful ease pervaded his senses and shattered again when she said, "You are my wild boar from the prophecy, which you have already fulfilled by saving me from Marcus. I have no idea what else can be expected of you."

Unable to sit still, Mtombe rose as he said, "Except you do not see the spirit animals of every Protector, just those of your . . . "

"Husbands. Yes, I know." Her sadness returned. "You are too young for any such commitment, and I'm not sure I want one, either."

Mtombe grabbed Jasirey's shoulders and pulled her resisting body toward him. "Please relax. I would never hurt you." He cradled her head against his shoulder. "You do not say, as I would have expected, that you reject the idea."

When she did not reply, he simply held her.

Eventually, she patted him on the shoulder and stepped back. "I'll see you in the morning to say goodbye. You have your work. I have a trip to England to prepare for."

Mtombe smiled. "Plenty of time to contemplate our futures." His brow furrowed. "We shall see each other soon, though?"

Jasirey reached up to kiss his cheek. "We will. I promise."

After prayers that evening, Jasirey told Ian, Lee, Liu, and Fael that Mtombe fulfilled prophecy as her wild boar.

"We saw plainly that you cast your spell over him," Fael said.

Jasirey sighed. "I wonder if that's a good thing or cruel."

England

During the latter half of August, Fael borrowed Nikolai's team to assist in the larger farm fields. Mirai helped Jasirey harvest her garden and plant seeds in the greenhouse for cool-weather greens to transfer to the garden after they returned from England.

Mirai suggested adding honeybee hives for propagation. She knew one of the people at the compound had studied beekeeping.

The town contacted the family with their belief that a beaver dam on the family's property must be destroyed, since it blocked a culvert meant to prevent flooding of a town road.

Jasirey studied the species and various compromises when their natural behavior became problematic for humans. The pond created by the family of beavers provided a home for blue herons and other water birds, turtles, and who knew how many other species. She suggested running a pipe through the dam and out the culvert that could be capped when water levels remained unthreatening and opened when they rose.

As Ian offered to assume the cost, the town agreed.

While researching their property lines, Jasirey discovered that one corner bordered Quabbin Reservoir, the world's largest manmade reservoir devoted to providing public drinking water. At dinner that night, she talked about the four towns leveled and more than two thousand citizens and even graves displaced to allow a dam and dikes to hold back the waters of the Swift and Ware rivers to be delivered by gravity and cleaned through natural filtration as drinking water to Metropolitan Boston. She found the teens' reactions interesting glimpses into their personalities.

Fire in his eyes, Michael said, "They can't do that. How can they do that? Take people's homes and everything?"

Head canted as though searching for answers, Bazir said, "That's a lot of people to move, but the number of people needing the water was much greater."

"In class last year, we learned about the Nipmuc Native Americans," Christopher said, "who lived here in the Pioneer Valley and in central Massachusetts and Connecticut. We took the land from them first. Quabbin is their word for the meeting of many waters."

"An engineering feat," Kirani said, "the reservoir took years to build and seven just for it to fill with water."

Jasirey decided to take them to see the beaver family. Mirai and several of her squad accompanied her—Christopher, Michael, Kirani, Bazir, Zubeena, and a few of the people off for the day—on a hike to the pond near the outskirts of the property. Everyone enjoyed Jasirey's stories of the animals not found on the island of the Devoted, animals that mated for life and nurtured their offspring for years, older siblings helping with the younger along with continual dam and lodge repairs.

As they neared the pond, Mirai directed everyone to move quietly and stay behind trees. The beavers ate poplars and other softer wood trees. It kept them from overrunning the forest and allowed hardier maples and oaks to thrive.

Christopher managed the courage to join Zubeena behind the trunk of a pin oak wide enough to hide both teenagers. He mentally kicked himself when he realized he couldn't talk to her. Then she smiled at him, an image he would carry for a long time.

Yearling beaver cavorted around a lodge made of branches and mud. In the pond shallows, a mother moose and calf pulled up water weeds that provided nutrients they could no longer glean from the forest. After late spring, trees produced a substance that made their leaves indigestible. The adult moose kept a keen eye on the beavers hauling young leafy branches to their lodge and anchoring them underwater as food for the winter. The beavers kept a wary eye on the moose who would find their larder a tasty snack.

The husbands brought Jasirey into Boston for an overnight stay for clothes shopping and invited Lizzie, partly as a consolation gift for her having to miss the trip to England. She knew designers, trends, what was fashionable, and what most definitely would not do.

Jasirey truly had no idea what constituted fashion. She knew the styles, colors, and accessories she found comfortable and decided that was what mattered.

A chance in a lifetime, Lizzie thought. She had long despaired of ever eliciting Jasirey's interest in haute couture. *Well, more coerced by her husbands.* It worked for Lizzie.

Jasirey went along good-naturedly but put her foot down on items priced outrageously simply because they sported a famous name on the label. Lizzie pouted, but Jasirey held her ground. She did agree to a large-brimmed sunhat Lizzie insisted everyone wore in England.

"Good." Jasirey grabbed it. "It would look very cute on Ian." She wrestled it onto his bald and easily burned head.

He evaded and with a hand on either side of the brim, secured it on top of her silver waves to pull her in for a kiss. "Yes, the perfect hat," he said. "We'll take it."

Lizzie loved bling. Jasirey thought the word had gone out of fashion, but Lizzie adopted it as if she'd invented it. Jasirey absolutely refused any more jewels or clothing loaded with sparkly stuff except for one evening gown. Relieving the plain black of a square neckline and wide shoulder straps, brilliant crystals flowed down the skirt in vertical lines close together at the waist and widening to two handbreadths apart at the hem.

When Jasirey stepped out of the dressing room, "Oh, baby," Lizzie reacted in chorus with her husbands' whistles. Only the length needed adjustment.

They bought Lizzie a cerulean dress with lighter blue and clear glass stones across the bodice and up the multiple, thin shoulder straps that met at the back in a large oval of rhinestones. The deep tone of the skirt made Lizzie's bright blue eyes pop. She loved it even before she tried it on and gave only a token protest at the cost. The dress required substantial adjustment to the length and padding in the bodice.

Later that night, dressed in conservative dark suits, white shirts, and ties, the men escorted the women to an elegant restaurant that included a dance floor and live orchestra. Jasirey left her bracelet at home and wore her fire opals surrounded by rubies and diamonds with the burgundy dress she had worn for the legal marriage to Ian. The jewels overwhelmed the new black dress she hadn't expected to buy and wanted to save for England.

Lizzie goggled as they rode the elevator down from their rooms to the lobby. "Now, that's what I call bling."

Jasirey smiled serenely. "No, it's called elegant."

"And lovely," Ian said.

"Whipped," Lizzie stage whispered.

Ian endeavored to appear intimidating. "See if I give you your present."

Lizzie drew up her two-inch-heel-bolstered five feet. "It'd take a crowbar to get this rig off my bod. Mine." Her brows drawn in what she intended as a menacing frown, she looked as threatening as a lamb.

Ian laughed. "I meant your other present." He leaned down as her attitude shifted with a bat of eyelashes. "See my wife, Lizzie? Think any other woman has a chance to sway me?"

Lizzie deflated. "Pooh. Nobody can compete with her." She watched people in the lobby staring at Jasirey with admiration, some of them fascinated, all under the thrall of her smile. "She isn't the youngest or the most beautiful woman here, but it doesn't matter when she zeroes in on you like you're the most important person in the room."

Ian lightly draped an arm over Lizzie's shoulders. "She has power, a great gift. As you pointed out, she's meant to interact in the world."

A shiver of fear Lizzie didn't understand prickled through her. "You'll always be by her side, right?"

He squeezed gently. "Always." From his pocket materialized a choker of small diamonds and a pinkie-nail-sized sapphire that he clasped about her neck. Ian turned her toward a mirror.

Lizzie's eyes became huge. "Holy shit, Ian." Desperately wanting to ask while knowing it rude, she grabbed his arm and blushed furiously. She didn't ask.

Jasirey joined them and hugged her friend's waist. "Yes, they're real." Tears filled Lizzie's eyes. "Brace up," Jasirey admonished, "or you'll ruin your makeup."

Lizzie sniffed. "It's waterproof."

"Oh, well, go ahead then. Personally, I'd rather eat. I'm starving."

"Yeah," Lizzie said, "me, too. Thank you, Ian, so much." She tiptoed to kiss his cheek.

He still had to bend. "Your friendship is thanks enough."

A limo transported them to a restaurant with enough elegance and fanfare to intimidate Lizzie. At least she knew which utensil went with what—for the most part.

On the dance floor, Lizzie preferred Liu and Fael for height compatibility and felt like an Irish fairy with Lee. Despite his grace, her feet occasionally left the floor. He set her down gently each time. After the third time, she suspected he did it on purpose. Too bad for her, smacking him was not an option in such a swanky place. She tired faster than desired and may have pushed herself, but Ian noticed and escorted her to their table.

The party soon returned to the limo. Lizzie sighed contentedly. "Do you remember, Shannon, when we first met? Bobby called us Mutt and Jeff, and my kids thought he was calling us a couple of dogs." Her husband had been gone nearly two years, and she reminisced with more fondness than regret, though what she wouldn't give for one more dance with him.

Back at the hotel suite, Lizzie wanted a long soak in her bathroom's jet tub and hoped to sleep soundly. Going by the constant touches and gooey glances, she judged the men had other ideas for Jasirey.

Lizzie hugged her friend. "I'm tired," she said. "I'm gonna love you and leave you." She snickered as she waved a hand at the men. "Bet your salivating pack's planning on loving you and not leaving you alone anytime soon."

Jasirey laughed and drew her husbands to the master bedroom. The bed was too small to hold them all, so the men got creative. Clothes were removed and hung up. Jasirey wore a one-piece corset that pushed her breasts to an enticing fullness and had a slit opening at the crotch. Fingers, tongues, and the male anatomy fit through fine—against the wall, her body draped over an upholstered chair, legs over Lee's broad shoulders, and kneeling on the bed.

Every nerve ending tingling and too wiped out to open her eyes, Jasirey gladly let her men remove the undergarment. Two of them cuddled her between them.

She woke up in the morning with Liu and Ian. She considered rubbing against them and teasing them awake but really had to pee. She came out of the bathroom to lay a gentle hand on Liu's shoulder. Her soft voice woke both men instantly. Not worried, she figured they'd just gotten a little rowdy the night before.

"I don't think it's anything serious, but I'm spotting, and it's not time for my period."

Liu had her lie down and pressed on her abdomen. "Any pain?" She shook her head. He retrieved his bag and some gloves. Lubricating two fingers, he examined her for swelling or abrasions. A tiny amount of blood pooled in the canal, nothing else amiss. "I think you are fine, precious one. Since we are here, however, I shall call for Jesse's opinion."

To be on the safe side, Jesse asked his office staff to set up an appointment for him to examine her.

Jasirey, Ian, and Liu joined Lee, Fael, and Lizzie in the sitting room for breakfast. The plan had been to visit a few more stores before heading home. Lizzie plotted and suggested that Lee and Fael take her to pick out the casual outfits Jasirey still needed and everyone meet at the airport.

Jasirey pulled Lee and Fael aside. "Don't let her buy anything outlandish."

Lee hugged her. "Don't worry. My size intimidates her—sometimes."

Jasirey laughed and kissed them both. "Good luck."

Jesse's eyes crinkled at Jasirey. "And what were you up to last night?"

"Nothing you and Lill wouldn't do."

"We're not into the group thing," he whispered. "I might come off second best."

Jasirey eyed him fondly. "Highly doubtful."

"Any abdominal cramping or other pain?"

"No," she assured him.

"I read in your records that your family history includes uterine cancer. I'd like to take a biopsy of your uterine lining to rule out any problems."

Jesse explained the procedure and inserted a speculum. He first took a pap smear, then introduced the biopsy instrument into the cervical opening. Jasirey breathed through immediate cramping. The procedure required less than five minutes.

"All done," said Jesse. "You did fine. Feeling okay?"

"It wasn't really any worse than what I experience with my period."

He patted her shoulder. "Go ahead and enjoy your day. There may be some spotting and cramping, so nothing too active. I'll call with the results. I don't see anything out of order. Spotting is common in perimenopause."

The three adults joined the others on the plane back to the compound. The men pushed worry aside and kept the conversation light and positive.

The only one completely unconcerned, Jasirey knew her destiny did not include cancer—for the moment anyway.

Lizzie enjoyed embroidering her own tales of shopping victories and disappointing woes when prudish husbands interfered. She showed off the jewel-toned skirts and slacks she'd purchased along with several blouses in lighter hues. Jasirey complimented her friend on a job well done. She especially liked a white bolero jacket that would make casual clothes dressier.

On the ride to the compound after another of their drivers left to bring a happy and tired Lizzie home, Lee and Fael wanted clarification on what perimenopause entails.

"Simply," Liu said, "it is the time before menopause when symptoms of changing hormones begin. It may last years before cessation of menstrual cycles, though those cycles often become more sporadic as menopause approaches."

"Surely Jasirey is too young for menopause," Fael said.

"The average age is from the late forties to early fifties."

"And fertility?" Lee asked.

"Drops dramatically in the forties."

Jasirey watched Fael and Lee ruminate over that with troubled faces. Ian looked out at the scenery. "You worried I'm getting too old for a second pregnancy?" she said.

Fael's gold eyes washed over her. "No beloved, not in the sense of becoming pregnant since you have done so once already. I am concerned about the physical repercussions to you."

"The council told me that because I saw the second pregnancy, it's a done deal. I'm not convinced. I don't want more kids."

"More children or more lovers to father them?" Liu asked.

"Either." Her arms crossed over her torso.

Sitting beside her, Lee pulled her against his chest. "Little one, do you fear our reaction or not trust our support for the choices you must make to further your mission?"

“Would you be as opposed,” Liu asked, “to a pregnancy through in vitro fertilization?”

That caught Jasirey off guard, and she had to admit, no, she wouldn’t. “Could I do that?” she asked.

“A poor option, precious one,” Liu said. “My intention was to point out that your true aversion to a second pregnancy is needing other fathers.”

“Be clear, beloved,” Fael said, “we do not object to the necessity of other lovers.”

Ian caressed her troubled face. “Lee, Liu, and Fael have made it as plain as they can that they support your destiny. I introduced you to this life and have no right to sway you with my ambivalence, which isn’t about more kids. It’s the role of the fathers in the family that throws me, and we can work that out.”

* * *

Jesse called Jasirey with her test results—negative—a welcome relief to her husbands.

Jasirey researched weather in the UK to figure out what to pack for four teenagers, four babies, and four husbands. During September, temperature in the UK county of Surrey where Reginald lived ranged from fifty degrees to nearly seventy with about eight and a half inches of rain. That sounded heavenly to Jasirey after wilting over the summer through several brutal heat waves in New England.

Delicately broaching the subject of clothes for Kirani and Bazir with Kharia, Jasirey described the weekend party planned in England and traditional clothing worn to such an affair. She suggested that since the family had invited Kharia’s sons, they should buy suits and casual wear for them at the same time they purchased Michael and Christopher’s.

Used to bartering goods and services on the island, Kharia accepted without a qualm. The farm and compound generated many jobs her sons could do in return.

A week later, everyone climbed aboard Ian’s private jet. He had decided to pilot the plane in order to leave one more seat for security, which included Yusef and Mirai. Kimika and Nikolai’s team had flown over the week before. Devoted from the island or nearby countries would be deployed as required, especially for the party.

"Poor Reggie, he may feel like the barbarian hordes are descending," Jasirey said as she watched people filling the plane's seats.

They made a short stop in Boston for an excited Jesse and Lill, and then the party was off. Teething and unable to crawl and explore as usual, the babies fussed. The adults and teens took turns entertaining them and were considerably relieved when they finally napped. Many of the adults and the teenagers also slept.

Out of sorts and edgy, Jasirey paced. Liu pulled her down onto his lap, rubbed her back, and nibbled on her ear and neck.

"There's no privacy on this plane, mister," she said. "Knock it off."

"Let us see what can be done about that." Mischief simmered in his eyes. He grasped his wife's hand and pulled her along to the bathroom.

"You're kidding. Everyone's going to know what we're up to."

"Most are sleeping. Those who are not can find their own partner." Liu plopped her derriere on the counter and wrapped her legs about his hips. His lips grazed over hers. His dexterous physician's fingers kneaded, stroked, and coaxed her resistance into the erotic adventure of the moment.

For access, they removed or realigned clothes, and Jasirey drew Liu closer with legs and arms until their bodies joined. He kept to a gentle pace, sunk in deeply, and rotated against her clitoris.

Plucking her nipples, he thrust in time to Jasirey's escalating breaths. Her lips pressed together to prevent her sweet sex noises. Liu laughed softly and plunged harder. She clamped her teeth onto his shoulder, erupted around him and he in her wet, heated body.

Liu leaned on her while waiting for his legs to steady, then carefully withdrew and removed a condom.

Jasirey glanced at it in wonder. "I didn't even notice you put that on."

He lifted her down. "You feel the hormonal changes of ovulation, precious one."

"Huh, glad you knew that."

Liu kissed her affectionately and handed her paper towels to clean herself while he cleaned the counter. "Your cycle has not yet evened out since the birth."

Jasirey twined her arms about his neck. "Never was what you'd call regular." She grinned impishly. "I'm embarrassed to go back out there. It was worth it, though."

Liu's kiss expressed definite agreement.

Jasirey kept her eyes glued to the floor as they returned to their seats.

"Problem?" Lee drawled.

"No comments from the peanut gallery," Liu said, pleased with himself. His wife had relaxed sufficiently to sleep.

Lee closed his eyes. "I call dibs on the way back."

"Oh, good God." Jasirey cringed in her seat as Lill and Jesse snickered.

Later, the babies woke, ate, and chewed contentedly on teething toys.

Jasirey brought sandwiches to Ian and his co-pilot.

"I was beginning to think we'd been forgotten," Ian said.

Jasirey nuzzled his ear. "Not a chance." She handed the copilot his lunch. "You guys will be awfully tired by the time we arrive."

"Probably," Ian said, "but we'll get some rest at the hotel and be fine."

While not an overly long drive from Fair Oaks Airport to Reginald's estate in Mole Valley, it was too much on top of the seven-hour plane trip. They'd decided to wait for morning.

"Kiss me and go back to the babies," Ian directed.

She complied and did a thorough job of it.

The co-pilot, also a Protector, appreciated the lovely image of her bending over her husband.

* * *

The airport lay less than five miles outside Woking, one of the largest cities in Surrey, the county with the most forested land and the UK business center for many corporations, including Ian's.

A car waited to take Everett to his family in London. The rest of the group piled into rented vans that soon delivered them to their hotel. After tea and a short rest, everyone wanted to exercise muscles complaining from sitting too long.

When planning the vacation, the family had decided to stay in and explore London on the way back to the States. That left one afternoon for sightseeing in Woking.

Centuries ago, the beginning settlement of the city, Old Woking included the ruins of Woking Palace, a royal residence during the Tudor period. Kings Henry VII and Henry VIII, and Queen Elizabeth I had all resided in the palace at times during their reigns.

Jasirey had studied the Tudor dynasty in college and wanted to visit the ruins. Part of a park, the area would also have plenty of grassy areas where her toddlers could run around. She also wanted to see the Shah Jahan Mosque built in 1889 and the first building purposely built for Muslim worship in the UK. It included a central prayer hall roofed by an onion dome and topped by a crescent finial.

Jasirey, Ian, Fael, the toddlers, Jesse, and Lill rode in one van followed by Mirai and several of her security squad in an SUV. Yusef followed Lee, Liu, and the teenagers who chose to see the statue of the author H. G. Wells unveiled in 2016 and one of the Martian tripods unveiled in 1998—used in Wells's book *The War of the Worlds* to transport Martians on earth.

Written in the 1890s, much of the *War of the Worlds* takes place in the Woking area. Lee and Liu admired the book. The teenagers had seen the movie with Tom Cruise several times.

Both groups agreed to meet up at the Living Planet Centre opened by David Attenborough in 2013. The building provided headquarters for the UK branch of World Wide Fund for Nature, was noted for a barrel-vaulted roof over its atrium, and contained a learning zone open to visitors.

After returning to the hotel, everyone had dinner together in one of the hotel's private dining rooms.

Christopher and Michael enthusiastically described for their mom the old buildings they'd seen that reminded them of movie versions of *A Christmas Carol* she loved and watched every year.

The adults had packed legless highchairs with the baby gear they had brought with them and attached them to individual dining chairs for the babies who barely managed to get through the meal before falling asleep. If they slept to a reasonable morning hour UK time, they'd be well on their way to adjusting to the time difference. If not, the next day would prove difficult.

Lee and Fael stayed with Jasirey in the master bedroom. Lee's dimples deepened. "I fear I may need a sleeping aid, it being so early our time." Apparently apprised by Liu of her cycle's status, he dangled a condom at Jasirey.

She smiled in mock sympathy. "You must have endured a great deal of discomfort to find one that fits."

“You start, little man,” Lee said, ignoring Jasirey’s comment.

Fael understood Lee’s intention and felt sorry for his beloved, but friendship also required loyalty, so he cooperated and began a slow seduction. He trailed whisper-light fingertips over her skin followed by nipping teeth. He soothed the faint marks he left with his warm, versatile tongue.

Jasirey’s lips parted to ease her heightened breathing, and Fael covered them with his, nudging them farther apart as he plundered the soft depths of her mouth. He nestled between her thighs, slid through her slick valley, and felt her clitoris swell. He entered gently, then rapidly built their rhythm until her hips rose and fell in frantic need. He let himself go and left her writhing on the brink of release.

Lee brushed away Jasirey’s clutching hands and held down her torso, which bowed up with the need for completion. He teased—light touches and kisses, lazy swipes of his tongue over her breasts and lower as he waited for her to calm before beginning another torturously slow build-up that had his wife mewling. He thrust deeply as her nails bit into his back and red-hot lust surged through his veins. The viselike spasms of her climax hurled Lee into a realm of pure sensation where he registered nothing but their bodies clasped together.

Afterward, Jasirey sprawled between her men, dewed in sweat, too sated to move or speak. The men thought it a good look on her.

Reginald's Estate

The babies' sleep varied between eight and nine hours. Jasirey woke feeling fine. The rest of the adults and the teens dragged themselves to breakfast.

Liu made a large batch of his restorative drink with herbs he'd brought along. Even the babies had a small amount in their sippy cups. The group repacked the little they had unpacked and stuffed bags into a cargo van. The travelers fit snugly into two passenger vans.

Most napped on the drive and, along with Liu's drink, felt better. They passed through London's urban sprawl until it dwindled, and they entered a lush forest that eventually thinned and opened to wide expanses of lawn, hedges, and gardens. An enormous building rose in the center. The road ended in a circular drive that continued around to the back of the manor. Wide granite stairs led up to the entrance.

Reginald came down the steps followed by a butler in a suit with coattails that Michael had once hoped Everett would wear.

Kimika, Nikolai, Chen, Andwar, Favian, and Sajan greeted everyone and helped unload the luggage.

Well acquainted with the stress of traveling, Reginald kindly suggested they save the introductions for inside.

Jasirey kissed his cheek as he offered his arm and ushered her into a cavernous entrance. "Reggie," she said, "the house is amazing."

A broad central staircase lent itself to romantic visions of elegantly dressed people sweeping down for a ball. Ornately carved brocade-upholstered chairs and accent tables sat between numerous doorways. Paintings and objets d'art looked to have been in the house for generations.

Her pleasure washed over Reginald and made him see his home anew. Pleased the house did not disappoint, he led the group to a massive parlor.

With knee-high sills, windows stretched up close to the ceiling and dominated the room. The teens gawked at a marble fireplace easily three times the size of the one in the living room at home and the focal point of the main sitting area where Reginald had everyone congregate. Trays with teapots, a coffee service, and a pitcher of lemonade and glasses sat on a spindle-legged coffee table surrounded by a leather sofa and chairs with legs that matched the coffee table.

Sitting beside Reginald on the sofa and without specifying the men's connection to the family, Ian followed Master Kai's advice and introduced Lee, who chose to stand holding Colin while warily eyeing the fragile looking chairs; Fael who sat in a chair far enough away to prevent Jaimie from grabbing valuable ornaments; and Liu, also opting to stand as he held Safia. He introduced Jesse, Lill, Kirani, and Bazir as friends and Christopher and Michael as Jasirey's children.

Holding Sun Li, Jasirey sat on Reginald's other side on the sofa and presented Colin, Jaimie, Safia, and Sun Li. Not one of the young ones resembled another. He considered the possibility that the babies might be adopted. They appeared to be the same age, however, and had Jasirey's smile. One boy looked a great deal like Ian, the rest like each of the men in the mysterious trio comfortably holding them.

Sunny—and what an apt name that was—beamed and held his arms out to Reginald. At Jasirey's questioning smile, Reginald bravely reached for the fine little fellow.

Sunny explored his new playmate's glasses with spellbound concentration.

Despite Sunny's tiny fingers straying into his line of vision, Reginald managed to direct the butler, helped by a maid in a dark dress and white apron, to serve the drinks. Since the staff would soon serve lunch, they offered no snacks to distract Jaimie, Colin, and Safia. They struggled to get down and explore.

"Perhaps we should take the babies to the nursery," Jasirey said, "so they can crawl around without breaking anything."

Reginald kept a firm one-handed grip on Sunny trying to peer into his glasses and risked letting go of the glasses stem he held on to in order to wave his hand at the room. "Let them have at it. Surely, they cannot reach anything dangerous."

Jasirey grinned. "Haven't been around babies much, have you?" Nonetheless, she motioned for Lee, Liu, and Fael to let Jaimie who was perilously close to wailing, Colin, and Safia down to explore.

Sunny noticed his brother and sisters, patted Reginald's cheek, and reached for the floor. Reginald set him down and marveled at the surprising speed the youngsters managed on hands and knees. His hands flew to his face. Grateful Sunny hadn't taken them with him, Reginald scooped his glasses from off the floor.

Jaimie's short arm stretched toward a glass bowl swirled in rainbow colors as she pulled herself up at a table. Colin headed straight for the fireplace. Jasirey, Lee, Fael, and Liu ran interference.

Taken aback that such little beings could create so much chaos, Reginald congratulated himself on being childless.

Ian had remained seated with Reginald, his British CEO, to answer any questions their host might have.

"They all seem to possess your wife's lovely smile," Reginald said carefully.

"Colin is the spitting image of my baby pictures, except for his mouth."

"Shall I introduce you and Jasirey at the party and leave the rest to your discretion?"

"That's probably best, and please introduce Jasirey as Shannon. Her nickname is used only among family and close friends. She counts you as the latter."

"I'm honored."

The butler announced lunch within the hour. The dining room could seat five times their number. High ceilings, crystal chandeliers sparkling in the sun pouring through windows that occupied most of the outside wall, and a fireplace at the far end reminded Jasirey more of a ballroom, which Reggie told her was on the second floor and burst her fantasy of sweeping down the staircase for a ball.

The family secured the babies' booster chairs to dining chairs.

Jasirey gave the babies small pieces of softer food to pick up by themselves and sippy cups of formula. They usually wanted bottles only first thing in the morning and before bed. The husbands helped a great deal, but Jasirey knew she would miss Satoko and Mashita and the ability they afforded her and her men daily free time together. She'd gotten spoiled and made a mental note to be sure to tell the older couple how much she appreciated them.

Reginald watched Jasirey and the four men handling the children with an unspoken, synchronized efficiency that indicated a long-standing, intimate knowledge of one another. The doctor and his wife, the older children, and the security personnel obviously knew of their familiarity. While talking with Ian, Reginald had found out the four older boys had been tutored together and that the friends of Jasirey's sons belonged to a woman working for the family.

Liu noticed their little ones nodding over their food and asked Kimika to choose a team to take the children to the nursery for a nap.

Reginald took Jasirey's arm and guided his guests on a tour of the bottom floor. The first floor included his office, one less formal sitting room, a den with a large entertainment center, the kitchen and dining room, and a two-story library. Reginald noticed Jasirey's wistful expression as she gazed at the books and determined to set aside time for her to browse.

Along with the ballroom, he told them, the second floor held many guest rooms. The third floor housed the nursery, master bedroom, and more bedrooms. Servants' quarters comprised most of the fourth floor. He led the group outside.

A garage sat at the back of the manor along with a stable across from a large paddock. Reginald owned five riding horses. As a center for equine activities, the county of Surrey and Mole Valley where Reginald lived had well-kept scenic footpaths and bridleways.

The teenagers stood in awe of the large horses, and the adults let them stay to explore in the care of a stable hand.

"If you've no objection," Reginald said, "the young gentlemen can be given riding lessons while here to keep them occupied and give my horses some welcome exercise."

"They'd be in seventh heaven," Jasirey said. "It's very sweet of you to offer."

"Not at all."

"Do you mind a personal question, Reggie?"

"Not from you." Her brilliant smile sent waves of warmth swelling through his heart.

"The financial upkeep of this place must be astronomical."

"Most of the house is kept closed. With work, I rarely have visitors or host functions such as this weekend's party. Family money was left in trust for the upkeep, and a good portion of the acreage not sold off is forest, which requires fewer resources to maintain."

"I assume you're the oldest child." She remembered he had a niece and a nephew.

"Quite. My father held to the old-fashioned notion that the firstborn male should inherit property. As neither my brother nor sister had any interest in living in the country, it worked out well. They inherited sizeable sums of money and were content."

"You must not get to stay here much, either."

"Actually, Surrey has more company headquarters, including Ian's, than any other county. I stay here year-round."

"It's beautiful, Reggie."

They continued the tour.

Other than several multicolored rose gardens, the grounds consisted of lawn, ornamental shrubs, and small trees, some of the flowering variety. Designed for decoration rather than use, a three-foot high box-shrub maze sloped up a small hill.

The group returned to the manor for tea. Jasirey discussed the riding lessons with her husbands and gave Reginald the go-ahead to suggest it to the teenagers who agreed with pumping fists and a loud chorus of "Sweet!"

* * *

Jasirey figured she'd made enough personal inquiries of Reginald and questioned Ian the next day about the upcoming party. They walked the grounds while the other husbands watched the babies. "Does Reggie have all the resources he needs for the weekend party?"

"Is that the politically correct way to ask if he can afford everything?"

"I knew I married you for more than your money."

Ian drew her close. "Did you, now?"

She nipped playfully at his chin. "A two-day party—I assume people will stay overnight, which means extra meals and hired hands. Any idea how many have been invited?"

"I didn't ask. I'd say a full house. A caterer connected to the corporation will handle meals and teas. Extra help cleared by Kimika has been hired and financially taken care of."

Jasirey burrowed in and caressed his long back. "That's what I guessed, my thoughtful fella. It's a good thing none of your other women knew how sweet you are."

His eyes narrowed at the impishness in hers. "I've warned you about that word." He propped his foot against a low stone border and flipped her over his knee. "Apologize."

She laughed, then yelped as he paddled her bottom between bouts of arousing fondling. The sensual and powerfully erotic attention soon had Jasirey writhing against Ian's large hand.

Arm in arm, Jesse and Lill strode into view. Jesse lifted a casual brow. "Does that work?"

Ian grinned. "It does for me."

"As I thought. Carry on." He steered a goggling Lill back around a hedge.

Struggling in vain, Jasirey yelled "Traitors" and squealed as Ian's hand snaked up her skirt. "Ian, someone else might walk by."

"They'll have to stand in line. I insist on coming first."

He pulled her behind a hedge, pushed down her panties, and held her firmly bent over as he first lightly paddled then firmly ran long fingers over her sensitized skin until she was warmly wet and ready. Intense, plunging minutes later, his wife genuinely yelled out. His own limbs trembling, Ian helped her sink to the grass and gently caressed her delicately pink cheeks. Once able to stand, he righted their clothing and tipped up her face. "I am never sweet."

Jasirey felt disposed to overlook his getting the last word.

By the next day, everyone had adjusted to the time difference and decided to take in some of the sights. Reginald brought them to an outdoor village market that displayed pottery, wooden instruments, and jewelry along with fresh foods.

Jasirey carried Sunny and handed him to Reginald. The little boy had an affinity for him that their host seemed not to mind in the least.

Jasirey checked out a guitar. Pleased it was mostly in tune, she fiddled with the tuning pegs, strummed, and picked a few chords.

"I only play chords to accompany myself singing," she said. "It's been a while."

The music had sounded good to the rest of the adults.

"I'd like to hear you play while you sing," Lee said, gently grasping her hand. They'd become accustomed to Reginald's presence and forgot to be discreet around him.

"Does she sing well?" Reginald asked Fael.

"She has a lovely voice but is shy in front of strangers. Not with the people, though." At Reginald's perplexed look, Fael said, "Let Jasirey explain."

"Safia is your child, isn't she?" Not usually so bold, Reginald surprised even himself.

"They are all our children." Having added to Reginald's confusion, Fael said, "Ask Jasirey."

Still looking at musical instruments, Jasirey watched Kirani pick up what he considered a stick-like wooden flute. Jasirey told him it was a recorder. He produced some melodious notes, blushed at Jasirey's praise, and bought it thinking the recorder might add some interesting sounds to his and Christopher's band.

Reginald knew of a family-friendly pub within walking distance. The large group sat at tables placed outside the old building that had once been a coach stop. The teenagers knew chips meant French fries and got a kick out of ordering fish and chips and getting their soft drinks in tankards. Lill decided to try a pint of local stout. It did not occur to Reginald to warn her that in Great Britain a pint was twenty American ounces.

"Oh, this hits the spot," Lill said after a tentative sip. "The sun is warm today." She swung her sweater over the back of her chair and nearly finished the dark beer before the British version of shepherd's pie arrived.

Jessie pushed his pint toward his wife. "Too strong for me."

Jasirey set out the blander foods she'd brought with them for the babies and enjoyed her lamb stew and dark bread. Halfway through her meal, her attention snapped toward Lill, who had flushed an unnatural pink. Distress—not her own—clawed at Jasirey, and she quietly laid a hand on Lill's shoulder. "Come to the ladies' room with me."

Lill bobbled as she rose. "Don't let the kids see me like this," she hissed.

Jasirey linked arms with Lill and led her to the pub bathroom. She sat her light-headed friend on a bench outside the door and went in to wet a paper towel she then lay on the back of Lill's neck.

Lill's embarrassment flooded Jasirey's mind and seemed worse than the effects of the alcohol. Jasirey did not possess the gift of healing, but she could deal with strong emotions.

Lill became teary with self-disgust. Jasirey hoped countering with a ridiculous memory might help and projected the possibility to Lill. She hadn't intended to intrude but sat mesmerized as Lill recalled a memory of her and Jesse's dating days. Jesse had taken Lill to a lake for a picnic and, carried away with romantic ideas, rented a small rowboat he hadn't the least notion how to propel. They never made it past twenty feet from shore and drowned their lunch basket when a paddle accidentally knocked it into the water.

Jasirey withdrew from Lill's mind as the couple slinked back to their B & B room and headed for the shower. Lill's moony grin indicated she remembered just fine on her own. Still floating but calm, she allowed Jasirey to guide her back to the tables.

❦ ❦ ❦

After returning to the manor, everyone retired to their rooms until time for tea. The husbands volunteered to put the babies down for a nap. Only Reginald and Jasirey showed up in the downstairs parlor.

"Shall we go for a walk, then have our tea?" he asked.

She happily agreed.

When they entered the rose gardens, he held her hand companionably. "They handled that quite well."

"Handled what?" Jasirey asked as they strolled comparing different types of roses—climbing dark red blooms twining about arbors, stately shrubs in shades of red and peach, and sprawling bushes saturated with smaller flowers of dark pink. Jasirey breathed in the wonderful scents.

"I asked Fael some rather prying questions, I'm afraid. He directed me to you."

"I really admire your patience waiting this long. I'd have been prying the first day."

"My dear, you do it with such sweet concern, no one minds."

She laughed and kissed his cheek. "Before you start, let me ask one thing?"

He fondly deferred to her.

"Do you have any kind of mystical bent, or do you consider your sensibilities more proper, no-nonsense British?"

"That's rather stereotypical and doesn't leave much option for anything between."

She smiled impishly, an expression he hadn't seen before. The odd notion occurred to him that she probably made an exceptional bed partner. Embarrassed, he turned to cut a lavender rose and handed it to her. "Mind the thorns."

Jasirey slipped her hand in his and continued walking. "Our story includes elements of the fantastical. Even if you find the story unbelievable, I need your word you won't repeat it."

"Certainly." His curiosity far outweighed any trepidation at the secrecy.

She described the Devoted, their missions, Jasirey's overall purpose, and the prophecy of more children. "You've already figured out Liu, Fael, and Lee fathered my babies with Ian."

Reginald sat on a bench and tugged her down beside him. "You make it sound as though these people consider you some sort of broodmare. I've seen their regard for you, from your sons' friends to your security and, of course, your men. Devoted is the perfect adjective."

Jasirey laid her head on his shoulder. "I know they love me. I love all of them."

Overcome by an urge to protect her, though from what he couldn't imagine, Reginald placed an arm about her. Was her story plausible? Considering her effect on him, he already believed Jasirey special, so her story didn't seem out of the realm of reality. *How strange.*

"Forgive me, dear heart, but you don't seem enthusiastic about having more children."

"My last pregnancy took everything I had. Doing it again . . ." She sighed.

"You feel pressured to endure another?"

"Everyone supports whatever I choose to do."

He sniffed. "Indeed. That leaves all the responsibility on your shoulders and leads to the question, 'Do you fulfill your perceived duty or disappoint everyone?'"

"Exactly. I can't really blame the Devoted or my husbands for being in that position. I only had to say no to everything, although initially I wasn't sure what I might be called upon to say no to. I adore my husbands, the kids, and my people. I wouldn't give them up for anything, but there have been serious bumps along the way. I pray every day for guidance and faith that I'm following the path meant for me."

"How long have you been carrying this—I shouldn't like to say burden—but . . . ?"

"You may be sorry you asked," Jasirey said. "My period started again in June. It brought everyone's expectations and hopes back to the forefront."

"I see." Unaffected, he had never cultivated the notion of regarding bodily functions as something one should not talk about in public. Jasirey stood and held out a hand. Reginald let her pull him up.

"You haven't said what you think. You don't appear shocked or skeptical."

"I'll share my own family secret. We had Druid ancestors. Totally hush, hush in previous generations afraid of scandalous whispers by intolerant people who associated the religion with wizardry and witchcraft." His gaze became serious. "I do want to ask you one thing. These missions, what makes the Devoted equipped to determine what should be done for—or, more importantly, to—others?"

"I haven't thought about that in a while." Jasirey's eyes took on a faraway cast. "Who decides between intervention and interference, appropriate actions when dealing with cultures having vastly different points of view? I wondered in the beginning. I suppose I've become complacent, sidetracked by the pregnancy and spending time with the people, seeing so many different races and cultures working in harmony." She nodded to herself. "I should know the checks and balances in the decision-making process. I'll find out."

"Is that wise?" Reginald had no desire to stir up trouble for her.

She patted his arm. "The Devoted aren't a fascist state. They may evade or leave out details when trying not to worry me, but no one refuses my outright requests for information. It's one of the perks, and I'm pretty good at getting details once I set my mind to it."

"I imagine you are. I shall remember to be on my guard."

Her laughter bubbled out and clearly insinuated he didn't stand a chance against her. It never occurred to him to take offense.

⁂

After dinner, everyone gathered in the parlor where Reginald determined to find out precisely how Jasirey's husbands perceived her role.

He cornered them by the fireplace. "Please tell me you believe your wife is of more value than simply to incubate children."

Lee glowered as an image of the harrowing birth of the quadruplets played in his mind.

Ramrod-straight, Reginald braved their ire. "She has so much to offer, but to be burdened with the notion that she is responsible for the world's welfare—rather unfair, really."

"Did she say that?" Ian asked quietly.

A shiver ran up Reginald's spine, and he realized he hoped never to have Ian's wrath directed at him. He waited.

"We do not dictate to Jasirey," Liu said. "We support and protect her in every decision she must make."

"She mostly says the same," Reginald said, wanting to be fair but still concerned that many decisions rested on her shoulders alone. "I wonder if something might be done to open avenues less fraught with world-shaking consequences."

Ian relaxed. "Here is the very reason why we visit a new friend she wants in her life, who helps to introduce the promise of Jasirey to the world."

Lee's eyes crinkled. "I think she's found a new Protector as well."

Reginald covered a cough with his fist. Jasirey had explained the Protector's role.

They all turned to watch her playing on the floor by the windows with her babies—hugs, tickles, and talking to them as though they understood every word.

"I must admit," Reginald said, "she and her little ones make a lovely picture. I don't suppose she wishes her life were different."

"Mm, maybe less complicated," Ian said. "It's our job to nudge her out of her comfort zone while providing a safe harbor for her."

"A tightrope act." The line of Reginald's shoulders eased. "And you four are her safety net. I'd be honored to assist in whatever small capacity I'm able."

"Hardly small," Fael said. "The party you plan is the most involved affair I have ever attended." He caught Kimika's eye and gestured for him to join them. "Jasirey has revealed herself to our host," he said to the young man. "Explain to him how the people regard her."

Kimika's eyes shone. "She is our most precious lady, chosen to bear the children who will one day aid in stabilizing the world." That had been taught to him by rote.

Reginald studied the young man. With Asian features, Kamika also had pale skin, tawny eyes, and a no doubt fascinating story.

Kimika simmered with passionate conviction. "We learned the stories, the history, and waited for Jasirey to appear. No one expected a person of such love, compassion, tolerance, and fortitude. She has more courage than anyone I've ever met, a very powerful person."

Reginald frowned. "Powerful?"

"She guides people to their destined paths in ways they don't always recognize and seldom resent—me, my friend Mtombe, another Protector of Jasirey. With no prior knowledge of him or his circumstances, she knew his destiny lay beyond the Devoted and released him from his duties as a Protector. He has recently found his place in the world and is profoundly grateful. Her children are blessed to have such a mother and we, to have her as our lady."

Jasirey followed Sunny and Jaimie as they crawled to their fathers while Lill and Jesse kept an eye on the other two. "And what are you telling Reggie?" Jasirey asked with a smile.

Gripping Liu's pant leg for balance, Jaimie stood. He scooped her up. She mouthed his nose, and he nuzzled her silky curls. Sunny crawled toward the hearth where Lee intercepted him. The baby happily pulled on his papa bear's dreadlocks.

Jasirey hugged Kimika. "I haven't seen much of you. I know you're busy with the weekend's preparations, but try to join us occasionally for tea when you're not on duty, okay?"

"As you wish." Kimika bowed, ruffled Jaimie's curls, and nodded at the men.

Reginald puzzled out the interaction. Kimika was a Protector, a prospective husband, yet Jasirey regarded him with a motherly love the young man obviously basked in. Being a Protector apparently encompassed emotions besides duty and sexual attraction.

"What is that gesture?" he asked. "I've seen your security start it and stop abruptly."

Jasirey smiled. "Poor people. It's an ingrained, difficult habit to break, a sign of respect for me—Jasirey. We've asked them to refrain in public. It calls risky attention to me."

Reginald hadn't thought of Ian's security as primarily for his wife, but he then realized it was. *Well, no doubt also for the children.* He couldn't imagine harm coming to her at his home. Still, once considered a mild nuisance, the security people became most welcome to him.

Jesse and Lill wandered over with Colin and Safia in tow. Safia cocked her head to get a better view of Reginald and held out her arms.

He held her. "Hello, bonny one."

Safia bloomed with her mother's beautiful smile.

The teenagers wandered up, hoping to catch Reginald's ear to talk horses. He could describe the characteristics of each breed.

Jasirey joined Ian and Colin playing with blocks on the floor. She asked Ian to pick Reginald's brain about an appropriate horse for a new rider.

Ian's brow rose. "Are we in the market for a horse?"

"It would make a very nice birthday present." She smiled winningly. Michael had deferred a birthday present for their trip.

"Don't use your wiles on me, woman. You hardly need my permission."

"Help then?"

He kissed her forehead. "I can do that. I'll e-mail the groundskeepers to start plans for riding trails and probably a stable. You can't expect one horse to accommodate four boys."

Jasirey's warring expressions brought home to Ian exactly how his words might be construed. "Not one comment," he said. Eyes dancing, she mimed zipping her lips. "You've experienced that spanking is not an idle threat."

"I let you get away with it," Jasirey said and evaded his grasp by shoving Colin at him. She tossed a wicked grin over her shoulder. His answering predatory gleam whapped her in the heart and coursed down to her toes. She stumbled on a rug.

Ian had turned his attention to Colin. Only Kimika noticed the small bobble. Mouth quivering with suppressed laughter, he discreetly gazed elsewhere.

❧ ❧ ❧

The rest of that week, Reginald guided his guests in exploring the surrounding country. One larger estate, open to the public, had a real evergreen maze that took the teens nearly an hour to decipher. Another day, the group picnicked at a castle ruin with a magnificent view of rolling green interspersed with stands of trees, all intersected by a thin winding river of sun-glinting silver.

After an excursion to a deep blue lake framed by dark firs, they stopped for an early tea at Reginald's closest neighbors ten miles away. The property boasted row after row of dog kennels and a large house—not an estate. Jasirey didn't catch why.

A middle-aged couple greeted them with a great many dogs they bred and sold for bird hunting. The fathers held fast to babies wriggling as hopefully as the dogs. The owners assured their guests the breed made excellent family pets.

Jasirey diplomatically explained that the babies weren't yet dog friendly and would poke fingers into canine eyes and nostrils or pull fur, ears, or whatever else came to hand.

Intrigued, the couple obligingly removed the animals from the parlor. Reginald's guests were outside of his usual crowd. The couple looked forward to his party.

Weekend Party

Many of Reginald's weekend guests planned to arrive Saturday morning. Those having farther to travel trickled in throughout the afternoon on Friday. The staff kept tea available until two hours before dinner.

Though most of the guests were couples, one family included twin sixteen-year-old daughters, a deliberate choice by Reginald, Jasirey concluded.

Christopher and Kirani nudged each other forward for introductions and invited the girls for a walk in the gardens. Jasirey wondered where her shy little boy had gone. Another family brought a son, an experienced horseman Michael and Bazir's age. The trio disappeared to the stable.

Many of the guests went to their rooms to rest in the late afternoon. Knowing dinner and after-dinner socializing would not end until late, Jasirey, her husbands, and the four teens used the time for family prayers. Mirai and several people from her squad had volunteered to care for the babies for the rest of the night.

Jasirey had seen little of The Five since arriving at Reginald's home and suspected that, since she was supposed to be on a relaxing family vacation, Kimika deliberately assigned them duties away from her.

That evening in the dining room, conversation flowed continuously through a simple dinner designed to contrast with the next day's more formal menu. Everyone continued to converse comfortably as they moved into the parlor after dinner.

Mostly business associates, those gathered considered the evening an excellent opportunity to network with Ian. Jasirey gave them an hour and then moved to Ian's side. She skillfully turned the conversation toward more entertaining topics, which to her mind meant personal.

Reticent at first, the guests soon laughed together over exploits of their children, embarrassing moments at work, hobbies, and romantic foibles.

Jasirey had taken command and subtly led the guests where they would not ordinarily go.

Reginald marveled at the success she made of the evening.

Lee, Fael, and Liu had never seen their wife in such a setting, and glad they'd heeded Ian's advice to encourage her to branch out from the family, watched with wonder and pride.

After family time the next morning, Jasirey and her men dressed casually for lunch in the garden. Jasirey wore a periwinkle blue dress, the bolero jacket that flattered her figure, and her sunhat. She had Ian take a picture and send it to Lizzie. Her friend would have been in her glory with the Old World flavor of the weekend.

Reginald personally introduced Jasirey and thereby set her apart as the guest of honor. She did not recognize the social protocol and felt no pressure to make a good impression. The husbands wandered off to find people with common interests. Their wife found everyone interesting.

She talked to a group of avid gardeners, all aware Reginald worked for Ian, a powerful corporate leader. It surprised their TV-inspired ideas of rich American wives that Jasirey dug in the dirt and tended vegetables. Her extensive knowledge of organic techniques convinced them she did, and they liked her for it.

Reginald's warm glances and a continual hand on her arm also surprised them. He had never been demonstrative with his emotions and thoughts. They enjoyed getting to know another side of him.

Jasirey noticed a slight, attractive man regarding Reginald with curious puzzlement and wound her way over to him. "This party is unlike anything I've ever attended," she said.

Darkly blond, he had a pleasant smile and mild blue eyes. Bryant introduced himself. "Have you known Reginald long?" he asked.

"No, we met at a party for Ian's corporation and quickly became friends. You?"

"Business associates primarily, though we often attend the same social functions."

"Are you here with someone?"

Startled at first, Bryant relaxed his usual reserve as Jasirey smiled warmly in apology. His eyes crinkled. "I'm alone, an old bachelor."

She laughed. "That's what Reggie says."

Reggie? No one else Bryant knew used the nickname.

She gave him a mock frown. "Neither of you are older than I am. I refuse to believe our best years are behind us."

Their host joined them, and Jasirey linked her arm in his. "Reggie, Bryant seems to think he's too old for love. Assure him he's still an attractive man."

Reginald understood exactly what Jasirey was up to and glared at her in warning. She pinched his bottom, forcing him a step closer to Bryant, and laid her free hand on the other man's arm to keep them close.

Jasirey's eyes sparkled with irrepressible mischief. "Don't you think Reggie's still attractive and has a lot to give a partner, Bryant?"

Bryant gave Reginald a bemused smile. "Something of a force of nature, isn't she?"

Reginald attempted sternness. "Indeed. She has decided my life requires managing."

Jasirey kissed his cheek. "I'll leave you two alone. Can Bryant call you Reggie?" She laughed at his grimace and blended into the crowd.

❧ ❧ ❧

More people arrived and conversed in groups over tea. Kimika kept in continual contact with squad leaders while he and Mirai stayed close to Jasirey. Yusef, Nikolai, and Favian watched the babies while Sajan, Chen, and Andwar monitored the rest of the children having their own party in the smaller sitting room.

Ian searched for his wife to inform her that Everett's family had arrived. He found two finance power couples goggling at her. He had been a consultant for both couples on Anglo-European trade and knew they espoused opposing sides of a trade agreement with several European countries critical for ensuring fair wages and the integrity of water usage.

"Ian," one of the men said, "I did not realize your wife is also an astute businessperson. I do believe she has given us a path toward compromise that may allow an agreement to go forward this year."

Both couples continually clasped Jasirey's hands until Ian managed to extricate her. "I can't wait to hear that story," he said to Jasirey as they made their way to Everett's family.

"Honestly," she said, "they all knew they needed to acknowledge each other's valid points. They just needed a path to bypass their entrenched positions—mostly ego-induced."

Ian did some goggling of his own. "They're involved in complicated negotiations. How could you know which path would be best?"

Jasirey's brows puckered in a faint frown. "I study environmental issues, especially their impact on people. The couples each represent a corporation looking into building manufacturing plants along a minor river prone to flooding and running through six countries."

"Serious flooding that could damage any facilities built along it," Ian said.

"Yes. One side believes building a large dam at the river's headwaters will be the most economical way to solve the problem. The other side argues that the expense is prohibitive and that such a dam would cause unacceptable land and habitat damage downstream—and they're right. But instead of looking for a solution, the first side recommended scrapping the project."

"That area needs the economic growth." Ian tried to relax as he waited for her solution.

Jasirey shook her head. "I don't offer solutions. I suggest options, in this case that cities and groups of towns where the businesses would be located might have the incentive to help pay for smaller, less invasive dams—for instance, giving the land needed to the corporations while reaping another source of jobs for their citizens. The man wanting to end the project disliked dealing with the ethnic groups in some of the towns."

Jasirey had given the project opponent a strong nudge to look past his prejudices. Fortunately, the businessman's wife did not share her husband's bias, liked the compromise, and prevailed in conversation with him.

Ian exhaled a long breath and gave Jasirey a broad smile.

"I think this is part of the job I'm here to do as Jasirey," she said. "Have faith in me, Ian."

"Baby . . . !"

They reached Everett's family. Ian silently berated himself. There they were to encourage Jasirey to take a step deeper into her destiny, and at the first test, he had allowed his training to fly out the window.

Jasirey hugged and kissed Everett.

He returned her greeting and introduced his family, all acquainted with the sentimental side their father would deny having and his deep affection for Jasirey.

She plainly regarded them as family and, before they'd finished their tea, learned their life histories, including anecdotes about Everett's parenting.

The din quieted noticeably as people drifted off to rest before the more formal dinner and dance that would go into the wee hours. Jasirey and her husbands spent time with the babies before taking naps.

Liu stayed with Jasirey. He truly meant to have her rest, but the bed seemed intended for only one and a half people and he found her silken underwear—her bra and panties all she wore—snugged into his crotch. He doubted any heterosexual male could resist such temptation. He fondled the soft cloth while trailing his lips and tongue up and down her spine.

When Jasirey pushed into his hand, Liu mouthed his way to her derriere and dragged her panties down and off her legs. He pulled her to her hands and knees, then licked and nibbled her inner thighs while slowly pushing them wide apart.

"Liu, now," Jasirey entreated.

He rose, clutched her hips as he lightly bit her cheeks, then returned to her thighs. "I am not ready," he said primly.

"Well, you better get ready, buster, or I'm going to flip onto my back and put your head in a leg lock."

Liu slapped her heart-shaped bottom and taunted, "Had I known you to be a fan of wrestling, precious one, I would happily have accommodated you."

That did it. Jasirey twisted her upper body to face him, lunged, and wrapped her arms around his head. She collapsed and let her weight drag him to the bed.

Liu's mouth opened at the distinct feeling of a paddle smacking his ass. "Hey! That is cheating."

Jasirey assumed a look of innocence. "I don't remember any rules against using my gifts."

Instead of struggling to break her hold, Liu levered her upper leg straight up—her hips and legs still twisted to the side—and surged forward to seat himself deeper than he'd ever managed before.

Eye to eye but with her bottom still facing Liu, Jasirey gave a startled *oomph*.

His warrior's grin flashed as he drew back and fully buried himself over and over.

Pinned and unable to move in counterpoint to Liu's piston-like plunging, Jasirey cried out with the intense sensations when he circled her clitoris with his thumb. She was aware only of her and Liu's mating, striving bodies as a tidal wave of pleasure swept them up and over.

She slept only fifteen minutes but awakened with energy to spare.

At the dinner, Reginald seated Jasirey, wearing her burgundy gown and fire opal jewelry set, next to Lord Spotiswood. Ian and Lady Spotiswood sat across the table. Jasirey judged the couple to be in their eighties.

On her other side with silver-streaked dark hair pulled tightly back and wearing an unadorned black gown featuring long sleeves and a high, rounded neck sat a large-boned woman in her fifties. A classically handsome younger man escorted her. Roberta laughed often at what she called her set's rigid ideas of propriety, which she enjoyed trampling. That contingent esteemed her astute business sense despite her acerbic wit, Roberta explained.

"Mr. Henry Biggerstaff," Roberta identified a man several seats down who loudly proclaimed the success of his investment firm while darting pointed looks at Ian. "Dated him before he married the current Mrs. Biggerstaff. The name is a misnomer financially—I found out from my background check on him—and in bed, which I can personally attest to."

Lord Spotiswood possessed a gentler sense of humor and good hearing. He stifled a laugh, and when Roberta turned to her date, he described his estate for Jasirey. "The land has belonged to Spotiswoods for centuries. I'll never sell it, though I recognize the possibility that my heirs might."

Jasirey's undivided attention made the old gentleman feel younger. He intended to congratulate Reginald on his clever seating arrangement. Jasirey's sweetness and warmth contrasted to great effect with Roberta's flintier demeanor and minimalist appearance. Lord Spotiswood appreciated feminine appeal while remaining faithful to his wife—at least after he'd grown up sufficiently. Quite taken with Jasirey, he decided Reginald's guests must attend the annual Spotiswood Ball scheduled for the next weekend.

Dinner ran nearly two hours and included meat, fowl, and fish courses. Roberta warned Jasirey to pace herself. She heeded Roberta's advice, limiting herself to a few bites from each plate. Nevertheless, Jasirey finished overly full. She barely sipped at the wines—flavored vinegars, to her palate—offered to complement each course.

She managed two bites of a treacle tart and regretted the waste as servers removed many food-laden plates until Roberta remarked, "Our porcine neighbors will dine well tonight."

Reginald escorted Lady Spotiswood to the ballroom, and Lord Spotiswood offered Jasirey his arm to climb the elegant stairway.

As long as the dining room and three times as wide, the ballroom featured a fireplace that took up nearly a third of the far wall. A small fire crackled to show off its light effect on the polished wood floor. The room warmed rapidly as the guests filled it. Wait staff circulated continually, offered trays of champagne, and fetched other drinks as requested. A small orchestra played from a balcony opposite the fireplace.

Claimed for every dance, Jasirey had the eerie sensation of eyes licking up and down her body. She tried to pinpoint the source, but the crush of people was too great. Giving up the search, she sought out Everett for a reel and set up a time for the families to meet at breakfast.

For the last dance, a waltz, Reginald swept her around the floor until they had it to themselves. At music's end, their audience clapped in appreciation as Reginald bowed and kissed her hand.

Jasirey had enjoyed the evening but would have preferred more time to talk with others. Her feet hurt. In her and Ian's bedroom, Liu massaged one foot and Fael the other as they all sat on the small bed to discuss the evening. She'd seen very little of her men.

"I promised to have breakfast with Everett and his family at ten," she said. "That should give us some time with the babies first."

Fael kissed her hand. "We have been impressed, loved one, with the impact you have on people you interact with."

Jasirey laughed. "What impact?"

Lee hung up his wife's dress. "I heard nearly all the partygoers buzzing about you—your warmth and how you made each one feel special."

After the others left for the room they shared, Ian rocked Jasirey lightly to and fro. "I'm sorry, love, about my reaction to you speaking with those two business couples."

"Don't be silly," she said on a yawn. "I have doubts myself. Why shouldn't you?"

The revelation brought him no comfort. He resolved to be more supportive. She fell asleep, and he spooned her to keep his feet from dangling over the bed.

❦ ❦ ❦

The little ones fussed when their parents prepared to leave the nursery in the morning. The teens had gone to the stable for a ride.

Jasirey crooned. "Oh, poor babies." Even Sunny cried. "You guys go. Ask Everett's family if we can get together in London."

Lee kissed the top of her head. "We'll go down and ask them to join us here for breakfast."

"Thank you, teddy bear."

Jasirey sat on the floor with her sons and daughters, sang to them, and held up one or another happy baby to dance. The others bounced on their padded bottoms or stood, supporting themselves on their mother and dancing to her beat.

Everett gestured for quiet as he opened the door for the wait staff carrying trays and stealthily led his family in to watch.

Reginald had marched up to reprimand Jasirey for her desertion but was entranced by her lovely voice.

Sunny warbled along, lost his balance, and plopped down with a laugh. He saw his fathers and waved his arms. Jasirey glanced over and instinctively dimmed her joy to a softer welcoming light.

Reginald withdrew before Jasirey caught sight of the devious smile he couldn't contain.

"Are you hungry, babies?" Jasirey remained on the floor and accepted a plate from Everett. She tried kippers—*not bad*—but couldn't quite think of fish as a breakfast food.

Everett's family sat on extra chairs brought up by the staff and watched Jasirey's family on the floor assist their young ones. They were lovely children and caused the sons and their wives to miss their own children, left at home. They anticipated Everett's explanation of the unusual dynamics of his adopted family.

Ian made it a point to invite them to America for their holiday the following year. They had been accustomed to visiting Everett every year when he and Ian lived in Boston. What with finding Jasirey, moving to the compound, and Jasirey's difficult pregnancy with the quadruplets, it had been nearly two years since their last visit.

Everett's daughters-in-law asked to hold the babies, and Jasirey held out Sunny and Safia. Jaimie and Colin had begun to show stranger anxiety and took longer to warm up.

The babies' fathers worried the first time Jaimie and then Colin burrowed into them instead of interacting. Jasirey reminded them it was a normal part of their development as the babies realized they were beings separate from their parents.

When the babies contentedly played with their security caregivers, the adults went downstairs—Everett's family to mingle, Jasirey and her husbands to find Jesse and Lill. They'd hardly seen the couple since lunch the day before.

Lill linked arms with Jasirey. "Reginald passed the word that you needed to spend time with the children. Quite a few people had to swallow their disappointment at not having a chance to say goodbye. More than half have already gone."

Many of those who remained cornered Ian to discuss business. Jasirey, Lill, and Jesse spent the time before lunch talking to people walking the grounds.

Ian, Lee, Liu, and Fael joined Jasirey, Lill, Jesse, and Everett's family in the dining room for lunch. They talked about places and things to do in the Pioneer Valley where Jasirey's town lay that Everett's family might like when they visited—perhaps a riverboat cruise of the Connecticut River launching from Northfield Mountain.

The remaining guests left after the meal. Jasirey kissed Everett and his family.

"I really like your sons and their wives, Everett," she whispered. "I'm sure your wife's proud of the job you've done raising them."

Words inadequate, he kissed her cheeks.

Reginald waited for afternoon tea to sit with the family and discuss invitations they'd received, mostly in person since the family would not be with Reginald long enough for mail service. He showed them the ornate, formal invitation for the next weekend delivered by hand from Lord and Lady Spotiswood.

"This, we must accept," he said. "An invitation from them after such short acquaintance is quite an honor. It would be considered bad manners to refuse."

Jasirey perused the invitation. "Just an evening affair, not overnight, right?"

"Precisely. Dinner, dancing, and performances from anyone local, proficient instrumentally or vocally, and perhaps one professional of their acquaintance to highlight the hour. The ball continues well into the morning, though one may leave any time after the hosts retire. They usually do so quite early."

"We ought to leave fairly early," Ian said. "We return to London on Sunday."

"Quite right. As to the rest of the invitations, most are for tea or dinner from business associates hoping to forward some agenda, others from friends wishing to be hospitable."

"Anyone you'd particularly like to get to know better?" Jasirey asked.

Reginald's color heightened, and the husbands wondered what she had been up to.

"As we are introducing you," Reginald said, "we should decide what's best for you."

Puzzled, she asked, "Who's being introduced? Doesn't everyone know Ian or at least of him and the corporation? Ian, you choose. It's your business."

Ian kissed Jasirey's temple. "I can always acquire business contacts. We're here to visit Reginald and give you the opportunity to spread your wings."

"And fly where? I'd have been happy just to spend time with Reggie. Why all these other people if it's not for business?"

"We enjoy showing you off. You have quite an impact, love, more than I think you're aware. We wanted to bring it to your attention."

Jasirey no longer laughed at nor disparaged her destiny, but she saw no reason not to have a little fun. "So, I'm supposed to choose." She rounded on Reginald. "Did we get an invitation from Bryant?"

"Don't you have enough on your plate without adding matchmaker?"

"He's really nice—and cute."

"An impossible woman." He appealed to her clueless men. "Gentlemen, steer Jasirey on course, please. We must answer these people, preferably today. And yes," he grudgingly said to Jasirey, "he invited us to tea at his club."

"Ian, take that one, and I liked Roberta if she offered. Jesse and Lill, anyone you'd like to get to know better?" When they said they were happy to go along with any choice, Jasirey said, "You decide about the others, Ian."

* * *

Together with Reginald, the husbands devised a light schedule with emphasis on family and one day for the library.

The men cleverly planned social visits near sites of historic or scenic interest. Jasirey enjoyed those smaller get-togethers—tea with childhood friends of Reginald, a local play featuring a corporate executive's daughter and dinner afterward with real conversations.

Midweek, the adults joined Bryant at his golf club. Reginald was an avid golfer, Ian and Jesse played fairly well, and Lee more enthusiastically than well. The rest of the party enjoyed the trees and ponds along the fastidiously tended course.

Satisfied with the relationship developing between Bryant and Reginald, Jasirey kept her mouth shut. She offered only one thing. "Are you attending the Spotiswood Ball, Bryant?"

"I am not personally acquainted with His Lordship."

"Would you care to go if asked?"

Bryant blinked in confusion, not sure if she were asking him to accompany her family.

Reginald stepped up, placed his hands on Jasirey's shoulders, and pointed her at Ian over by a grove of trees. "I believe your husband requires help finding his ball. I trust you're good at that." She burst out laughing and obediently left the two men alone.

"Unusual woman," Bryant said.

"She fancies herself a matchmaker."

"I don't seem to mind." Uncharacteristically direct, he asked, "Do you, Reginald?"

"Please call me Reggie."

❧ ❧ ❧

That evening, Jasirey tried to mind her own business. For about two minutes. She plopped down beside Reginald on the sofa. "What happened? Did you invite him?"

"You do realize what an interfering woman you are."

"And you like me despite my gauche faults."

"Do I indeed? I shall have to think about that." Though his lips firmed in a disapproving line, the corners twitched upward. "And yes, he graciously accepted my invitation."

She gave him a brief, hard hug. "I truly hope this works out for both of you. You have a lot to give."

Reginald kissed her cheek. "Thank you, my dear. I'm happy to have you think so. I believe I like you tremendously."

Destiny's Sharp Edge

The following evening, Reginald led Jasirey, Ian, Jessie, and Lill into a pub in a nearby town for drinks with the head of an accounting firm that worked as a retainer for the London branch of Ian's corporation. Lee, Liu, and Fael along with Kimika, Mirai, and Andwar spread throughout the cozily crowded space. As Reginald led Jasirey to a semi-private table in a back corner, she halted and pressed a hand to her chest where it felt as though an anvil had landed.

Ian rubbed her rigid back. "What's wrong?"

Breathe, just breathe. "Not sure." But she was. "Later. Let's not make a scene."

A couple in their mid-thirties stood when they saw the group. The woman's eyes latched on to Jasirey's and punched hard at her calm façade as Jasirey recognized the unhealthy light emanating from the woman and the man beside her.

"Ian," Reginald said, "you know Samara. This is her husband, Jackson, legal counsel for their accounting firm as well as co-owner, of course. Samara and Jackson, you met Ian's wife, Shannon, at the party."

Jasirey turned as though she hadn't seen Samara extend her hand and introduced Jessie and Lill. Aware of the maneuver, Ian sat Jasirey across from his business associates and between him and Reginald. Lill and Jessie sat beside Samara and Jackson.

"Are you enjoying your holiday, Shannon?" Samara asked.

The woman had brown eyes as warm as a dark hole. Jasirey instinctively knew she had been the one watching her at the party. Training had honed Jasirey's ability to project pictures and emotions and to probe another's psyche, but she found doing so with volunteers or friends vastly different from confronting the couple's . . . evil. It was the only word that fit.

Under the layer of polite interest, Jasirey felt the couple's cold glee at her obvious uncertainty in their presence. And that killed any reluctance she felt at prying into the couple's psyche. "Ian has his business-related duties," she said. "I've enjoyed becoming acquainted with a few people." She waved a careless hand. "Feel free to talk shop." She noted Reginald's start of surprise.

Jackson's reptilian smile cooled beneath simmering eyes. Samara subtly elbowed him, and both angled their faces toward Ian.

Reginald raised a questioning brow, and Jasirey gently squeezed his knee to convey a need for silence as she set out on a fishing expedition.

Reginald felt a pulse of energy emanate from Jasirey. The prickly feeling heated to a sense of danger, though Jasirey remained outwardly calm and still.

Alert to the power pouring from Jasirey, Ian relied on his training to keep his attention focused on his business associates.

Samara and Jackson lacked that discipline. Their awareness of something amiss becoming more evident with each pass, their eyes strayed several times to seemingly oblivious Jasirey. Their poise shattered when an Asian man and woman approached and flanked her.

"The bartender," Kimika said to his lady, eyes hard on the couple, "recognized the gate you projected to me—it's quite distinctive—and the people who own the property it guards. The local authorities have been notified."

"We should leave now, lady," Mirai said. "Ian will deal with the police."

Like that of an annoyed bull, Jackson's head swung between Mirai and Kimika, who moved around the table to pull out Lill and Jesse's chairs. His voice hissed. "What is this?"

Samara began to rise and stopped at an imperious flick of Ian's hand. Lee, Liu, and Fael joined the group to lead Jasirey from the pub. Kimika remained to fill in Ian.

❦ ❦ ❦

An excess of residual energy goaded Jasirey to pace Reginald's parlor. Not sure how to aid their lady, her husbands and people kept watch.

"I don't understand," Jessie said. "How can you be so sure people were in danger?"

On the sofa beside her husband, Lill flicked at his arm. "I told you she's psychic."

Jasirey had to smile but let it die as she realized she could not protect them from the ugliness she'd seen. "Samara and Jackson pay traffickers to smuggle immigrants here—slave labor. She has a family vineyard. And for . . . " She rubbed at her temples. "Let's just say the two of them feed each other's perversions."

Liu stepped into her path and helped her sink down onto an ottoman.

"I'm okay," Jasirey assured him and everyone else. "We'll ensure that those poor people aren't simply deported to avoid any political embarrassment." It wasn't a question.

"As this information came to the police via an anonymous source," Fael said, "we are not legally involved, however . . . " He looked pointedly at Reginald.

"We will certainly see to it that they are sorted out," Reginald said. He lowered himself beside her and took her hand. "You somehow saw the immigrants, their location." He hesitated. "Saw what was done to them."

Jasirey's face went blank. "I felt confusion, terror, pain. A few are only teenagers."

"Enough." Reginald's ravaged eyes sought the men. "Don't allow her to do that. She cannot be expected to do that."

"I've never had such clear and specific pictures and feelings before. I guess this time off cleared my head, allowed the training to gel."

Lill clutched at her husband. "What does she mean? She actually feels . . . ? Jessie?"

Jasirey telepathically eased the horror twisting in her friends' hearts but ran out of energy to do the same for her husbands and people. She resigned herself to the knowledge that, as she met her destiny, they would have to handle any repercussions to themselves as they witnessed her doing so.

⁂

Reginald had fortunately set the next day aside for the library and the children. Their parents carried the babies outside to a lovely warm morning. The children struggled to get down and then walked holding on to adult fingers, their favorite new activity. Jasirey tired less easily at the task. As her husbands archly pointed out, she didn't have that far to bend. Lill scoffed at their excuses and lent a hand or two.

They returned to the house for lunch and found Mtombe waiting in the parlor. A happy welcome in her eyes, Jasirey hugged him.

Mtombe chastely kissed her on each cheek and stepped toward Ian to shake his hand.

Ian introduced him to Reginald as a family friend and associate.

"I am sorry to interrupt your holiday," Mtombe said. "A matter of some import has come to my attention and requires Ian and his security's input. I shall not take long."

Reginald offered his office. Kimika and Yusef joined the men as they made their apologies. Mirai had taken Nikolai's team to scout out the Spotiswood estate. Jasirey harbored no illusions that Mtombe had arrived for a casual visit.

Lill, Jesse, and Reginald helped feed the babies lunch. Afterward, Jasirey asked a few security people to take them to the nursery.

The men still huddled in the office, and the rest of the adults went to the library. Jasirey had almost managed to immerse herself in a copy of Dickens's *Bleak House*, the one novel of his she had trouble getting into, when her husbands joined them minus Mtombe. As afternoon tea would soon be served, they declined Reginald's offer of a late lunch.

Ian led Jasirey out to the entrance hall. "I'll explain later. Mtombe is waiting to say goodbye at the garage."

She hurried out and found Mtombe, who clasped her hands in his.

"I've missed you, loveling," he said. Jasirey's smile imparted such love and belonging that everything askew in his mind righted. "I asked, and your men agreed, that I might join the family during your stay in London."

"I'd like that, but why have you come here?"

"Let your husbands explain." He looked sheepish. "I came to London for business and could have simply called, but I wished . . . needed to see you. I want to hear about being your wild boar. In London. There is not time now." He cupped her face for a second. "Back you go to your family."

"I think you realize you're part of my family as well."

Mtombe grinned, gave Jasirey a hug, and jogged over to a battered sedan. He waved and drove away from the manor.

Not ready to face whatever Mtombe had brought with him, Jasirey paced in a rose garden. She suspected it had to do with the lava-like colors flashing nightly in her dreams. She knew she should inform the Imperiat but had nothing concrete to share.

Lee came searching for her and engulfed her in his big arms.

"Lee, are we endangering Reggie by being here?"

"Doubtful with our security."

"But possible. I think we should talk to all the adults."

"All right. Let us first tell you why Mtombe came." Lee held her hand as they returned to the entrance hall, then left her to bring out Fael, Ian, and Liu.

They all agreed to include Reginald, Jesse, and Lill since they deserved to be told of any danger that could affect them. As he brought in Kimika and Yusef, Fael asked their friends to sit on the couch with Jasirey.

"Jesse and Lill, you remember the attack on Jasirey," Ian said.

The couple nodded and clutched each other's hands. They had seen the aftermath of Marcus's attack but weren't told the details.

Reginald placed an arm about Jasirey.

"A man named Marcus peddles humans—mostly for the sex trade." Ian's level tone clashed with his harsh expression. "The four of us have interfered with his sales or acquisitions a few times. I won't go into that, but his abduction of Jasirey was rooted in vengeance."

Reginald's head reeled. *Why would anyone wish harm to such a lovely woman? And what in the bloody hell did Ian mean by interfere?*

"Marcus arrived in the country two days ago," Lee said. "As the young men Mtombe works with have at times run afoul of Marcus, he monitors the trafficker's activities and has uncovered no intel of any business the man means to conduct here in the UK. We therefore believe his agenda of revenge remains the same."

Eyes glinting with deadly purpose, Fael sent shivers down their spines. "Profit no doubt also motivates him. He would not believe Jasirey's legend. Others do, and her children might be used to gain wealth, perhaps even power."

Lee growled. "Marcus is the foulest sociopath we've ever dealt with. He cares for no one and uses people in whatever way achieves his goals."

"Meaning us." Jesse's voice remained calm, though he pulled Lill closer.

"I doubt he's looking at people traveling with us," Ian said. "Not with our security forces. Reginald, you he might exploit through family or friends."

"Consider," Fael said, "that you make a less attractive target simply by our leaving."

Reginald drew in a steadying breath. "I have never cared for conceding to bullies."

"Reggie, please." Jasirey's voice rose in pitch. "If you got hurt or Bryant . . . "

Reginald's back stiffened. "He couldn't know Bryant. I barely know him."

"He has someone watching us." Jasirey glanced at Fael who nodded in confirmation. "I think revenge became secondary when I challenged his sense of authority on that boat of his and became his obsession. I've been dreaming of danger coming. I should have informed the Imperiat, but there was nothing specific in the dreams to report. Everyone would be safe if we had stayed on the island."

"Beloved, keep in mind your prophecy," Fael said. "It is meant to be."

Though privy to some of the details of Jasirey's vision quest in the Imperiatu and her prophecy, Lill, Jesse, and Reginald had trouble following the discourse. However, they certainly recognized Jasirey's distress.

Reginald had ordered an early tea for the men and poured Jasirey a cup of Earl Grey with her preferred lemon, a bit stronger stimulant than the green tea she usually drank in the afternoon.

Reginald handed Jasirey a teacup as he asked, "Ian, can you protect Jasirey and the children here?"

Lee signaled Kimika to answer. "We don't sit helplessly waiting for an attack. Marcus is not a wanted criminal in Great Britain, but neither is he here legally, which lessens his ability to move freely in the country. He'll need to rely on associates, a weak spot we can exploit."

"Scotland Yard will come into play there," Fael said.

"I agree that running from threats is not a feasible plan," Kimika said, eyes on Jasirey. He did not like to see her worried. "Lady, what kind of life would you have confined to the island?"

"You don't have children," she said fiercely. "You can't endanger children."

Lill rescued Jasirey's untouched, badly trembling teacup.

Kimika squatted and cradled his surrogate mother's hands in his. "I have loved ones I'd give my life to protect. Is it so different?"

Reginald handed Jasirey his handkerchief despite needing it himself. He reached for a napkin. "Right," he said, "it's decided. Stay here, continue your holiday, and trust your security to keep us safe. I have every confidence. Let's have that tea." Reginald patted Kimika's shoulder. "Thank you, son."

Kimika kissed his lady's damp cheek.

"There now, my dear, I think we all need a little time. I will cancel tomorrow's engagement. Roberta is quite flexible about last-minute changes. Saturday, we attend the Spotiswood Ball, and Kimika shall provide impenetrable walls of defense around us."

Lee recognized the fight before them to convince Jasirey to leave her children for a dance. "Gentlemen, we know full well how stubborn our wife can be. How do we assure her the situation is under control?"

"Lee," she said quietly, "don't make light of this. I trust you all, but sometimes the bad guys win. I'd like to talk to Kai after dinner."

"Not a problem, little one."

She stood. "Jesse, Lill, you probably are safer with us but take time to talk while we get the babies ready for dinner."

Lill jumped up to vise her arms about her friend. "We don't need to talk. I know Jesse agrees we won't be dictated to by a maniac. We're family. We'll stick together and be fine."

Jesse added his arms about both women. "And that answers that."

Reginald patted Jasirey's shoulder. "All will be well. Why not speak to this Kai person before dinner? Perhaps he can ease your mind so you eat more heartily than you managed at lunch. Jesse, Lill, Kimika, and I can handle the children for a bit."

With a watery smile, she heeded his advice and borrowed his office once more. Master Kai came onscreen immediately. He and many of the Imperiat had spent much of the previous few days in the security center. The Imperiat understood the signs of stress Jasirey exhibited. They did not have to like it.

"How are you, dear one?"

Glad to see Master Kai despite the circumstances, Jasirey smiled. "Worried. Our lives have spread out. So many can be affected by people who might hurt them to get at us. It makes me leery of making friends. How many can we protect?"

Master Howard, an expert in defense strategies, stepped close to the screen. "As many as need be." He turned and pointed the web cam at the physical map she'd seen on her tour of the island's security center when she'd last visited the island. He used a pointer to highlight areas in the States that corresponded to where her parents lived, her sisters, and Lizzie. Yellow magnets surrounded each location. He tapped them. "Our people."

He moved toward Boston. "As your friends are with you, most of those who were stationed there are now here." The pointer moved across the Atlantic to England. Magnets, too many to count, surrounded Heathrow Airport and Everett's family. Others congregated southeast where Reginald's estate stood and dotted various cities and ports.

"Lookouts," Master Howard said. He touched a cluster of red magnets. "Marcus's location. We expect he has considerable intelligence and a planned means of escape. Known and suspected associates are under surveillance."

Jasirey sat abruptly. "I had no idea. How long have you been at this?"

"From the moment you became Jasirey," the man said cheerfully.

"It is what we do, why we are here," a councilwoman said. "Your welfare is of utmost importance to us."

Jasirey buried her face in Liu's side.

"I hope these are tears of relief rather than further stress," Master Kai said gently.

Jasirey rallied. "So, we attend the ball, sort of like Cinderella and her friends."

"Friends?" asked Lee. He didn't remember any friends in the story.

"Movie version, animal friends turned into coachmen and horses . . . Never mind."

"What else weighs on you, dear one?"

Jasirey sighed. "I promised to tell you about my dreams." Council and Imperiat members stood quietly attentive, and Jasirey described what she'd been experiencing.

Her revelations troubled Master Kai, though he kept his expression neutral. "How long have you been dreaming in this manner?"

"Pretty much every night since we arrived in England."

"Perhaps related to the current whereabouts of the trafficker." He regarded her speculatively. "There is more, yes?"

Needing the answer but feeling ungrateful, Jasirey blushed.

"Jasirey, you shall piss us off if you refuse to confide in us."

Jasirey burst out laughing at his borrowing of one of her phrases. "It doesn't seem very important now."

Master Kai merely raised an eyebrow.

Jasirey barely refrained from casting up her eyes. "Marcus is an obvious case of someone needing to be stopped. In other cases, missions . . . "—she didn't mention but had certainly noted all the other red magnets on the map—" . . . what safeguards do we employ to prevent any harm or mistakes? How do we follow the ripples that might spread out from an intervention and maybe cause a more destructive future reaction?"

The leaders converged, all intently concentrated on Jasirey. The husbands instinctively closed ranks as her eyes widened.

"Hurting or offending you is the very last thing I intended," she said. "I'm just curious about the checks and balances."

"It is a wise and insightful concern," Master Howard said. "Years back, long before your husbands' time of service, an incident occurred where the Devoted freed a village from a tyrannical ruler. Within weeks, aware of the power void, rival villages attacked and virtually destroyed the village. Many died or were enslaved."

Ian, Fael, Lee, and Liu had been trained with the iconic tale that underscored the minute attention to detail demanded for planning and conducting missions.

"We created a series of committees designed to thoroughly examine mission plans. Completed missions are monitored for any unintended—ripples—as you concisely interpreted it. Indications must be positive to proceed, and minimum intervention employed."

"Such as calling in local authorities." Tension eased from Jasirey's body. "I'm amazed by all of you, by your dedication and caring. Thank you."

"You are the whole," Master Kai said, "the force that binds us. We are blessed to have such a person to serve."

Jasirey's hand brushed the screen.

"I will consider that an embrace, dearest one," Master Kai told her. "Your husbands will no doubt be happy to give you ours."

Reginald ordered an early dinner. The men hadn't eaten. The teens had theirs and video games in the lesser sitting room with a returned Andwar and Chen for company.

"We thought it best to keep them occupied elsewhere tonight," Lill said.

Jasirey smiled brightly as she described the thoroughness of protection the Devoted provided. The husbands watched and waited for their wife's reaction, overdue since Marcus's attack on her.

Jasirey's spate of words cut off, and a surge of heat hit everyone in the room. Her anger boiled. *That rat bastard.* And erupted.

Reginald took a step back with the dish of potatoes he'd been feeding Colin.

Lill instinctively rushed to her friend but stopped at the ferocious gleam in her eyes.

Jesse joined his wife. "Let her husbands deal with it," he said.

"Oh, yeah," Lill replied in awe.

Reginald didn't care if his retreat over to Jesse and Lill looked undignified. "There's that saying," he whispered. "If looks could kill."

Jasirey's men guided her out to the grounds. She didn't run, exactly. She vaulted over flowers, benches, even a low hedgerow at a graceful, rage-driven speed. They blocked her access to the thorn-laden rose gardens and otherwise let her be. Jasirey ran out of breath before running out of anger and collapsed in a heap.

Right on her heels, Lee sprang into a flying leap to keep from crashing into her. Her blouse stuck to Jasirey's dampened skin as she gulped in air.

Lee followed his gut, tore the blouse and bra from her heaving breast, and clamped onto one. Her back arched off the ground in an immediate orgasm. The men gave her no time to come down. Her clothes disappeared and hands, fingers, and mouths caressing or entering her body catapulted Jasirey back to the peak.

Several sets of strong arms supported her as the husbands flipped her onto her hands and knees. One entered roughly, the others continuously stimulating sensitized pleasure points. Jasirey reveled in the plunging friction and let worry and rage melt away. Her lungs burned despite the cool air. Her body gathered to the point of pain, and a finger eased up her ass ripped a scream and a massive eruption of release from her.

Gentler orgasms followed as the men withdrew. A phalanx of warm male bodies preventing hers from cooling too rapidly, they cuddled Jasirey. They wiped her down with her ruined blouse, then bundled her into Liu's large shirt. She twined about Lee's neck as he lifted her onto his lap. Scattered thoughts left her tongue-tied, so she beckoned her men with outstretched arms.

The husbands understood precisely what their wife wished to convey.

Reginald heard the group return and poked his head into the entrance hall. Jesse and Lill craned from behind him. All three ogled their friends' disarray. Grass in her hair, Jasirey looked small in Liu's shirt with her face buried in Lee's neck. She remained oblivious to the gawking trio while the men grinned unabashedly and climbed the stairs.

"I guess they took care of her," Jessie said. His hand ran down Lill's shapely behind.

Jasirey and her men showered, dressed quickly, and returned to their once more delayed meal. When the little ones became sleepy, Mirai and security took them to bed.

Lill cornered Jasirey in the parlor. "Thank you in advance for tonight." Her eyes gleamed. "I expect my husband's in the mood to outdo himself."

Jasirey smiled ruefully. "Good luck with that. Personally, I'm a little sore."

Lill had no sympathy. "And otherwise, you feel like a million bucks."

Jasirey's grin didn't deny it. Jesse and Lill bade everyone an early good night.

Jasirey sat beside Reginald. "I'm sorry for today's hullabaloo. Are you okay?"

"With all the bloody pheromones about, I feel rather the odd man out."

"Oh, poor Reggie, I'm sorry."

He patted her hand. "I'm pleased to see you back on form."

She linked arms. "I talked to the Devoted about the missions. Their concerns mirror yours. They take substantial precautions in investigating each potential action to minimize unintentional consequences."

"And this all done for you, which unites them. I can think of no one else I'd serve so devotedly. Perhaps your gift is to bring people together in common cause, something the world truly lacks right now."

The Spotiswood Ball

According to Reginald, the Spotiswood Ball ranked several social steps up from his weekend shindig. Lill wore a sparkling silver sheath with spaghetti straps that showcased strong shoulders and well-defined arms. Jesse's black and white was very handsome and called further attention to his brightly contrasting wife.

Jasirey wore her new black *bling* gown that needed no jewelry save her wedding band and engagement ring Ian had given her for their legal marriage in the US. She had borrowed a blow dryer, and her hair waved in pixyish abandon. Her eyes and face glowed with softly applied glamor.

Ian slowly twirled Jasirey. "A—maz—ing." He shunned tradition and wore a black shirt and pewter satin tie with his formal black suit.

Jasirey kissed him to acknowledge that he'd dressed for her. Black and white didn't suit his pale complexion. It looked wonderful on the others. She'd have wolf-whistled if she knew how.

Reginald met them in the parlor and complimented both men and women. Lacing his fingers in Jasirey's, he excused the two of them from the group, guided her to his office, and opened a small wall safe. He handed her a shallow hinged box.

"These belonged to my mother. She would have been happy to let you borrow them." On a glossy bed of satin lay a necklace that graduated from small diamond clusters to bigger stones, the largest at the center.

It flamed in the light and, lying flat, reminded Jasirey of a tiara.

Reginald carefully draped it around her neck. "It's perfect for this dress, my dear."

"Reggie, it must be priceless. Are you sure the clasp is secure? I'd hate to lose it."

"Foolish woman." Under the top tray sat another, which held long earrings in like style and a cuff bracelet with stones of equal size. He attached the screw-back earrings to Jasirey's small ears and pushed the cuff into place on her right wrist. "More magnificent than any constellation in the heavens."

"Now who's being foolish? Thank you, Reggie. I'll take good care of them."

The office contained no mirror, which mattered not one whit to her. She was the least vain creature Reginald had ever met and would probably notice only how the diamonds sparkled if she did have one. When they returned to the others, their reactions satisfied him.

"Wow!" Lill goggled.

"Shiny," Jesse said with a twinkle.

"For plain diamonds," Jasirey said, "these are especially beautiful, aren't they?"

Reginald shared an amused glance with her husbands, who teasingly told their friends about her unsophisticated preference for amethysts. Jasirey stuck her tongue out at them.

❧ ❧ ❧

Kimika and Yusef stayed behind with the children. Nikolai's team, Mirai, and three more women from her squad accompanied the adults. Others worked as waitstaff at the Spotiswood estate. Ian procured a limousine for the partygoers and stopped for Bryant. They arrived promptly. Lord and Lady Spotiswood had little tolerance for the notion of being fashionably late.

The manor was easily three times the size of Reginald's. The grounds contained multiple flower gardens, a tennis court, and topiary—geometric shapes rather than animals. One circular shrub enclosed in a shorter hexagonal wall fascinated Jasirey. She wondered how the gardeners found room to prune it.

The elderly lord and lady formally received their guests in the broad entrance. Several couples—Jasirey assumed the hosts' children and spouses—stood alongside them. The line moved rapidly. Jasirey expected to smile, greet their hosts, and move on.

Lord Spotiswood grasped both Jasirey's hands and held them apart to get a better view. "Perfection, my dear. Welcome."

She smiled at his sweet, gentle charm. "Thank you for the invitation."

Lady Spotiswood leaned forward confidentially. "You must save a dance for my husband." Her eyes crinkled. "He is quite taken with you."

Jasirey grinned and moved on to their oldest daughter who was much like her mother. "I understand what my father sees in you," she said nicely. "Your smile is indeed memorable."

The daughter's husband curled his fingers about Jasirey's wrist. "Indeed," he echoed. Her smile dimmed to polite attentiveness as his eyes raked up and down.

Ian felt the change in his wife's body and zeroed in on the son-in-law's man-on-the-hunt gaze. Ian answered it with a cool warning the arrogant man attempted and failed to brazen out. His eyes skittered away as he pouted.

Past the reception line, people entered a parlor the size of Reginald's ballroom for drinks. Jasirey's group reacquainted with many couples from the previous week's party, including Roberta, again in unrelieved black but on the arm of a different, equally handsome man.

"I was disappointed to lose the opportunity for a tête-à-tête," Roberta said in her straightforward way. "I visit the States once or twice a year. Let us make it a point to get together then, shall we?"

Jasirey lifted her glass of iced tea to seal the bargain. "Definitely."

Dinner was announced. Lord Spotiswood sat at the head of a gargantuan table, a well-known soprano to his right as guest of honor. Jasirey and Ian were seated to his left.

"I understand you sing," Lord Spotiswood said. "Please favor us with a song later."

At a loss, Jasirey blinked.

Ian smoothly interjected. "I doubt the accompanist is familiar with the songs Shannon prefers." He squeezed her hand when she flashed him a grateful smile. "If an acoustic guitar is available, she could accompany herself." His smug smile slipped as color drained from her face.

"I shall see to it." His Lordship greatly anticipated the sweet lady's performance.

"Betrayed by my own husband." Jasirey's whisper rose in pitch. "Do you realize how long it's been? What if I can't remember anything?"

Ian hadn't considered that. He gave her a feeble pat. "Maybe it's like riding a bike."

She cast a withering glare at him, set a hand on her fluttering stomach, and mournfully eyed her plate. "I won't be able to eat."

"I imagine singing's easier on an empty stomach." Ian waited out her struggle not to whap him and believed it a good thing she was unaware of the soprano's fame.

Jasirey appreciated none of the lavish meal and cursed the fact that she had to continually wipe her sweaty palms on the linen napkin. The party at length returned to the parlor where a wide semicircle of chairs had been set up before a grand piano.

Ian's arm circled behind Jasirey as she took an involuntary step backward. "Courage, love, you'll be wonderful. Choose something you'd sing to the people and pretend they're in front of you."

"Ian, don't ever do this to me again."

"I didn't do it this time," he growled.

Jasirey's eyes narrowed. "Where's Reggie?"

Oops. "Never mind, you can berate him at home. It's too late now."

"Shit."

"Shannon Rose," Ian said with a hushed laughed.

"I'd like to see your reaction if you were dragooned into singing."

"It's hardly that drastic. Face it, baby, you're talented. Don't be selfish. Share your gifts."

Although his comment stung, Ian bathed her in love with dark eyes that calmed the anxiety roiling in her stomach. A brass quintet and then a cellist performed, both excellent. One of the Spotiswood daughters introduced Jasirey, and Ian escorted her to the piano. He fetched a chair at her request, and she sat facing the audience.

Someone handed her a guitar. Cradling it on her lap, she strummed to ensure it was in tune.

Smiling with childlike anticipation, Lord Spotiswood sat directly in front. On impulse, Jasirey switched from the golden oldies medley she'd decided on to a love song and sang to him. She played chords, and her fingerpicking provided a rich accompaniment.

Jasirey chose a folk song with a range and emotional depth that stirred her audience. The guitar music complemented her tone beautifully, and the diamonds and her voice sparkled about her as brightly radiant as her face. She ended on a sweet, floating note.

The audience applauded loudly and called, "Brava."

His Lordship rose and kissed her cheeks. "Enchanting, my dear. Absolutely enchanting."

Ian returned her to their seats. "Hauntingly beautiful, my love. I'm glad you did it."

She held his hand lightly as her tension drained.

The audience quieted for introduction of the main attraction. The soprano had a commanding presence and a powerful voice that exuded technical excellence. Jasirey recognized the expertise regardless of not caring for heavy vibrato. The soprano sang an aria from *Madame Butterfly* and received enthusiastic applause and a standing ovation.

The entertainment concluded, and the guests were ushered to a ballroom lit up by three barrel-sized crystal chandeliers. A large orchestra played on a dais.

Wisely not wishing to compete with the crush of admirers he knew awaited, Lord Spotiswood claimed Jasirey for the first dance. He stepped slowly and pivoted gracefully.

"What did you think of our opera star?" he asked.

"She's very proficient," Jasirey said.

"I don't care for such a heavy voice, myself," he said, eyes shining merrily. "I much prefer one easy on the ears. Being easy on the eyes doesn't hurt either, eh?"

Lord Spotiswood's son-in-law Harris stepped up and asked to cut in. Jasirey drew back at the breath of alcohol in her face, but something else caused the overly bright gleam in the man's eyes.

Lord Spotiswood's grip instinctively tightened as Jasirey's body stiffened. "Surely, Harris, you do not intend to interrupt an old man's one dance of the evening."

Harris's eyes glittered. He bowed stiffly and moved off.

The old gentleman zeroed in on his partner's unusual eyes the color of blue spruce trees. "Don't care for him, do you?"

"No, I really don't." Jasirey felt compelled to add, "I don't think he much likes you, either. You might want to be careful of him."

Sincere concern in her eyes touched him. "Thank you, my dear. I may take a closer peek at him. In the meantime, if Harris bothers you, sic your husband on him. He'll do a creditable job of protecting you, I'm sure."

To His Lordship's delight, Jasirey kissed his cheek.

"I like you, young lady. Thank you for the dance." He escorted her to her husband.

Oblivious to the striking couple they made, Jasirey followed Ian onto the floor.

After his dance, Ian handed her to Liu, who ended his dance in front of Fael. He in turn brought her to Lee.

"Perfect choreography," Jasirey said. She failed dismally at dimming her glowing eyes.

Lee winked. "Jesse and Reginald are next." His eyes softened. "You sang and played beautifully, little one." His wife instinctively moved closer, and he spun her into Jesse's arms.

The doctor quickly detoured away from other ardent admirers.

Jasirey laughed, then became serious. "Are you and Lill enjoying this vacation, Jesse?"

"Very much. The different culture, though you'll never persuade me the English know what pudding is—the people we've met—it's been fun. We haven't relaxed like this in some time." At Jasirey's incredulous look, he said, "Admit it. Most of this trip has been wonderful."

She briefly pressed her cheek to his. "Admitted."

"Lill and I enjoyed your song. You have a more powerful voice than we realized from listening to you sing to the babies."

"Ian refused to let me chicken out."

"Good for him." Jesse saw Reginald waiting and steered her toward him.

Reginald masterfully twirled her back onto the floor.

Jasirey frowned at him. "I should yell at you for putting me on the spot like that."

"Since you'd never do anything so nefarious. You were brilliant, by the way."

"Bryant was for your happiness," she said with exaggerated dignity.

"And what I did made even more people happy, therefore I win."

Jasirey laughed at his absurd logic.

"And this way, you spent less time being anxious."

"And had less time to get out of it." What little annoyance she'd harbored melted.

Her beautiful eyes filled with a loving light that inexplicably brought Reginald back to childhood memories of his family roasting marshmallows at the fireplace.

"Are you happy, Reggie?"

"I am, my sweet, never more so. Thank you for being interfering." Blinded by the joyful light in her eyes, he missed a step and covered by handing her to Bryant.

Bryant smiled down at Jasirey. "I hope you don't mind. I think Reggie wishes us to be friends. He's quite fond of you and oddly proud of your accomplishments."

"He takes credit for pushing me into the life of a social butterfly."

Bryant considered a moment. "Perhaps you've brought out the best in each other."

"No doubt about it. I treasure his friendship."

"As do I." Bryant's gaze fluttered from her face to over her shoulder.

"I've been praying for the two of you. You're good together."

He blinked at the unexpected reassurance her sweet words brought him.

The rest of the evening was a free-for-all to capture the charming newcomer for a dance. Some flirted, which Jasirey returned within bounds. Others tried wangling her favor as a conduit to Ian. Those she ignored with polite, inoffensive firmness. Most, to her dismay since younger, prettier women abounded in the ballroom, simply wanted her company.

After two hours of continual partner changes that prevented her from flagging the circulating waitstaff, Jasirey grew tired and dehydrated. Posted specifically to their lady by Kimika, Mirai noticed signs of physical distress and ordered Andwar to intervene. He bulled his way forward and steered her outside to a wide veranda. A waiter, obviously one of the people, brought her an iced tea and a plate of hors d'oeuvres. Mirai asked Andwar to inform Jasirey's husbands where she was.

"It feels good to sit. Thanks, Mirai."

"My pleasure." She smiled, bowed, and retreated to an out-of-the-way corner as the husbands joined Jasirey.

"Tired, precious one?" Liu sat with her.

"Warm and thirsty. This cool air will revive me."

"Having fun?" Ian asked.

"Honestly, not so much. Small gatherings are more my cup of tea. Dancing's fun with my handsome men. You guys don't trample my feet. That gets old after the fifth or sixth time."

"Did someone actually step on you?" Lee asked in concern.

"Several someones—toes, instep—one even bashed my heel as we left the floor."

Liu stripped off her sandal and found the injury. "He produced quite a bruise."

"I'm fine."

"Yes, you are." He kissed the swollen spot. "Beautiful and charming."

"Well, in that case, I'll let more of them trample me."

"Your feet are done for the night."

Jasirey smiled at Liu's take-charge healer's voice. "Good luck getting through the horde in there, and I don't want to drag the others away if they're not ready."

Fael sent Andwar to find out.

Jasirey winced when Liu's fingers hit a sore spot and sighed as Ian leaned her back into a soothing kiss. "So much better than dancing," she murmured.

Jesse, Lill, Reginald, and Bryant joined them. "Oh, can I sit, too?" Lill wilted onto the bench. "Aren't there enough women to go around in there?"

Jasirey commiserated. "Did you get trampled, too?"

Jesse obliged his wife and rubbed her feet.

"Oh, yeah. Thank you, honey." She regarded the men suspiciously. "Were you guys dancing all this time?" Unlike her, she was sure, they didn't appear the least bit frazzled.

Jesse's eyes twinkled. "Apparently we aren't as charming and desirable."

"Says who?" Jasirey's chin lifted.

"Every man determined to dance with the two most beautiful women here."

Jasirey gave Lill an arch look. "Means the women were too conservative to ask and our men too involved elsewhere to offer."

Lill scoffed out a laugh.

"Quiet," Jesse said, "or no more massages for you."

Lill's voice wheedled. "Sorry."

Jasirey poked her friend. "You're easy."

"Says the woman with four husbands to take care of her."

"Four—what?" Bryant whispered to Reginald.

"I'm sorry," Lill said, truly contrite.

Jasirey patted Reginald's arm. "Use your best judgment."

"I'll explain later," he said to Bryant.

"I thought you two were together." Bryant pointed between Lee and Fael.

Lee guffawed and pulled Fael in under an arm that dwarfed the smaller man. "You *are* awfully cute."

Fael slithered away and deftly pinned Lee's arm to his back. "What did you say?" He applied a bit more pressure.

"Okay, okay. Sorry."

Jasirey walked over and laid her cheek on Fael's. "I may want that arm later."

"I shall ensure mine suffice."

Lee whipped around and engulfed them both. "I don't think so," he said softly as he kissed his wife and knocked Fael on his backside.

Fael popped up instantly.

Jasirey stepped between them. *Pent up,* she supposed, *from too long having to be circumspect about their true role in the family, they certainly meant no harm.*

Fael lifted her into his arms and nuzzled her neck. "Shall we play American football to move our beloved through the throng?" He tossed her to Lee.

"Hey, watch the dress and the expensive jewels," she cried.

Bryant watched the horseplay in fascination. "Are they always this familiar?"

"They're family." Reginald laced his fingers in Bryant's. "Ladies and gentlemen, Lord and Lady Spotiswood retired. I suggest we make our escape before everyone decides the same."

Lee set Jasirey down for Ian to escort through the ballroom as propriety dictated.

❦ ❦ ❦

Jasirey hated to say goodbye to Reginald. "Promise you'll visit us soon."

"My word on it." Reginald kissed her cheeks.

The group returned to London but stayed at a mid-range hotel much like many others and used nondescript vans to travel in the city. Kimika, Yusef, Mirai, and Nikolai's team went everywhere with the family. Yusef and Mirai's squads blended in with other tourists and Londoners.

Jasirey received a disappointing e-mail from Mtombe. He found himself unable to join them after all. Business, he said, and promised to call when free.

The group rented a private catamaran for a restful afternoon cruising on the Thames, which the babies mostly slept through. The adults enjoyed seeing the Tower of London—a historic castle with several buildings centered within two rings of defensive walls and a moat. Among other official capacities, the Tower had been used as the royal residence, a prison, and home of the Crown Jewels of England. They passed the Palace of Westminster where the House of Commons and the House of Lords met. The teenagers mostly enjoyed the boat ride.

The next day, they toured Kensington Gardens and its Round Pond, actually more of a rectangle and home to the Model Yacht Sailing Association. The boys stayed there. Jasirey and Lill went to the Dutch Garden showcasing geometrical plantings of many flowers and edged by clipped, dense hedgerows and low walls—no tulips as the women had expected.

The women also went to the contemporary art galleries Serpentine South and, a five-minute walk away over the Serpentine Bridge, Serpentine North.

The following day, Everett and his family, including his seventeen-year-old and twelve-year-old grandsons and fifteen-year-old granddaughter, joined them to tour London Zoo. Bazir and the granddaughter loved tigers and huddled together at the Sumatran tiger enclosure.

Jasirey shared their sad dismay at the near extinction of all tigers. She would give a great deal to be able to affect the likely outcome.

The babies loved the high platforms in the Africa-themed section that afforded up-close views of giraffes. All enjoyed the aquarium. Jasirey refused to take the babies into the butterfly enclosure where their little fists could grab and crush fragile wings or the Tiny Giants section—formerly called B.U.G.S.—with its bird-eating spiders. Her sons teased unmercifully. It was the first her husbands learned of her arachnophobia.

The family, Jesse, and Lill had dinner in a private room off the hotel's charming pub-like restaurant. At Jasirey's pointed look, her teenagers bit back their adolescent humor as Everett's grandchildren ordered bangers and mash and recommended the steamed pudding spotted dick to them. Also, she didn't spoil Everett's grandchildren's fun and let on she knew they were having a joke at her teens' expense.

As dinner ended, Jasirey became still. Sitting beside her, Everett leaned in. "Are you all right, my dear?"

Jasirey quietly drew Fael's attention. "Something's wrong. There's plenty of security for Everett's family?"

Fael, Lee, Kimika, and Mirai led her from the room to a hall that entered the lobby. "What is it, little one?" Lee asked.

A man weaved drunkenly in the lobby. Jasirey tensed, and Mirai automatically stepped in front of her. The man sneered at the women and entered the elevators.

"You know him?" Mirai asked.

"Lord Spotiswood's son-in-law Harris."

"Do you believe him to be the source of your disquiet?" Fael asked.

"Maybe. I disliked him instantly."

"Let us go back in and say goodbye to Everett's family. Security shall keep them safe."

"I'll give Reginald a call," said Lee. "See if he's heard anything."

Reginald had a great deal to report. Lord Spotiswood had indeed investigated his son-in-law. Not particularly clever and arrogantly sure of his position in the family, Harris had barely covered up his peccadilloes, as he called them when excusing his behavior. Harris's position in the family business required him to oversee rental properties in London. Hired auditors found evidence of his penchant for raising rents without putting the new rate on the books and then pocketing the extra revenues.

Reginald said that Lord Spotiswood immediately sacked his son-in-law and sorrowfully informed his daughter Julia that, while her husband would not be prosecuted, he had lost his position. To the old Lordship's even greater sorrow, Julia begged him to reconsider having Harris charged. An official record of wrongdoing enabled her to enact their prenuptial agreement and more easily extricate herself from a miserable marriage. Lord Spotiswood felt a failure that his child had not felt free to come to him for help before then.

"Harris is now persona non grata," Reginald said, "to every social and business connection of the family and no doubt in a financial pinch."

Jasirey found it difficult to dredge up sympathy for the cocksure man.

We Learn By Doing

Fael and Mirai with her squad stayed in the next day with Jasirey and the babies while the rest went to a wax museum, Madame Tussauds. Jasirey had little interest in figures of sports or film stars and infamous murderers. The teenagers hoped the displays showed the murders.

"Little heathens," Jasirey said.

Mirai's lovely face lit in remembrance. "My brother used to be blood-thirsty in his teens. My mother was sure he'd wind up a mercenary. My dad laughing at her worries didn't help. She'd have worried less if she knew how patient he was with his pestering little sister."

"You said he's a boat mechanic?"

Jasirey's memory impressed Mirai. "Yes. And a gently sympathetic parent to a son who can't stand to step on an insect and a daughter who more often than not comes home scraped and bloody from one adventure or another."

"Jaimie's so much larger than her siblings," Jasirey said. "I'm hoping she doesn't take to terrorizing them."

Fael realized the light comment stemmed from ambivalence over her own compelling nature that she feared translated into the bullying control of others. He snuck in a kiss to his beloved's neck. "Her mother would never allow it."

Fael asked Mirai to assign several security people to put the babies down for their nap and, holding Jasirey's hand, led her to the suite's master bedroom.

First, her lavender blouse floated to the floor, then his dark brown loafers launched toward a chair. Fael draped Jasirey over his shoulder to push off her beige sneakers and unbuttoned her light charcoal gray slacks as he helped her slide back to the floor. His light yellow short-sleeved shirt and faded pair of blue jeans fell neatly on top of her slacks.

Gliding along the polished wood floor in thin cotton socks, they danced in their underwear—an ivory lace bra and panties and navy boxer briefs—to a radio station playing easy listening oldies from the 70s and 80s.

Jasirey sang along to Barbra Streisand's song *Evergreen.*

Spellbound, Fael stopped dancing to listen and found himself holding his breath on the amazingly long end note.

Jasirey watched him and laughed as they both gasped in air while Ms. Streisand's voice soared on.

Fael lifted and swung her around. "My beloved, I love and adore you." He carried her to the bed and proved his words.

Relaxed physically and mentally, Jasirey snuggled into Fael, but too soon felt the need to dress and pace as her brain clicked and clacked.

Fael understood that her struggle with looming decisions again crowded her mind since their vacation would soon end. Master Kai had asked her to come alone to the island for a two-week intensive training course with masters.

"Take a walk with Mirai," Fael said. "Think of nothing save the sights of the city. Clearing your mind may give you a better glimpse of your path."

"Like meditation, which I've sorely neglected."

"You have had little time. Go enjoy the different culture."

❧ ❧ ❧

The city retained more warmth than the countryside. Jasirey didn't bother with a sweater. Fewer people crowded the sidewalks on a Sunday afternoon. She recognized some of their security blending into the populace. They walked to an older section of the city where the shops were dark and narrow.

Jasirey entered a used bookstore. Hardcover books lined bookcases with paperbacks strewn on narrow tables, lending her a nostalgic peace. Interested to see the differences between the English and American versions, she bought a set of Harry Potter books.

Mirai wordlessly handed the heavy set to one of her team and steered Jasirey to an outside café for tea. They sat at a tiny table. Scones and homemade jam were served alongside a ceramic pot, cups, milk, and lemon. As she poured a second cup, a man jostled Jasirey as he took the table vacated by a couple beside them.

"I beg your pardon." The innocuous phrase rang with gloating menace as something hard that Jasirey assumed was a gun pushed into her ribs.

"Interfering bint. Now, now." Harris wagged an admonitory finger at Mirai. "Don't be foolish. You don't wish your mistress hurt. Leave the tab on the table and rise slowly. We'll be going to the street just ahead."

Jasirey didn't move and kept a bland expression as her stomach churned. Harris reeked of death. "Whatever he promised you, Marcus won't deliver. He intends to kill you," Jasirey told Harris.

Harris's bravado slipped. "How . . . ?" He snorted a nasty jeer. "You know nothing."

"Quick work on his part getting to you. He wants me alive. I'm not moving."

Fury sparked in the man's drug-dulled eyes. "Haven't a choice, have you?" The gun bruised. "Quite the whore from what he says. He has the African you lured into helping you escape his ship." Harris fumbled in his pocket, drew out a phone, and with surprising dexterity, pulled up a picture of Mtombe tied to a chair and glaring through swollen eyes at the camera. "Not looking his best, is he?"

Mtombe, no, Jasirey's mind moaned. She could have brazened through and escaped Harris. Marcus might not kill Mtombe, but her wild boar would wish himself dead long before Marcus finished with him. She said to Mirai, "Hold back security. I trust you and my husbands to find me and Mtombe."

"Is Mtombe's welfare more important to you than your children's?" Mirai asked brutally. "Let us save Mtombe."

"You can't. Harris has been told only what Marcus deemed necessary. He won't live long enough to take me to Mtombe."

Harris hissed. "Conversation's over. Get up."

Mirai subtly moved into position. "Mirai." Jasirey's soft voice lured, soothed. "Remember, I'm not defenseless."

The picture she often saw in the young woman's mind surfaced in Jasirey's. Mirai had been married and bore a son, Dickens, who became ill with cancer at the age of three. The marriage fragmented under the stress of their child's chemotherapy and its failure. After the funeral, her husband had almost ended his service to the Devoted. The marriage did not survive.

"I'm sorry, Mirai." Jasirey touched Mirai's arm and hated herself.

❦ ❦ ❦

Mirai could not push the memory away as it repeated in her mind. *Three-year-old Dickens lay in his toddler bed, tubes sprouting from his thin arms. No, no longer.*

They'd unhooked everything but the heart monitor, the lines and beeps erratic, fading. Dickens's father had to leave the room. Mirai, her parents, and Master N'yuwen kept vigil, waited . . . waited . . .

A man from Mirai's squad shook her shoulder. Jasirey had gone with a stranger. Security realized something amiss with Mirai when she simply sat at the café table staring at the street. Two members of her team rushed their dazed squad leader back to the hotel while the rest searched the area.

Fael seated Mirai at the suite's dining room table. "She hurt you." Mirai gazed into those glowing eyes in bewilderment.

"What happened?" Kimika asked her as Ian, Lee, Liu, and Yusef gathered round them.

Her elbows braced on the table, Mirai's head rested in her hands. "I'm not sure. One minute I planned to launch at Harris and the next, I was caught in . . . in a memory. I don't remember Jasirey leaving. Nothing until one of my team shook my shoulder. That's never happened to me. I don't understand."

"You do," Fael said. "What did Jasirey say just before?"

"She said Harris wouldn't have been told where Marcus was and wouldn't live long enough to bring her to Mtombe."

"True enough," Yusef said, devoid of sympathy for the fool.

"No, Mirai." Fael laid an insistent hand on her arm. "Remember. What did Jasirey say as you prepared to attack Harris?"

"She said, 'Remember.'" Mirai pushed up straight. "She put her hand on my arm, too, and said, 'Remember, I'm not defenseless.'" Mirai's eyes became unfocused. "She caused the memory, did that to me."

"Yes. I am sorry."

Mirai raised as tall as her stature allowed. "I had no idea of her power. She should have left Mtombe to us, but her abilities give us an edge. Let's incorporate that into our planning."

Kimika knew that under similar circumstances his own reaction would have been far less composed. He squeezed Mirai's shoulder.

Yusef struggled with the idea of their lady permitting herself to be endangered. Remedies flitted through his mind—a course in discipline, training in proper procedure, a good hiding.

Though sensing Mirai's internal struggle, Fael did not interfere. It was for Jasirey to make amends. But first, they must find her.

From a nearby computer, Nikolai updated the status of the online tracer. "She's heading inland, north. I see no main roads in the vicinity."

"Their route suggests a fear of surveillance, not knowledge of the tracer," Kimika said.

They soon lost contact as Jasirey's coordinates began to lift into the air. Considering the area, it would have to be a small plane. Security flooded London's Heathrow Airport, other British airports, airports across the channel, and in Ireland. If they landed within Britain, they could pick up the tracer again. Everything was in place for instant mobilization.

Ian noticed Fael's scowl. "What is it?"

"They head for an island or why utilize a plane?" Fael pushed away maps to find one of the islands off the northwest boundary of Scotland. "Here, I am sure of it. I can see them."

The other husbands' fierce smiles mirrored Fael's. Their wife had used telepathy to broadcast her position to Fael. She was not helpless.

❦ ❦ ❦

Jasirey blocked out everything except her objective and kept the shield of her fury close. No one touched her. Entering a dark sedan unaided, she had spared one glance for Harris lying in the alley, permanently delivered from his troubles.

They traveled south to Salisbury, down to Christchurch Harbour, and boarded a shallow-draught boat needed to get past the area's sandbars.

Jasirey wished she'd brought that sweater. The craft hugged the coast, came inland, and they guided Jasirey to another sedan. She'd expected to be taken to Marcus's ship. Yet again, they transferred modes of transportation. A small plane brought them inland. Hours later, they flew over a large island, landed, and took a boat to a smaller one.

Throughout the journey, Jasirey formed mental pictures of what she saw and projected them to Fael. Whether it worked—they must have traveled some distance from London—Jasirey could not tell. She felt nothing from Fael in return.

Marcus had rented a house on a hill with an uninterrupted and uninhabited view of the sea on three sides, woods in the back. Landing at the Isle of Skye airfield for private aircraft, the plane labeled *Her Highness* carried Jasirey and Marcus's henchmen. The party then took a boat to Eriskay, one of the Outer Hebrides Islands housing few people and renowned for its wild ponies.

Connected to the larger South Uist Island by a causeway, the destination island lay forty-three miles from the mainland with a ferry terminal that provided a forty-minute ride to the southwest island of Barra. No boat or car could approach undetected, and Marcus's ship was a speedboat ride away if problems arose.

With the courtly manners it pleased him to affect, Marcus received Jasirey in a sunset-lit office one entered from a wraparound porch. She took the seat offered at a small table set for two with finger foods and a tea service. He'd remembered her preference.

Her stomach growled. She'd traveled most of the day without anything to eat or drink. She heard no other sounds of people, saw no door leading to the rest of the house.

"I am delighted to see you, highness. I thought your security would prevent this reunion. Mtombe must be more important than I realized. You will tell me the story, won't you?"

"We've been down this road before." Jasirey could just about feel the ice forging through the trafficker. He did not like being reminded of their last encounter on his ship where he hoped to break her will. She shrugged. "It's not a secret. He belongs to me."

Whatever he'd expected, Marcus's raised brow said that wasn't it. "And how do your other men feel about yet another man belonging to you?"

"They accept him."

"How very . . . unusual. Are there more?"

"Not yet."

Marcus's face darkened.

"I'm not being snide," she said. "It's part of the job description."

Marcus needed to process that. He gestured to the food. "Please."

Jasirey spread brie on some thin crackers and helped herself to a cluster of red grapes. Marcus poured her a cup of tea.

"So, what did you come up with in your research?" she asked.

"Now, now, don't skip the pleasantries, highness. You look well."

"And hoping to stay that way."

Marcus let loose a genuine laugh. "I do enjoy repartee and miss it when it's gone."

"You mean destroyed."

"I think of it as blossomed to—"

"Your will—everyone jumping to your tune." She noted a slight tightening around his eyes. *He honestly considers himself as some kind of architect,* she thought. "I'm sorry. I interrupted. Blossomed to full flower?"

Tell me, she projected, quickly forming a bridge from her mind to his using the bones that remained from the last bridge they had shared.

Marcus's eyes deepened to a darker yellow in the lamplight. "You live in privileged comfort. Most don't. Most won't, left to their own devices. But to receive, something must be rendered. What more can one offer than perfection?"

"Your clients don't find perfection, like beauty, subjective?"

"Physically, yes. Variations in style—saucy or school-girlish, prim to foul-mouthed. In attitude, the will to comply, no—the product must willingly provide exactly what is desired." Marcus's mouth shut with an audible click. "You're drawing me out, highness. Interesting, and leads us to my research. Nothing on the internet, a miracle of subterfuge in today's world.

"I questioned Mtombe," Marcus continued, "and am content he knows no more than the drivel he divulged. The Devoted reside on some unnamed island and conduct missions to bring order to the world. Rather a hopeless task, but there's no accounting for superstitious beliefs. And you are the hope of this organization. Tell me, what exactly do they hope from you?"

Jasirey gave a soft scoffing laugh. Marcus's eyes flared and then relaxed as he realized it was an involuntary expression of personal exasperation. She did fascinate him.

"I sow the seeds of stability in a precarious world—the Devoted's words—that my children bring to fruition. Just how I do that or what it entails is left totally up to me."

Marcus studied Jasirey's face. "Preposterous, but I think you believe that." Calculation entered his eyes. "It might be entertaining to watch you wrestle with such a task. At the moment, however, we have more pressing matters. Shall we say hello to Mtombe?"

He escorted Jasirey out the door, around the porch to another door that opened into the kitchen, and from there to a hallway with several doors. A man, evidently a guard, sat outside one. Marcus dismissed him and ushered her inside.

Jasirey hurried to Mtombe. His arms were bound to the back of a kitchen chair, and his head lolled on his chest.

Jasirey gently patted sweat away from his eyes. "Mtombe."

He jerked at the sound of her voice and awakened. Dull eyes slowly focused, and Mtombe's body convulsed away from the nightmare of Jasirey's presence.

"Not happy to see your . . . what? Queen, leader?" Marcus said. "And her highness so willing to sacrifice herself for you. So, perhaps paramour?" Marcus laughed at the burning hatred sparking from the younger man's bruised eyes.

Jasirey held back her love and concern. Anger better served Mtombe.

He sputtered at her. "Are you mad?"

Jasirey moved behind Mtombe and, with the cheese knife she'd palmed, sawed at the cable ties binding his wrists. Marcus let her proceed and held out his hand for the knife when she finished. Keeping an arm's-length distance, she gave it to him handle first.

Lightheaded from dehydration, Mtombe remained sitting. Jasirey chafed to return circulation to his cold hands. Marcus moved lightly for a beefy man, but Jasirey anticipated him and stepped beyond his reach.

"Not much room to maneuver," he said, lips lifting. They thinned at a knock on the door. "I believe Mtombe may need a moment to gather his wits. I'll leave you to reunite." He closed the door behind him.

Jasirey almost felt sorry for the person being berated by Marcus whose voice rose in anger at being interrupted as the two men's footsteps faded. She reached into her pants pocket for a small bottle of water she'd carried in London and saved for Mtombe. He managed it by himself. His expression remained dismal, and Jasirey knelt to lay her head under his chin. Mtombe's arms banded about her.

Jasirey let comfort and love wash over him and waited for his heartbeat to steady. "Don't worry, my wild boar. Fael will find us."

"Loveling, why did you do this? I comforted myself that he would be unable to get his hands on you. Your husbands let . . . ?"

Jasirey placed a finger on his lips and sprang up a second before the door crashed open. She tried to catch the battered little body flung at her. She recognized Mirai. Both women landed on Mtombe, whose chair gave out and splatted all three onto the floor.

Vibrating, teeth gritted, Marcus stood over them. "Where's the tracer, Jasirey? Must be sophisticated for my men to miss it."

Mirai didn't appear mortally hurt. Finger-sized bruises formed on her biceps, and strands of loose hair stood out from her customary braid.

Jasirey regained her feet and stepped away from her and Mtombe. "I'm not wearing a wire."

"Do not fuck with me. You'll watch them both die."

"No one's ever said anything about a tracer," she said truthfully. She'd known about the tiny device implanted in her arm while asleep after the Imperiatu test for some time.

"Unfortunately, we haven't time to assure your veracity or room for an extra passenger." The feral light in Marcus's eyes chilled Jasirey. "Choose which one will come with us. You have five minutes to decide." He stalked back out the door.

❦ ❦ ❦

Fael signaled his team—Kimika, Mirai, Yusef, Andwar, and Chen—into the water. Favian, Sajan, and Nikolai ran their boat without lights to wait offshore for Fael's signal to come as close as possible to the beach to pick up Jasirey.

What little moonlight lit the sky did not reflect from the teams' wet suits. Using snorkels, they stayed underwater, then let the waves wash them to shore near rock piles and boulders.

Nikolai had maneuvered a drone to pinpoint where Marcus's mercenaries lay in wait, their numbers lessened by Ian, Lee, and Liu's attacks from sea. Ian and a security team landed near the causeway from Uist to Eriskay where he met fierce resistance. They intended the incursion for well past midnight, and no locals hindered their efforts to keep Marcus's men occupied and away from the other groups.

Lee's boat engaged with a large rescue vessel that blocked the entrance into Eriskay's one boat-worthy harbor. Liu's shallow-draft craft met a boat too large to enter the lesser harbor itself, but large enough to block Liu's entry. Out-manned and out-gunned but faster, Liu played cat-and-mouse. The rescue was up to Fael.

Once on land, Fael's team split up. Yusef, Andwar, and Chen stayed where they had landed, a good position where they could help Jasirey into the rescue boat after Fael, Kimika, and Mirai found and brought her to the beach.

Kimika made his way inland to the tree line, where several snipers and their spotters had spread out through the forest to guard the beach.

Fael cleared the hill of those guarding the path to the house while Mirai dispatched the few remaining guards outside the house itself. Fael trusted her to bring Jasirey to the beach and avoid the traps he had to leave intact when Kimika texted that, mission accomplished, he required immediate backup.

❧ ❧ ❧

Jasirey sensed help nearby but doubted they could reach her in time. She had one chance at slowing Marcus and placed her hand on Mirai's shoulder. The young woman's mouth opened to protest the picture in her mind but tensed as the door opened for Marcus and another man.

Marcus's rheumy eyes gleamed. "Choose, Jasirey. Does this slip of a girl's life compare to Mtombe's?"

Jasirey took a step closer. "Have you noticed that you're calling me Jasirey?"

Those weird eyes ignited. "Kill him." The henchman beside Marcus lifted his arm.

The flat of Jasirey's palm smashed into Marcus's nose. A side kick to the ribs sent him sprawling over the gunman Mirai had felled.

Mirai grabbed his weapon and said to Mtombe, "Take Jasirey's arm and don't let go." Eyes cold as steel raked over her lady.

"I'll follow orders," Jasirey said. Pride bubbled up for her hellcat security expert.

Mirai flashed a warrior's smile and, gun leading, stepped out the door. She explained Lee and Fael's plan as she led Jasirey and Mtombe down the hill to the beach.

Favian, Sajan, and Nikolai wait for us on a rescue boat," Mirai said. "Ian, Lee, and Liu attack from three different points to pull away Marcus's mercenaries from the beach. Fael, Kimika, Yusef, Andwar, and Chen intend to pinch the mercenaries left behind from two directions. We must thread whatever hole they manage to open and swim out to the boat."

Mirai just hoped that hole was far enough away from bullets. She had been stripped by Marcus's people of her pistol and martial arts throwing stars. She dug into her braid and retrieved a miniature phone and flashlight. She read her texts.

"Excellent," she said. "Fael secured the hill. There are traps, however, for unwary feet. Lady, stay behind me and follow my footsteps exactly. Mtombe, follow our lady."

Mirai stopped twice to climb over ankle-high razor wire strung across the path.

Jasirey stopped when she saw a wire curled up to one side of the path and a trail of blood heading into the trees. Jasirey shook her head when Miral stepped in front of her to prevent her from following the blood into the woods.

"I feel his pain," Jasirey said softly. "He's young and fears bleeding out." Jasirey's face hardened. "He revels in the life Marcus provides, the violence, hurting women. He's beyond our help. Let's continue on."

When they reached the beach, Mirai waited with her phone for Yusef's signal, then pointed to a haphazard line of rocks and boulders. "Drop to your hands and knees and crawl behind those rocks toward the water. Yusef is about halfway down. I'll have your backs."

"Can you crawl, Mtombe?" Jasirey asked. "The rope cuts on your wrists looked deep."

"No worries, loveling. Go."

Sporadic gunfire sounded from their right. They held their heads low. Flakes of sea-sharpened stone scraped at hands and knees. Mtombe soon had enough, grabbed Jasirey's ankle, and lay on his back. He began to scoot on elbows and feet covered by a jacket and sneakers until he drew even with Jasirey. He pulled her on top of his chest and kept going.

Jasirey tried not to become dead weight, an effort made more difficult with Mtombe frequently pulling her head down. They passed Chen, who saved his ammunition for when Jasirey's group would have to make a run for the water. Their best swimmer, Andwar waited behind the last boulder at the water's edge to assist Jasirey. Chen patted Mtombe's shoulder in a gesture of encouragement.

Yusef and Chen fired continually when Mtombe reached an area of sparse cover until he and Jasirey reached the boulders where Yusef sat, Mirai following behind them.

"Well done," Yusef said to Mtombe. "Mirai, glad to see you in one piece. All right, lady?"

Jasirey gently kissed Mtombe's split lip, then contemplated Yusef's rigid jaw. "I see and feel things others don't," she said. "Part of my mandate as Jasirey." She knew her decision to put herself in Marcus's hands angered her husbands and Protectors. "I won't always have time to explain what I'm doing or why. Trust me or don't. I do as I must."

"Your training to meet hostile conditions is limited," Yusef said. "We have years of training to rely on. Why would you not trust us to do what needs to be done?"

"I have gifts that give me immediate facts you can't access as quickly." Jasirey's head snapped around, though she couldn't see much past the boulders they sheltered behind. "Kimika's in trouble."

Jasirey spoke aloud so Yusef, Mirai, and Mtombe could hear what she projected to Fael. "Fael, Kimika's behind the men shooting at us, but another group of Marcus's mercenaries have taken position behind him."

"Fael sees Kimika," Jasirey told her group. "He has a plan and says to be ready to swim to our boat at his signal."

⁂

A wild pony snorted near the second line of Marcus's gunmen, who had crept up behind Kimika. Jasirey clearly felt agitation and projected calmness at the animal. It daintily picked its way through the rocks behind the attackers.

His arms vised about its neck on the side of the pony facing away from the second line of mercenaries, Fael clung, his legs clamped about the small beast's rounded belly.

When the pony reached a large group of rocks, Fael dropped down and slapped the pony's hindquarters to move it out of harm's way. Then Fael slithered on elbows and toes between the rocks and, hunting knife in hand, reared up behind each gunman to silently dispatch them.

Jasirey's abilities allowed her to see the gunmen through images in Fael's mind, and she formed her bridge to distract Marcus's crew. Kimika also helped as he fired on the first line of mercenaries between him and Jasirey's group.

Her energy waned. Yusef and Mtombe helped her to the boulder where Andwar waited for her. He pinned Jasirey to his side, ran to the water's edge, and dove under the waves alongside Mirai, Yusef, Mtombe, and Chen.

Andwar surfaced, and Jasirey gulped air into her burning lungs. Her legs curled up reflexively as pain ripped through her abdomen. She sank back beneath the surface to muffle her scream.

Andwar and Yusef pulled her up. Yusef checked her for wounds as she coughed up sea water she had swallowed.

"Kimika!" she wheezed. "He's been shot."

"You aren't hurt?" Yusef whispered in a strained voice.

Jasirey shook her head. Staying to either side of her, the men immediately struck off swimming for the boat they could see in the distance.

They reached the speedboat where Favian and Nikolai hauled one after the other of the swimmers onto the deck. Piloting the boat, Sajan fought the current. When all the swimmers lay on deck, he headed full throttle for the more populated Inner Hebrides. Favian told them Fael had texted that, though seriously wounded, Kimika was stable. With his shallow draft boat that could get closer to shore, Liu headed to pick up the two men.

They sped through the dark night, clouds blocking the moon and stars, until a strong earthly beam sliced the darkness behind them. A larger, faster craft closed in on their position. Sajan set a zigzag course to elude the other boat.

Andwar covered Jasirey with his body. She didn't like it but realized the futility of arguing.

"We've notified Ian," he said close to her ear. "We can't outrun that boat. We're heading to a nearby uninhabited island to buy time until reinforcements arrive."

"Where are the others?" Jasirey's teeth chattered.

Andwar nestled her against him to warm her. "On their way."

A shot rang out. Chen raised his voice above the noise of the engine. "Jasirey, we're half a mile from shore. The sea is calm. Can you swim that far?"

"Easily. Mirai, Mtombe, are you well enough to swim?"

Mirai gave a quick nod, and Mtombe said, "Yes. Do not worry about me, loveling."

The Five, Yusef, and Mirai looked at one another. *Loveling?*

Andwar felt Jasirey's amusement at Mtombe's term of endearment and wished they had time for the story.

"We can't stop without alerting the other boat," Andwar said to her. "Wrap your arms and legs around my torso and hold your breath on my signal." Knowing her a strong swimmer, they also all knew Jasirey had never learned to dive.

Andwar lifted her and crouched low. She clung like a limpet. "Now."

Jasirey sucked in a deep breath as again she felt herself plunged into roaring cold. Andwar remained under as long as he dared and surfaced not a second too soon.

Jasirey's heart hammered. Mirai and the other men surfaced nearby as Sajan piloted the boat away. The other boat followed Sajan and fired whenever its searchlight hit Sajan's smaller craft.

Jasirey sent up a prayer for the safety of all her people.

Jasirey's group swam for shore. In a short time, Jasirey heard only their strokes through the water. The constant effort of swimming kept the cold at bay. Nevertheless, it took its toll. She worried most for Mirai and Mtombe, already depleted by their treatment at the hands of Marcus and his crew.

They neared the island and swam parallel to the shore as they searched for a clear spot to climb safely onto the narrow rock-strewn beach. Chen trained a small light low as they crawled over the rocks. They sprinted for the shelter of some dunes as a light washed over the shore.

"I don't know if that's the same boat that followed Sajan or another," Nikolai said, "but Marcus's mercenaries obviously have no intention of giving up. I think they're looking for a spot to access the island. We need to move inland."

Nikolai cupped Jasirey's face. "How are you holding up?"

"I'm fine. Cold. Moving will help."

Yusef chafed her hands for a little warmth and held one as they carefully pushed through tall grass and grasping bushes. The breeze picked up, and the temperature dipped.

It was slow going. Finally, Andwar said, "Let's stop and rest a moment."

Chen let Yusef access the waterproof backpack he carried so Yusef could retrieve a lightweight, heat-saving blanket. Yusef unfolded it and threw it around their shoulders with Jasirey and, at her insistence, Mirai in the middle. They all smelled of sea water.

The women shivered uncontrollably. Still dehydrated, Mtombe also trembled. Jasirey drowsed until awakened by voices.

Chen pulled off the blanket. "Let's move."

Brisk air slapped Jasirey wide awake.

She and her Protectors scrambled over treacherous terrain. In a tactic of intimidation, their pursuers made such a racket that it covered the noise of their flight.

Shots rang out, and Jasirey's group dropped for safety. Yusef tripped over Andwar and dragged Jasirey down with him face first into a bush of inch-long thorns. Faces tight with remorse, the men extricated her. Dark splotches appeared on her thin blouse as her forearms and chest seeped blood.

Everyone formed a perimeter about Jasirey. "They don't want you guys," she said, doing her best to breathe through the pain. "Leave me."

Mirai bristled. "Don't be ridiculous."

"It's not a suggestion," Jasirey said in a commanding tone she rarely used. "You run. They'll have me and feel they've won and won't be as guarded. Swing around and take them by surprise."

They all hated the idea but recognized the soundness of the strategy.

"I will not leave you." Mtombe punched each word.

Jasirey caressed his scratchy face. "I couldn't stand having to choose. Strength in numbers—go with the rest."

Emotion clogged Mtombe's throat, and he gripped her tightly.

She swallowed the surge of pain and gently pushed away. Her people's posture crumpled as if she'd physically crushed them. She let her love wash over and strengthen them before she turned away. She lacked the courage to watch them melt into the darkness.

Jasirey stood, fought for balance, and trudged out into the open.

"Don't shoot," she called out.

"Show yourself," returned a rough voice.

"I'm alone." Jasirey stepped into their light. Hurting hands grabbed her arms.

"Got yourself deserted, did you?" A greasy-haired man sneered, reached out to grab her and thought better of it. She looked capable of tearing out his throat. "Back to the boat."

A few of the men stiffened. "What about the others?"

"He wants this one. We got her. You wanna chase the rest through this shit, you're on your own." He turned back toward the beach.

Desperately tired and cold, Jasirey prayed she could summon up sufficient mental energy to help her people when the time came.

An explosion out at sea drew her captors into a tight ball around her. She preferred the cold to their fetid breath.

❧ ❧ ❧

Sajan hadn't held the attention of the larger boat after one of its beams washed over the deck and revealed only Sajan. He watched through binoculars as the pursuing boat stopped and sent two dinghies full of mercenaries to the island. Once the dinghies disappeared around the island, Sajan swam to the nearly deserted main boat, easily found the armory, and dispatched the half-asleep man guarding the door.

He helped himself to some interesting illegal devices that he set up in their empty engine room. Sajan returned to his boat without incident and circled the island without lights and at a slow speed to minimize engine noise. He signaled Nikolai when he found a spot where he could get close to shore.

Jasirey's group reunited with Sajan and strategized on how to retrieve Jasirey.

An explosion rent the air. Yusef had twisted his ankle when he collided with Andwar on the small island, so he piloted the boat after they found the mercenaries' beached dinghies. Nikolai, Favian, Sajan, Chen, Andwar, Mirai, and Mtombe returned to the island to rescue their lady.

When her captors pushed her onto the beach, Jasirey sensed her people nearby. She wearily found a rock to sit on as Marcus's crew goggled at their flaming boat out at sea.

"Wha' d' we do?" one of the men asked.

"Have a fucking weenie roast," the greasy-haired leader growled. A warning shot kicked up sand inches from his foot.

Nikolai's voice rang out of the dark night. "We have your position surrounded."

Favian sounded off behind them and then Andwar from the other side.

"Drop your weapons, take your boats out, and you won't be harmed," Nikolai said.

The man's eyes cast about the beach. "Okay, we're goin'." He nodded at his men. They dropped their weapons and slowly backed up to the beached dinghies.

Jasirey stood shakily, heard warning bells, and fought to focus. She screamed as Mirai and Nikolai collided in midair. The blast wave hurled her into the rocks.

Destiny Chooses

In ensuing gunfire after the launch of their grenade, Marcus's men scrambled aboard their small boats and headed for Eriskay. Favian and Mtombe buoyed Jasirey as the team returned to their boat.

Sajan dug out a first aid kit for Jasirey, who lay unconscious. Red and swollen, a gash on the back of her head still oozed. Mtombe cleaned the wound and applied pressure before smearing antibiotic ointment on a patch of gauze.

"We must warm her," he said. He pulled off his sopping clothes while Favian and Sajan undressed Jasirey. The thorn punctures no longer bled but had formed red, swollen welts. Chen curled himself around her back.

Mtombe followed suit on the other side and cradled her head. Favian and Andwar pressed themselves to her legs and held them above heart level.

She moaned softly, and Favian fretted. "She must be in pain." She shivered.

"That's a good sign." Chen breathed in relief. "Shivering stops with hypothermia."

Jasirey pressed into Mtombe. Mindful of the injuries, he held her loosely. "It's all right, loveling. We have you. Be at ease."

Chen rubbed her shoulders. Jasirey sighed, leaned back against him, and pressed her face into his chest. As she had when pregnant and in great physical distress, Jasirey again turned to the love she felt surrounding her for solace and relief from pain.

The Protectors glanced at one another with an undercurrent of knowing response.

"Sex releases beneficial hormones that might help her now," Yusef said. "Her body calls to us, and we must answer. Mtombe, you were a Protector and call her loveling. Has she accepted you?"

Mtombe stared at the men's earnest expressions. "She has made it clear that she expects me to find my personal destiny before taking on the responsibility of being the wild boar she saw in her prophesy."

The others gaped at him. Chen recovered first and said, "More than fifty of us vied to be her husband when she was found to be Jasirey during her test in the Imperiatu. Besides Ian, her fiancé and husband-protector, she chose only Lee, Liu, and Fael. We accepted it as duty dictated. According to her vision in the Imperiatu and as her wild boar, you belong to her. Will you stand in now as her husband-protector as Ian did during the husband ceremony and tell us if she accepts us?"

Mtombe's head ached. The others understood his reticence and gathered round to pray for their beloved. The heartfelt words and sincere emotions alleviated Mtombe's misgivings as he guided the other Protectors in ministering to their most precious lady.

"Okay," he said. "Well, obviously she accepts you, Chen. We won't—uh—follow the husband ceremony since this is not the same . . . as Jasirey choosing her husbands, I mean."

"Get to the point," Chen said.

"Okay. How about this? If I say she accepts you, kiss her lightly, hold her to give her your warmth, and gently pleasure her. Concentrate on her welfare, on not stressing her body any further. You have all wanted her since she was found, so you will likely not last long. I know I will not," he concluded under his breath.

Chen grinned but quickly felt the weight of a moment he had thought he might never experience. He angled Jasirey's mouth toward his and reverently pressed down. "I am yours always, adored one," he whispered. "I love you."

Chen nuzzled her neck and shoulder as he entered her from behind to avoid most of her injuries. Mtombe had called it correctly. Chen barely managed into a second minute. He nodded sheepishly when Yusef had to help him move away from Jasirey.

Yusef replaced him, cuddled Jasirey, and said, "I am yours always. Though her eyes remained closed, her hand lifted to caress his face.

"She accepts you," Mtombe said.

Yusef kissed her. "I love you, cherished one." He entered her wet heat while massaging her from neck to posterior. He tried to hold back, but his whole body gathered and burst in joyful ecstasy.

Mtombe also declared Sajan, Favian, and Andwar accepted. They, too, finished quickly. Mtombe recognized that Jasirey remained dissatisfied as she moved fretfully against him.

"I am yours always, loveling," he murmured. "I love you." Facing her, he left a few inches between his body and her injuries but nonetheless managed to wrap her in one arm as he entered her and used his other hand to coax her up, up, and gently over.

Afterward, a healthy rose color tinged Jasirey's skin as she snuggled into Mtombe.

"She feels warm," he said. The men breathed in relief.

"Let's keep her that way," Chen said and with Mtombe spooned a peacefully sleeping Jasirey between them.

❦ ❦ ❦

Jasirey stood quaking in the midst of swirling fog. In the distance, impossible to measure, emerged a pale oval. Two smaller dark orbs rode its surface. She recognized Ian's dark eyes. Ian, her safe place, her heart, but the dark depths of his eyes held no warmth, no indication of her presence. He drew alongside and swept past never sparing her a glance.

"Ian!"

Her heartbroken cry woke her men. They gathered up their thrashing wife.

"Baby, you're safe," Ian said. "Wake up now. You're dreaming."

Jasirey had dreamt badly every night of the past week. The men soothed with soft murmurs and caresses. For once, Jasirey slid back from consciousness to sleep. Her concerned men watched over their wife—treated by Jesse before he and Lill had to return home—as she convalesced at Reginald's estate from a gash to the back of the head requiring six stitches, a mild concussion, and infected thorn wounds.

Other than the brief moments when she demanded reports on Kimika recovering from surgery in a hospital, Jasirey floated in a haze of medicated twilight. She lacked any ambition to break free into the pulsing color of her rage and pain. Despair was less challenging.

Mtombe kept watch until Sajan relieved him. He went downstairs to Reginald's office. The husbands glanced up, and he shook his head—no change. Fleeting frowns crossed their faces, but they returned their concentration to someone speaking via Ian's laptop. Mtombe gestured at Liu to follow him into the library next door.

Mtombe leaned against a two-story bookcase. "Any news?"

Liu patted the younger man's rigid shoulder that belied his nonchalant pose. "Our data technicians found a doorway into one of Marcus's bank accounts, sabotaged it, and froze a hefty portion of his assets, which we hope will severely cripple him."

Mtombe nodded. *Unfortunate that Marcus himself wasn't crippled.* "And Jasirey?"

"Help is coming."

"She has yet to shed a tear. The longer she drifts . . . "

"We know." Similar in temperament, the two men had formed a quiet rapport. "We allowed her to drift after the babies' birth but have learned better communication skills since then." Liu slanted a look at Mtombe whose frown remained. "Do you wish to discuss what happened on the boat?"

Mtombe straightened and began to pace. "I know in my heart we acted as Protectors, mandated to serve Jasirey in any capacity she requires. My brain fears her reaction."

Liu smiled. "A prudent concern. And do you fear consequences?"

"She has been adamant that I fulfill my destiny before taking on whatever my responsibilities may be as her wild boar. Do you think there will be . . . consequences?"

Two days after the attack, Ian, Lee, Liu, and Fael brought the babies and four teenagers to visit Jasirey. In some respects, Kirani and Bazir, still healing from the loss of their father, most needed to be assured of their lady's welfare.

Liu had lessened her medication to increase her alertness. The only noticeable difference to the teens was an ingenious harness Fael made from wire clothes hangers that kept anything from touching and shooting acute pain through Jasirey's hypersensitive, inflamed breasts, the first part of her body to land in the thorns.

Unable to get warm despite the crackling fireplace, she sat wrapped in a plush robe in the bedroom's sitting area. The teens hugged her gingerly. She pressed her cheek to theirs and invited them to sit on the floor around her. The fathers held each baby up for a kiss. Jasirey rubbed their sweet faces cheek to cheek. Injury prevented her from holding them. The little ones eyed her quietly, patted her face, and set their heads on her shoulders, one on each side, taking turns. She sighed. It would do.

"I didn't know Mirai," Christopher said as he bounced Sunny on his knee. "Nikolai was a really good guy, really patient teaching the moves of martial arts katas."

Kirani placed a finger in each of Jaimie's fists to help her stand. "He helped me with driving practice here in England."

Christopher's lips lifted slightly. "Sucked at driving at home. Got confused on the turns—used to left-lane driving."

Bazir cuddled Safia and remained silent. Fael made a mental note to check on his state of mind but felt Jasirey's assurance that the boy was coping in his mourning. It reassured him that in her own mourning, she stayed in touch with her loved ones' feelings.

Colin and Michael had developed an affinity for each other. The little boy gnawed on his big brother's finger. "Hey, kid, I'm not a chew toy." That reminded him that he missed their St. Bernard, Nick. "Are we . . . can you go home soon, Mom?"

Kirani had classes at MIT, and Christopher, Michael, and Bazir needed to start school, so Jasirey decided to send the teens home. She asked Ian to inform the teacher who homeschooled them when the teens would arrive.

She kissed all the children's cheeks, and Lee, Fael, and Ian returned the babies to the nursery. Liu settled her in for a nap. A small dose of medication took the edge off her pain and facilitated sleep. Jasirey left the robe on. Lee returned, lay alongside, and, his massive arms providing warmth and comfort, cradled her gently against his chest.

"His left arm is under my head, and his right arm embraces me," Lee said.

"What?" Jasirey opened drowsy eyes to look up at him.

"My lover is like a gazelle or a young stag leaping across the mountains. See! The winter is past. The rains are over and gone. Flowers appear on the earth. The season of singing has come." Faint laugh lines showed around Lee's eyes. "That's me," he said, "a leaping gazelle, the lover, your lover."

"And what am I?" Jasirey asked, intrigued by Lee's whimsy.

"Your eyes are doves. Your hair is like a flock of goats."

"Seriously? Goats?"

Doing his best not to laugh, Lee nodded. "And your teeth are like a flock of sheep just shorn."

"Ok-a-a-y."

"*Song of Songs*, though I've heard many call the book *The Song of Solomon*."

Jasirey tried to look knowledgeable. "Old Testament."

"You have stolen my heart with one glance of your eyes. How much more pleasing is your love than wine. Your lips drop sweetness as the honeycomb. Love burns like a mighty flame. Many rivers cannot quench love; rivers cannot wash it away."

Jasirey resisted the tug of sleep a moment longer. "Thank you, teddy bear. I know you're here for me. I'll know it better tomorrow and even better day after tomorrow. Promise."

❦ ❦ ❦

Unable to tolerate shower spray raining down on her injuries in the morning, Jasirey allowed Liu to sponge bathe her. Everett, who had rejoined the family to help, set out breakfast in the manor's rose garden for her and Master Kai who had also arrived to help Jasirey. She wore a large sweater that didn't quite hide the odd shape of the harness.

"A bit better today?" Master Kai sat beside her at a table draped in white.

Jasirey embraced the comfort she felt so powerfully in his presence.

Pleased it satisfied their lady for the moment, he let the comfortable silence linger. "When you are ready, dear one, Mirai's parents wish to speak with you. They believe she died for the greatest of causes."

Jasirey pulled back, said nothing.

"We all miss her greatly," Master Kai said, "and Nikolai, a fine young man."

Jasirey heedlessly wiped her eyes and nose on her linen napkin. She had been properly circumspect in fending off Nikolai's feelings. What she wouldn't give to have a few moments to assure him how much he'd been liked and appreciated.

"Dearest one, can you speak of your ordeal? It is best not to let it fester."

"It's a haze of blasting sound, heat, sharp pain . . . I was too tired to stop him."

"Explain, please."

"The guy who threw the grenade. I was cold, in pain, and didn't sense his intention until too late. He'd already thrown it. Mirai and Nikolai saw the toss and dove for it. Must not have been much left." Jasirey's voice choked on the words.

"As you wisely told me, you are not God. Your gifts have limits. Your body and mind have limits. To subscribe to unrealistic expectations lessens your effectiveness."

Jasirey ate a few berries, sipped at her tea. "I traded their lives for Mtombe's. If I'd let Mirai handle Harris, she and Nikolai would be alive."

"You cannot know that. A rescue mission for Mtombe might have ended the same or with other losses."

Jasirey stared at her plate. "We wouldn't have known where to go, so no mission."

Master Kai patted her hand. "Unlikely. Marcus no doubt had an alternative plan. Grieve for their loss, dear one. Do not let guilt consume you. Neither Mirai nor Nikolai will rest easily if you stay too long in despair."

"So, buck up for their sakes, huh?"

"Something along those lines." Master Kai debated whether to make Jasirey aware of events after the attack on her. He believed that, in her heart, she knew and only needed coaxing to allow the knowledge into consciousness.

Ian, Liu, Fael, and Lee gladly gave their master permission to do so at his discretion. To their credit, they feared Jasirey's reaction more for her emotional welfare than her potential desire to maim the messenger.

"As I understand it, once rescued and on board the motorboat, the others treated your wounds. You were in danger of hypothermia. What do you remember of these events?"

Jasirey shrugged. "Waking up in the hospital."

"Your Protectors cared for you, warmed you." He thought she intended to accept it without further questions.

Instead, she averted her face and asked in a small voice, "How?"

"As only your Protectors have the mandate, as your body demanded of them." He quickly continued when Jasirey shifted uncomfortably. "You turned to them for comfort and relief from trauma and pain, and such the Protectors provided."

Jasirey's mouth opened, snapped shut, and thinned. "All of them?"

"You accepted them."

"I was unconscious."

"No, Jasirey." The Imperiat believed that her destiny included the events and the men on the boat. It was crucial to her mission and well-being that she acknowledge them.

The use of her name, so rare from him, halted her spiral into self-protective rage.

"Your men would never force themselves on you. You participated, albeit not fully conscious, yet with resolved purpose. I think you find that fact more unpalatable than the sexual act. They joined with you in love and devotion. To think ill of them is unworthy of you."

Jasirey blinked rapidly and stood to stretch her rib cage. It hurt to breathe. "What am I supposed to do?"

"Speak to them."

"My husbands know." It was a statement of resignation.

"They were informed, understand, and agree your Protectors followed their training and cared for you as required." Master Kai stood to take her hands in his. "Dearest one. I think you know destiny has relieved you from making the choice you find so difficult."

Jasirey turned away. "I want to spend the rest of the morning with the kids. I'll see the Protectors in the afternoon. Reggie won't mind us using the smaller sitting room."

"I shall so inform them."

"I'm not ready for another pregnancy, Kai. The babies aren't even a year old yet."

He remained silent. No words existed to console her.

❦ ❦ ❦

Jasirey made sure she arrived first in the sitting room but, unable to settle, paced around the deeply cushioned furniture.

Mtombe entered, walked straight to her, and cupped her face to kiss her warmly. He felt her body relax against him the best it could with the harness. "Are you well, loveling?"

"Can't quite get my bearings."

"I wouldn't change our actions. We helped you."

Jasirey reached up to caress his sincere face that had become very dear to her. Chen, Sajan, Yusef, Andwar, and Favian entered and approached tentatively, so woebegone she set her anger and confusion aside and opened her arms to them. She intended one hug.

Chen encircled her small form and, careful not to aggravate her injuries, twined his fingers in her hair, gently pulled her head back, and let relief, affection, and passion all ball up into one sweet, sensual kiss.

Yusef coaxed her to him, his fervent eyes never leaving hers, and kissed her tenderly. Favian lingered over brief presses of his mouth to her eyes, nose, cheeks, top lip, and that full bottom lip he always wanted to suck on. So, he did.

Andwar held her to him, cheek to cheek. He longed for a fuller, more intimate connection. He kissed the sheen of tears from her eyes. "Please, don't be sad."

The men laid a sofa cushion on the floor for their conflicted lady and sat about her. Yusef drew her back against his and Mtombe's shoulders. Sajan and Favian massaged her feet. Finding the ministrations too familiar, Jasirey disengaged and sat up cross legged.

"Do you think I belong to you now?"

Yusef met her eyes squarely. "As ever, we belong to you."

"I don't want that responsibility," she whispered fiercely.

"Then it is a good thing the responsibility rests on us," Favian said.

"What do you expect from me?"

Chen softly chided. "Do you not comprehend that you already are everything we want and more than we ever expected? It's our job to fulfill your needs and desires."

Mtombe cuddled her back against him. "You have an exceptionally loving heart, loveling. Put aside your unfounded fears and believe your wishes come first."

"Kai says that on some level I turned to you, and it's impossible for you to turn away from me. I accept that. I just don't know where that leaves us. I want to go home. And I'm sorry, but I just don't know what kind of relationship we'll have once things get back to normal. We'll have to take things one day at a time."

Jasirey wondered at the mix of relief and trepidation she felt from her Protectors.

"We were concerned that you might send us back to the island," Yusef said.

Jasirey sighed. "Keeping you near me, I'm not sure that's the kind thing to do."

"We are Protectors," Favian said sternly. "You sow seeds of change in people of influence, perhaps people of no discernible power, yet you recognize they shall one day be in position to affect change. We protect you in that endeavor. We live to fulfill our duty."

"Your children historically take on more direct roles," Sajan said. "We may also be useful to them."

"As a figurehead," Chen said, "Jasirey is in a sense all women, yet no one else compares to you. We believe you mean to accept no more husbands. Duty drives us, not personal needs."

"Even if you don't choose us as husbands or consorts," Yusef said, "we count ourselves most fortunate to have a living person to serve whom we all greatly admire. Generations of Protectors before us devoted their whole lives to only a dream. If the time comes, we'll marry elsewhere. For now, we are content. Do not fret on our account."

Jasirey recognized her symptoms of fatigue. Tears pricked at her eyes and throat. Probably unfair, probably wrong, but it felt right, so she hugged Yusef affectionately. "Thank you, Yusef. You're very kind." She kissed his cheek and repeated the gesture with the others. She smiled at her Protectors with a full heart though still uncertain whether it was cruel to keep them nearby. She dismissed them except for Mtombe, who drew her against him.

"Do you love me, loveling?"

Her arms banded around him. "You doubt it?"

"That is the question and the answer." He laughed. "Do not be troubled. I am secure in your feelings for me. So much so, I harbor no jealousy toward your husbands or your other Protectors' attention to you or your attraction to them."

"What? Who says—"

He placed a finger over her lips. "You care for them."

"Sure, but that's not the same thing."

He kissed her, whispered in her ear. "I think it is. Care, concern, affection—for you, they intermix with love and desire. Such is your nature."

Jasirey pulled back. "That makes me sound like a slutty—"

"Stop." Black eyes snapped. "You are the most sensually sexual woman I have ever had the good fortune to be close to. There is nothing wrong with who you are. Quite the contrary." His cheek rested on her hair. "No matter the number of others in your life, no one else can claim that piece of your exceptional heart kept solely for me. You fill my soul with happiness. Waiting to be with you hurts, but as you say, I must first finish the course I have set."

Ian woke Jasirey before dinner. "Marcus sent you a letter," he said. "Fael opened it for security purposes but didn't read it. Would you rather we handled it?"

Jasirey held her hand out. It remained steady as she read the note to Ian.

> My dear Jasirey,
>
> Well, well, so you don't totally depend on others for protection. That attack hurt. Oddly, I harbor no burning desire to return the favor. I don't believe I have ever been so challenged—such exciting possibilities. Tell me, the death of the little ninja, does it weigh on you or was she expected to forfeit her life on your behalf?
>
> I truly look forward to deciding how to deal with you.
>
> Your worthy nemesis,
>
> Marcus

Jasirey tapped the paper against the fingertips of her empty hand. "What he's really saying is he sees me as a nemesis worthy of him. Might be interesting to the council that he never asks about the guy Strafe we took from his ship. It's not because he doesn't care." She handed the letter to Ian. "Do what you like with it."

"Baby, how are you really?" Ian asked Jasirey. "Mtombe told us what happened when you talked to him and your other Protectors. Your ambivalence toward whatever relationship you may have with them from now on stood out to me. You understand that as Protectors they've been thoroughly trained in the art of seduction. It would surprise me if they haven't already begun their campaign to win your love."

Ian's hand skimmed his shaved head. "I worry about you being overly stressed. Coming to England was supposed to be a vacation. Instead, you've had a flood of difficult situations to deal with."

Jasirey laid her head on Ian's shoulder, returned his kiss, and snuggled for a bit. She could think of nothing to say to ease his anxiety. Telling him the original Five had started wooing her the minute Master Kai assigned them to help with her training at the compound seemed more likely to confirm his worries. It worried Jasirey that he didn't voice his deeper concerns regarding how her relationship with her Protectors at home would affect him, Lee, Liu, Fael, and the children.

* * *

At dinner, the men on Jasirey's security team captured Reginald's attention. Pleasant expressions nearly masked furtive eyes darting back and forth to her. In the parlor afterward, the security men gradually infiltrated the space around her, a clever feat of strategy. They used humor and Jasirey's natural curiosity and interest in everyone to engage her in an animated conversation.

Sweet, bloody hell. Unless Reginald was much mistaken, and he wasn't, the security men wooed her while conveying a yearning painful to watch. Jasirey's sudden starts—consciousness of the men's agenda—and her sad evident ambivalence evoked sympathy for her and the men he now realized must be Protectors. *But—bloody hell.* He nearly glared at Master Kai as the elderly man sat beside him.

"They're in love with her," Reginald said in an accusing tone. "Every single one of them, and it would surprise me greatly if that fact escaped your notice."

"Yes, most male Protectors have similar feelings. Jasirey says she told you about the prophesied second pregnancy, her Protectors, and the need for multiracial children. Those men are possible candidates for fathers."

Reginald gulped like a fish out of water. "Surely you comprehend what this is doing to her, having to make such a choice. It goes beyond the pale. I think you care for her—"

"Above all else," the old master said. "Everything is in flux for the moment. It shall be settled when what is best for her becomes clear. We have assured Jasirey that she is free to choose the details of her destiny, though the end results are immutable. Occasionally, however, destiny chooses."

Reginald had no idea to what Master Kai eluded. "I worry for her."

Master Kai offered a hand in friendship. "Trust her husbands to guarantee her welfare."

❦ ❦ ❦

Mtombe kissed Jasirey goodbye early the next morning. She joined her husbands and Master Kai in the nursery.

Safia crawled to the older man and hoisted herself up on his pant leg. He lifted her to his chest. She gave him an open-mouthed kiss and unexpectedly launched at her mother. He might have dropped her had Jasirey not felt the movement and grabbed hold.

Master Kai patted at the sweat popping out on his forehead and smiled as Jasirey unsuccessfully suppressed her laughter. "I fear I am a bit out of practice," he told her.

Safia bounced in her mother's arms and sprang toward Fael. "She may become a gymnast," he said as he deftly caught his little girl, "or a dancer."

Fael sensed his wife's love tinged with sadness. "Loved one, what is wrong?"

The husbands sat on the floor and placed toys next to the babies. They pulled Jasirey down beside them and offered a cushion to Master Kai.

"Talk to us, precious one," Liu said. "There is nothing you cannot say to us. Please tell me you do not still doubt our acceptance of every aspect of your destiny."

Jasirey placed her head in her hands. Ian pulled them down more roughly than he intended. He would not allow her to flounder alone and in pain. "Baby, don't withdraw from us." Tears stung his nose and throat.

Jasirey looped her arms about his neck and rested her forehead against his. "My Ian, my safe place." She sat back to include all her men. "You're my life and not the problem. I think Jasirey is my problem. I thought I'd accepted her, the mission. I . . . It's time to go home."

"Dear one, matters are converging faster than is convenient," Master Kai said. "It's all difficult to absorb. I have spoken with the Imperiat. We remain uncertain of the best course for you, but I have been charged with convincing you to visit the island and concentrate on your training, no other concerns to intrude. It may clear your mind for future decisions. After your injuries have healed, come to the island."

Lee cradled her to him. "Little one, go to the island for training and see Mirai's parents."

She burrowed in silence for a few minutes. "Did you know she had a child, a little boy who died of cancer?"

Their expressions and sounds of sympathy said they hadn't.

"I used that memory to distract her and get to Mtombe." Her eyes filled. "I never got to apologize."

Ian deliberately smirked at her. "And she would have known it was bullshit, that you'd do it again if you thought it necessary."

Lee gently pulled at a lock of her hair. "When you believe someone needs your help, you jump into it with no holds barred until you consider the deed done. Mirai understood that."

Jasirey pictured Mirai's fierce grin and almost smiled. "She and Kimika were friends. He says her parents were her rock as she grieved. I hope they have someone to lean on."

"Grieving for Mirai is a process her parents must complete for themselves," Liu said, "though your support may bolster them. I advise you to go. Concentrate on something totally different for a time and, as Master Kai said, clear your mind."

"I agree," Fael said. "Training helps you to focus on what is most important to you."

"You don't think I'm already focused on that?"

"Loved one, we, your family, shall always be your priority. Training gives you strategies for managing difficult decisions. Is that not what you seek?"

Pretty much in a nutshell, she thought. "Ian?"

Ian took her hands. "Go to the island." His eyebrow lifted. "Think of it as a power nap."

The other husbands laughed at the same words Jasirey had used when she wisely sent them to the island to shore up their flagging energy during her last pregnancy.

* * *

The relief Jasirey felt at the thought of getting away and setting down her looming decisions waned as guilt followed—guilt at leaving her babies who wouldn't understand her absence, at leaving her Protectors hanging, and not least, imposing on Reginald's hospitality as she healed.

Since the teenagers needed to begin school and Ian had to return to work, she decided to ease Reginald's burden by sending the children home with Lee and Ian. Chen, Favian, Sajan, and Andwar would also return to the western Massachusetts compound. Liu, Fael, and Yusef and his squad of security people would remain until she left for the island.

After saying good-bye to Master Kai as he left for the island that afternoon to prepare for Jasirey's training, Reginald escorted her on a walk through the rose gardens. Though autumn had begun and the occasional breeze brushing over them carried a decided nip, a killing frost usually did not descend until October, so the hardier varieties still bloomed.

"Did you have other plans for the end of your vacation, Reggie?" Jasirey asked bluntly.

"Other than lazing about reading, which I can still do, I did not or at least not until your interference brought Bryant into my life—something, or I should say someone I can also still pursue."

Reginald urged Jasirey to sit on a bench before a rosebush of particularly abundant shades-of-peach flowers.

"I don't believe I have truly thanked you for bringing Bryant and me together," he said. "Thank you, dear heart." Sitting close to Jasirey, he felt her shiver. "Shall we go inside?"

"I'd rather stay out a bit longer, if you don't mind." When he started to unbutton his coat, she stayed his hands. "I'm not cold, Reggie."

"Nor did you invite me outside to insult me by suggesting I think you have overstayed your welcome."

Jasirey sat upright, then relaxed when she saw only humor twinkling in her friend's eyes. "Creep," she said as she hugged his arm.

"You have been through the gamut on your holiday—rescuing trafficked immigrants, being kidnapped yourself, having to face the death of two people close to you. And still, life goes on, decisions have to be made. I am the one party not invested in your destiny, mainly because I don't fully understand it. Talk to me, my dear."

Jasirey stopped clinging to Reginald, though she linked one hand with his. "You've only known me as Jasirey. Before meeting Ian, I lived an average life—marriage, two sons, then divorce, and a job at a small business to support us.

"I met Ian and got engaged. He brought me to the island of the Devoted, and everything changed—engaged to one man, suddenly married to four; happy with two kids, then a vision predicting that I'll have nine more at an age when I'll soon enter menopause, plus five of the nine must have fathers other than my husbands to ensure racial diversity."

She drew in a deep breath. "The Devoted are an enclosed society, protected from outside scrutiny—even from those living off island—except for the one family most likely to draw attention and censure—mine—because of a mission I'm only now beginning to think of as possible."

Reginald recognized that Jasirey needed to confide in him as a stress relief valve rather than as an invitation to advise or console. He remained quietly attentive.

"And now that I'm coming to terms with my so-called gifts . . . " Jasirey noted Reginald's raised eyebrow. "Okay. I still need to work on that. Let's just say I'm more aware of the possibilities my gifts give me to bring about positive changes in the world."

Jasirey smiled ruefully. "I'm almost done." She looked down at their clasped hands. "I have a burning desire to help, and more and more, I see pathways to doing that, but this last attack by Marcus . . . Mirai and Nikolai. I was too tired to sense the intentions of the man who threw the grenade. Clearly, I have limitations."

"So, you blame yourself for their deaths," Reginald said.

"Logically, no. Emotionally? Of course—and probably always will to some extent."

"Why you?"

"Sorry?"

"Why did Ian take you to the Devoted's island?"

"Oh. He said he recognized traits in me that reminded him of Jasirey."

"Too vague. What specifically makes you Jasirey?"

"Well, I passed the Devoted's test, the Imperiatu—"

"No." Reginald waved away her words. "I doubt they would have asked you to take the test unless they thought you capable of passing it."

Jasirey's brow furrowed in thought. "I want to say my gifts, but back then, I didn't believe I had any. The Devoted did but didn't know what form they took."

"Why did you agree to become Jasirey if you didn't believe yourself capable of fulfilling their expectations?"

A soft light filled her eyes. "Lee, Liu, and Fael. Ian would stay with me whatever my decision. If I refused to become Jasirey, I doubted the other three would. I loved them and needed them in my life. No matter how bizarre that life might become, they were worth it."

"And," Reginald guessed, "it's not really that you don't want five more children. You don't want five more lovers to father them."

"Too late."

"What do you mean?"

"I was hurt, in pain and shock, close to hypothermia on the rescue boat as we got away from Marcus. I turned to my Protectors for comfort, and with their training, they had no choice but to give it."

"You mean . . . What are you saying?"

"This is the hardest part about being Jasirey for outsiders to understand. Me, too, until lately as I've worked more closely with my Protectors. When I love someone romantically . . . The Devoted say that person belongs to me, and a bond forms so strong that we cannot be apart for long periods, and if deprived of the physical and emotional closeness we need, we can suffer illness, depression, grief."

"I still don't understand what is too late." Reginald insisted. "A second pregnancy? More lovers?"

"The Protectors on the boat with me have bonded with me. Sex provides chemicals that combat pain and anxiety and give warmth to body and mind. I was in and out of consciousness but accepted them as I sought relief while they sought to help me. Mostly, I remember feeling loved."

Reginald sprang up and turned away from Jasirey. "It's too early to know, but you believe you are pregnant?"

Rage—Reginald's—washed over Jasirey. No words formed to answer him. She tried not to take his reaction personally. No words came to mind.

When Reginald finally mastered himself, he faced Jasirey.

Squarely, bravely, her eyes met his as she obviously waited for him to censure her.

He flopped back down on the bench and flung an arm around her shoulders.

"I've seen how your Protectors feel," he said. "They love you deeply. I'd still like to plant them a facer, every single one of them."

Relief, disbelief, gratitude—all and more tangled together in one staccato burst of laughter from Jasirey.

"Darling, I am your friend," Reginald said. "Even if I disagree with you, I will never judge nor abandon you. You are important to me."

"Be glad you're gay," she whispered with a suspicious snuffle in her voice, "or you might have been one of my gang of Protectors."

"Yes. I believe I would. And isn't it that, your irresistible pull and ability to inspire people's spontaneous friendship and loyalty to you that makes you Jasirey?"

Jasirey's Training

On the day of Jasirey's departure, Reginald kissed her cheeks. "Be well, my dear. Let me know how you fare."

Yusef and his squad, Lee, and Liu saw her and Kimika safely to a local airport for smaller craft and a plane piloted by a Devoted international businessman returning to visit family. Kimika, just released from the hospital, planned to recover on the island.

They arrived on the island in the early evening and trundled Kimika by cart to the infirmary. To shake out travel kinks, Jasirey walked to the Imperiat domicile where she would be staying.

Jasirey doubted she'd need the sweater she'd brought. Island weather stayed warm most of the year. She'd miss her island dresses left in America and her bracelet. Able to ignore her bare right wrist in England, on the island she found the lack of her bracelet glaringly obvious.

Master Kai greeted her warmly and over dinner talked about topics other than her training. "Dear one, you remember we took one of Marcus's men, on his ship during your first capture, at the time of your escape. Can you tell me why you sent him to us?"

"I had a brief introduction to him at the resort where I first met Ian."

Master Kai's expression vacillated between incredulousness and annoyance. "Since Ian did not mention it, I assume you neglected to tell him of the encounter."

"I told Lee and Fael as heads of security about him after his capture. I figured they'd tell Ian and Liu. At the resort, there wasn't any reason to mention Strafe to Ian. Marcus was in the future. I just saw a guy hitting on me."

"Hitting—slang, I assume."

Jasirey had to laugh. "Means a sexual invitation."

"I see. Well, Strafe wishes an audience."

"I told Fael to remind the council that Marcus hadn't asked about him. Seemed a significant slip. Why does Strafe want to see me?"

"We have been attempting to deprogram the young man. He believes Marcus liberated him from an uncle who valued him only as a laborer."

"At what age?"

"Six and no doubt destined by Marcus for the sex trade until he decided to train Strafe in computer coding. Strafe is the only name he remembers. You apparently made a strong impression on him."

"And you want me to press that advantage and indoctrinate him. What do you want from him?"

"The question is what do you want? You asked Nikolai to send him. The council suspects you had a reason to do so, that he may be of use to you in some undetermined way."

"I had the same feeling but don't know why exactly."

"If you care to see him, we shall leave his fate in your hands."

"Uh-huh. You didn't throw in the word care for nothing. Manipulative, Kai."

He kissed her cheek. "Will you see him?"

"Sure, why not?"

* * *

After The Five's, her husbands', and security's stories, Jasirey thought she was prepared for training. She went to bed at eight in the evenings, rose at four for physical workouts, and reported to the trainer of the day after a light breakfast. She lost weight under the strain. The Imperiat ordered Master N'yu-wen to monitor her.

Several days in, the no-nonsense healer confronted Jasirey regarding Mirai and Nikolai's deaths. The healer regarded her charge calmly. "Guilt wastes time. If you behaved inappropriately, learn from it. If not, Americans have a saying—get over it."

Jasirey stared in mixed humor and disbelief.

"I served as Nikolai and Mirai's healer," Master N'yu-wen said. "His parents are off island visiting their own parents. As you have enough burdens to bear, Mirai decided not to tell you about her son. She loved and admired you. Had she told you, perhaps she would have been better prepared to deflect the projections—the bridge—you used to incapacitate her."

The healer watched Jasirey pull into herself and said, "Had she succeeded, you would have found another way around her. For you, the choice between non-action and protecting a loved one does not exist. Mirai understood this. It was one of your traits she most admired. You are not responsible for her death. You cannot control everything. Nor do you possess the arrogance to believe otherwise.

"I have scheduled a visit for you with Mirai's parents. You are invited to dinner, and as you do not wish to appear rude, you will eat."

The older woman allowed herself an inward smile at the rebellious light in Jasirey's eyes. "I am curious. Was your memory projection to Mirai planned or an in-the-moment reaction?"

"It was a quick decision in the moment but thought out. I understood the emotional repercussions to Mirai."

Master N'yu-wen nodded. As she'd thought. "And you wish to strengthen the ability to prevent inadvertent use of your skills, do you not?"

Brow furrowed, Jasirey glanced away.

"Stop resisting the training. Learn the extent of your gifts. Only then shall you be in the best position to decide whether it is appropriate to utilize them."

Jasirey nodded. Somehow, Master N'yu-Wen's lack of sympathy relieved her guilt. "Thank you."

The healer stunned Jasirey with a brief embrace. "You have sufficient to prevail over without fighting your own nature. Think of nothing now except tonight. Both you and Mirai's family need this time together to move forward."

⁂

That evening, Jasirey gratefully wore one of the island dresses that had appeared in her closet. She linked arms with Master Kai as he escorted her to the home of Mirai's parents.

The trembling in her arm became more pronounced as they neared the small house nestled in a grove of trees. Jasirey stopped to draw deep breaths. She refused to show up a basket case at Mirai's family's door and add to their pain. She bent at the waist to force blood back to her head.

Kai rubbed her back.

"Sorry. It's all right." Jasirey said. "I'll get it together." She straightened slowly. "Appreciate it if you'd let me greet them alone."

"As you wish, dearest one." After a bolstering hug, he left her at the door.

Jasirey's knock sounded timid.

The door opened instantly, and Mirai's father, mother, and brother drew her inside. Struggling not to cry, they huddled about her.

Jasirey tried to offer comfort, couldn't manage it, and accepted that they all had to wade through the pain.

Mirai's brother recovered first and led Jasirey to cushions around a low table set with a large assortment of dishes. The setting sun glinted off an upright piano and drew her to a picture of a laughing Mirai holding a dark-haired infant under the arms. The picture caught the baby kicking in delight. Jasirey wiped her eyes and smiled at the family who politely waited for their lady to sit.

"I thought you might like to sample traditional Japanese cuisine," Mirai's mother said, "and chose white miso soup to begin, lighter and sweeter than red miso."

Jasirey listened with interest as the family described the various dishes. Most of the menu, she knew, had been kept on the mild side since they did not know her preferences—the soup, shrimp tempura instead of sushi. Each dish was served on small individual serving plates, which explained their number.

"One dish's seasoning should not be allowed to contaminate another dish's," Mirai's brother said.

Conversation gradually included stories of Mirai growing up and her son, Dickens.

As the dinner ended, Jasirey stopped fighting and gave in to a strong vision of mother and son, on sturdy little legs, frolicking through a landscape of maroon-leaved trees. "I see them running together through Japanese maples," she murmured.

Mirai's mother gasped. "Her favorite tree."

Jasirey sensed it would not be an intrusion. She held the family's gaze and built a three-pronged bridge—something new she had been considering—and simultaneously sent the vision to each of them.

⁂

Tired of being cooped up in the training building every day, Jasirey decided to meet Strafe mid-week at the outcrop, a shaded clearing where the council often met and seated themselves on a ledge of tiered stone benches. Jasirey waited on the lowest tier and stood when four Protectors ushered Strafe into the clearing.

Strafe stopped for a split second to take in the small figure in a teal sundress. He wore the comfortably cool, loose tunic and trousers many of the island people favored. The large men escorting him bowed to the woman he knew as Shannon while he looked on in amusement and then surprise as she returned the salute. It further surprised him when she gestured for him to sit beside her.

"I recognized you on Marcus's ship," Jasirey said, "from when you spoke to me at the resort. There to spy on Ian for Marcus, I assume."

"I've never seen anyone get to him before," he said. "Or me, either. He said you bewitched me. Is that what you are?"

"A witch? The superstitious might think so."

"Your people don't seem superstitious, but they believe you have powers."

Jasirey smiled mischievously, the last reaction he expected.

"Still spying for Marcus. He'd be pleased to have whatever information you could glean about me."

The man stilled.

"You've seen enough of the world to know other options exist. Were you satisfied with the life Marcus provided for you?"

"Key words—Marcus provided."

"Took advantage of an unloved, unwanted child."

Strafe realized Jasirey's blue-green eyes fired in righteous indignation for him. Yet he sensed no sexual attraction. *What did she care?* Her mouth—a mouth he had repeatedly dreamed about—dipped with a fleeting frown.

"Of course, we want you to help us fight Marcus, Strafe. What do you want? To return to him? No other ambitions, dreams, maybe hopes for a family?"

He grimaced. "God, no."

"You don't have to go back."

Strafe sneered. "You'd let me go, nothing in return."

Her eyes grew, engulfed him.

He couldn't move. Tears, pleading, cries of pain inflicted by him. He struggled, didn't want to see it through the girls'—so many girls—eyes. "Stop," he said hoarsely.

"Something in return," Jasirey said. "Stop hurting people."

He clasped his hands together. "I don't know what happened to them. Marcus handled that part. We just trained—" He flung out a hand. "It's what they were there for."

"To be brutalized, hammered into little more than animatronic slaves."

The sharp edge of her voice sliced at Strafe. "Kids get used all the time," he said. "At least where we sent them, they got shelter and regular meals."

"For how long? Ever ask what happened to them when they were too used up to keep entertaining? Would that life have been good enough for you? It's what Marcus intended for you until he saw your potential, a potential he could mold and use to suit himself." Jasirey signaled the Protectors away when Strafe reared up. "Would you have chosen the life of a sex slave over farming or a trade?"

Strafe stepped down from the outcrop. "Put me in jail if you're going to."

"What I see isn't evidence and no witnesses remain to testify against you."

"What do you want?" Strafe felt her physically and mentally withdraw from him. It was a relief yet agonizing. He wanted to grab on to her, to hope. For what, he did not know.

"Think about options," she said. "We'll talk again."

* * *

Their lady's anger filled the room. Two security trainees sprawled on their backs waiting for the walls to stop spinning. She hadn't touched them. The eyes of three standing youngsters flitted between her and Master Howard. Mindful reactions were the day's goal. Jasirey breathed heavily and, in turn, eyed the older teacher warily.

"Don't rely on dredging up anger," he ordered in a clipped tone. "It requires too much energy. Anticipate the attack and your counter to it—cooly, dispassionately. You've done it before. Again."

Jasirey breathed, centered, and projected *Boo* at the intimidated trainees who failed to conceal their laughter from an aggravated Master Howard.

He studied his most challenging student. "You've demonstrated the effectiveness of your humor on negative emotions. It won't stop someone bent on violence. Concentrate."

"Kind of a cleansing of the palate," she said equably and halted a more experienced man and woman sneaking up behind her with a vision of quicksand spreading out at their feet.

She held them for thirty seconds, maybe adequate to get away or take preemptive action. Unfortunately, she hadn't once been able to multitask, to physically react, while projecting that psychic energy. It took every ounce of her concentration to hold the vision, and she tired quickly. It gave her a headache.

Sensitive to his student's body language, Master Howard said, "Productive session. Niharu, see to our lady's headache."

A small room set aside for her held a massage table and a cot for resting.

Master Howard clapped his hands. "Thank you, everyone. You're dismissed until tomorrow. Niharu, when ready, escort our lady to the Imperiat domicile."

Everyone bowed to Jasirey. She wearily returned it and followed the young healer. She'd rather have skipped the follow-up step. Niharu exhibited nothing other than dedicated concern for her welfare, but the dislike for him formed on her first visit to the island increased at his unspoken disapproval of her actions. Many of the trainees found her stubbornness and occasional irreverence uncomfortable. Even if that was simply the case with the young healer, she kept their sessions short.

Niharu had her lie face up on an exam table to perform acupuncture. She tolerated the needles. She couldn't stand his hands on her. "I'm not sore," she said as he reached down to her legs. "Today didn't require much physical exertion."

"You may not yet feel knots forming. It is preferable to check."

"Not tonight. I'll let you know if there's a problem in the morning. Right now, I'm starving." Which was true.

Niharu masked his displeasure in a bow. Though he admired her more than anyone, he believed her willfulness got in the way of her best interest. It surprised him that the trainers so often allowed her disobedience to go unchallenged. Yes, she was Jasirey, but surely such lack of discipline needed to be addressed before trusting her leadership.

Outside the training center, Jasirey saw an Imperiat she knew heading to the domicile. She bowled over Niharu's objections, bowed, and joined the woman.

⁂

With two days left of training, Master Kai took over. Their lady had long ago learned to block her empathic senses. She could teach master classes if she knew how she managed it. Jasirey had made great strides in focusing her energies. The length of time she maintained that focus would grow with practice. He taught her exercises to continue at home.

"I cannot instruct you on what you call multitasking. We are not positive it is even possible. You are unique to our experience and must guide us. Experiment with acting physically while mentally projecting a vision but do not focus on that area. Let it come as a natural progression."

⁂

Jasirey asked the Protectors to bring Strafe to the Imperiat domicile on the morning of her departure. She offered him multigrain croissants and tea in a small interior room, a skylight the only natural light. One wall held growth-medium pockets full of ferns. Over a year ago, before the fealty ceremony to welcome her as Jasirey, she had lunched in the same room with Kai and retained fond memories of it.

Strafe picked at a croissant. "The guards said you're leaving."

"Yes. Going home. I thought I'd give you a parting gift."

"I'm no longer an ignorant, unwanted boy," he sneered. "I know how the world works. Gifts come with strings."

"Oh, sweetie, your restricted view of the world comes from one narrow, grimy window."

He relaxed and let his legs fall open. "The present goes to the one leaving, doesn't it?"

"That will be up to you."

Strafe's face tingled where soft fingers caressed and soothed. Though he refused to admit it, Strafe had experienced Jasirey's bridge to his mind on Marcus's ship the first time the trafficker had kidnapped her. The bridge felt similar, but the message couldn't have been more different.

He didn't know which he liked better, the touch that whispered, "I care," or the soft, lovely voice singing nonsense words into his ear. The tone more than the words said, "I love you, sweet boy, my pride and joy."

When Strafe reluctantly came to himself, Jasirey had gone, and he was left with a bittersweet jumble of pictures, emotions, and perhaps memories of what it felt like to have a mother who would protect you, be proud of you, and love you all the days of her life.

⁂

Everyone living at the western Massachusetts compound gathered in the living room of the main house to welcome Jasirey home. She looked well but fatigued.

Liu gave her his herbal remedy for jet lag, and after an hour, her bedtime on the island, he insisted that she nap. She didn't argue.

Several hours later, her husbands brought her a late lunch in bed. The wonderful smell of turkey soup wafted around her, and accompanying crusty bread and peanut butter constituted her idea of heaven.

"How did it go, meeting Mirai's family?" Lee asked.

"They're lovely people," Jasirey said. "I saw Mirai running in a grove of trees with her son and shared it with them." She recounted the story as if it were an everyday occurrence. "I think it helped. I'd like to plant a Japanese maple in the garden in her memory."

Jasirey satiated her hunger, then let other needs unmet the past two weeks shiver through her. She lowered her eyes and planted erotic scenarios in her husbands' minds.

"Is that you?" Liu managed a strangled whisper.

"Find out." Jasirey's eyes danced with desire.

The men had intended slow seduction. Feeling their wife's very real curves pressing into their bodies as her passion scintillated inside their heads, they gave in to frenzy.

Jasirey blissfully lost track of the number of orgasms. Afterward, too undone to cuddle, the men sprawled in a state of torpor. Jasirey nested in their midst, recovered first, and ran soft hands down muscular backs and legs and up flat stomachs and firm chests. She settled in with each in an easy twining of tongues, nip of lips, caresses given and taken. She loved being home.

In the days that followed, Jasirey kept busy touching base with everyone—a visit to Lizzy thrilled with the video Jasirey had asked her husbands to make of Reginald's weekend party; calls to her parents and sisters; and with various members of the people, lunches or teas, a custom she wanted to adopt from England.

"Loved one," Fael said after two weeks, "Mtombe joins us tomorrow, and Yusef, Chen, Favian, Sajan, and Andwar have asked for an audience at your convenience."

Jasirey made a scoffing sound that made Fael smile. "Perhaps the wrong word," he said. "When you believe it prudent to stop punishing them."

"Hey . . . I'm not." She closed her eyes, opened them, and sighed. "Am I?" Her breath huffed out. "Fine. Tomorrow afternoon in the library with Mtombe." She wanted him as a buffer. "Today I want to speak to Satoko and Mashita, remind them how much they were missed while we were in England."

❦ ❦ ❦

Jasirey set up tea for Satoko, Mashita, and herself. She poured their preferred oolong. "I asked the groundskeepers to plant a Japanese maple in the garden for Mirai," she said. Is there anything similar you'd like done in memory of your family?"

"We attended to that in Japan," Mashita said. "We went to pray at a Shinto shrine not far from our home and left our Ema. While perhaps not easing the pain altogether, it did bring a measure of peace."

Satoko explained Ema. "Around the shrine, one places small wooden plaques with written wishes. For us, that meant the well-being of our family in the afterlife and our family here." She nudged her husband.

He handed a small box to Jasirey. "An Inuhariko, a paper dog that blesses births." Like all the Devoted, Mashita and Satoko knew the prophecy of the second pregnancy.

Jasirey shook off the dread the gift sent through her and hugged the couple. She sensed their need to talk about their family and encouraged them.

"We know so little," Mashita said. "After the tsunami, we stayed with my sister for many days before we were allowed back to our town."

"I remember she lives inland," Jasirey said, "so the tsunami missed you."

"Our son and son-in-law would not have sought higher ground without their families," Satoko said. "Their children were too young to attend school, safer because schools were built on higher ground. Many students became orphans."

"We have been told," Mashita said, "the tsunami washed away several shelters meant to protect us. We assume our families had the misfortune to choose one of them. We are grateful that their bodies were found and cremated with proper ceremonies. Thousands remain missing, and in places, mass graves provided the only alternative."

"I truly cannot imagine such devastation," Jasirey said.

Usually shying away from eye contact, Mashita allowed his gaze to level on his lady's. "Nor should you. Do not take on our burden. We shall ever be grateful that you have lightened it, but you must concentrate on your own destiny."

❧ ❧ ❧

On the following day, Mtombe arrived after breakfast. Jasirey walked with him in the garden pruned for winter, autumn leaves raked and added to compost piles.

She turned and clung to him. "I'm so glad you're here."

"What is it, loveling?" To look into her troubled eyes, he cradled her face.

"Still don't know what to do about my Protectors."

"You worry too much," Mtombe said in a dismissive tone. "Why must everything rest on your shoulders?"

He knew he had put his foot in it when Jasirey stepped back, her expression difficult to interpret. "I meant no offense."

"It's okay. They aren't your concern."

Mtombe took her hand. "What concerns you concerns me, and they are my friends. I prefer, however, not to let other concerns interfere with the little time that is ours. Fair enough?"

Her lips twitched as the imp entered her eyes, and she said, "You can't expect a wild boar to shed his tusks for touchy-feely sensitivity, I suppose."

He drawled in her ear. "We shall perhaps see about touching and feeling after the meeting."

Her shiver of anticipation raised a look of satisfaction on his face.

That afternoon, as much as she wanted to, Jasirey refrained from holding Mtombe's hand upon entering the library.

Sajan, Favian, Chen, Yusef, and Andwar stood waiting and bowed. They worked so hard to hide their anxiety, her heart melted. She hugged them and bade them sit around the small sofa she and Mtombe occupied.

"I'm sorry I've left you in limbo," she said. "Fael says—" Every bit of color leached from her face, and Jasirey bolted off the sofa.

Chen grabbed a nearby trash can and then her shoulders as she lunged toward it and vomited rather spectacularly. He helped her back to the sofa and gave her some water.

Liu walked in wheeling a tea service with small iced cakes and sandwich triangles.

Jasirey knew the real meeting had begun. She straightened her shoulders. "I'm pregnant, aren't I?"

Liu had already informed the Protectors that Jasirey had been ovulating the night of Marcus's attack. They waited with bated breath.

"Considering your prophecy," Liu said, "I believe destiny has been fulfilled. I also believe you already know this."

Jasirey choked back a curse. "The babies aren't even a year old. I thought I had more time, that the decision would be mine."

Liu sat beside her, enfolded her in his arms, and gently rocked. "As you found the decision so difficult, I suspect destiny chose for you. You still, however, must decide how your Protectors shall fit into your life."

Liu relinquished Jasirey to Yusef, who took Liu's place on the sofa. "It is not critical to work out everything today," Liu said. "Perhaps you might decide on a way to be comfortable together. I shall stay if you prefer a mediator. What is your wish, precious one?"

Jasirey drew a deep breath and slowly released it. "We'll be fine."

With something he meant as respect, Liu bowed to her but that coming from her husbands always disconcerted Jasirey.

Yusef gazed steadily into his lady's eyes. "I am yours always. Lover or friend—you know I wish both. Father or protector of your children, I am here for you, most cherished one."

Andwar clasped her hands. "I am yours always, my heart. Whatever your decision, I will love you all my life, but your well-being will always be my paramount concern."

"I am yours always, treasured one," Favian said, "for love, comfort, friendship, intellectual challenge—anything you need."

Chen cupped her face and kissed her forehead. "I am yours always, adored one. I love you. Please don't stress yourself. The answer will come to you."

Sajan crouched to Jasirey's eye level. "I am yours always, sweet lady, ready and willing to do whatever you require to help you remain well."

Jasirey needed time alone to process. The demands on her body of another pregnancy frightened her. She stood, and the men rose. "I didn't expect to talk about a pregnancy today. I want to talk to my husbands and Jesse about that first. Meet me here again tomorrow, same time."

Yusef kissed her cheeks. "Whatever we can do to ease your burden will be done. None of us wishes to further distress you. I believe our actions the day of Marcus's attack were warranted. I wish I could spare you any unpleasant consequences."

Jasirey managed a wan smile. "Other than pregnancy."

Unsuccessful at stifling their joy, the men bowed reverently and left.

Mtombe steered her back to the sofa. "All right, loveling?"

His guarded expression drew her attention. "I'm sorry, Mtombe. Are you ready for possibly becoming a father?"

Too many emotions flitted over his face for her to interpret.

"It's okay. You're bound to be ambivalent."

He pulled her into an ardent kiss that soon gentled to tenderness. "You misunderstand, loveling. You are ambivalent. I . . . "

The brightest grin Jasirey had ever seen on his face spread and made her breath catch.

"I am ecstatic. A child of you and me, I want it very much. I am sorry it upsets you so."

Jasirey rained kisses over his face and down his neck.

Mtombe had never more desired her as she stood in the sun, hair sparkling, eyes darkened. He leaned in to nibble on her ear and neck, cupped her face, and just looking, filled his heart. "Such an adorable face," he said. "I love you. I am yours always."

Jasirey let Mtombe believe she put off having sex with him because of not feeling well, but truthfully, she wanted his options to remain open until he settled into his new life. Once they became consciously, truly intimate, he would belong to her and need to be with her as often as possible.

Black Hole

Mtombe had to leave the next morning but promised to return soon. Jasirey wanted her wild boar with her during her pregnancy. The real possibility that he couldn't sliced at her heart.

After seeing Mtombe off, the husbands coaxed their wife into a walk. Lee draped an arm around her waist. "We assume this pregnancy is the quintuplets of the prophecy."

"Our house no longer seems so large," Ian said. "There are two options—an additional floor or a new wing."

"I'd prefer all the children on the same floor with us."

"A new wing then."

Wary of Jasirey's expected sensitivity to the next item on their agenda, the men drew instinctively closer. Fael had lost the coin tosses.

"Loved one," he said, "along with the extra rooms for the children and the people necessary to help us care for them, we think it logical for you to have a room set aside for your time spent with Mtombe or any other of your choosing."

Jasirey's cheeks reddened. Lee's arm hampered her from moving away. She bit down on the compulsion to yell at them for interfering. At least she kept back the blaze of heat she knew people often felt when she didn't have control of her anger.

"Shall you not wish to give the new fathers the opportunity to know their children?" Liu asked.

Jasirey deflated into Lee. "Meaning they have to be in my life, our life."

"They love you, little one," Lee said. "Have you no affection for them?"

She sighed. "Of course, but it's nothing compared to what I feel for you. I don't need anyone else. And nine babies? You'll be lucky if I have time or energy for you guys."

"We'll make sure you do," Ian said, determination tightening his expression.

Jasirey sighed. "I don't know how to fit them into our lives. It isn't fair for me to decide everything. It affects you, too."

"Yes, it does," Fael said. "Hence, we offer suggestions. For now, you have your craft room. Not ideal, granted, but it shall suffice. We prefer to leave dinner and prayer time for the core family, at least until the quintuplets arrive. Then, perhaps, the fathers should be incorporated in some way. We shall work that out."

"And will these children be yours or theirs?" Jasirey couldn't quite mask the snark.

"As your husbands," Liu said, "we shall be their fathers. The others understand this. Their relationship to the family must be carefully orchestrated."

Jasirey curled up against Lee's chest. "I can just see it. Everett, please set up lunch in my tryst room for my lovers. Lizzie, come meet the fathers of my next batch of kids."

Lee shook her gently, cradled her face, and gazed sternly into her eyes. "Stop."

"I didn't want . . . I just needed more time," she whispered with such abject misery, her husbands' hearts clutched.

"Apparently, a higher power stepped in to ensure your destiny," Fael said softly. "It is meant. All that remains is for you to accept it."

Though the men literally knew no one stronger nor more bravely resolute, they vowed to be a wall of strength for their beloved to lean and rely on as her husband-protectors in all things.

❦ ❦ ❦

Jasirey felt stuck in a revolving door with no exit. Her world was off, wrong, and she couldn't figure out how to right it. Uncertain of his reaction, she avoided Everett and requested that Isa follow British customary practice and arrange a tea cart for tea for her meeting with her Protectors.

Against the cool of the autumn, Jasirey built a fire. She stared at it as the men entered. Yusef went directly to her, bowed, and leaned down to kiss each cheek. The others followed. He sat beside her on the sofa, the rest on chairs.

She served the tea and stared at her cup. "I'm sorry, but I don't want any more husbands or lovers."

That was emphatic.

"Neither do I want to deny you the right to be part of your children's lives. I can't see a clear way to juggle everything and not wind up in a . . . " Her hand spiraled aimlessly in the air. " . . . a heap of broken pieces or something."

"Cherished one," Yusef said, "do you not want us personally or do you believe it wrong to have feelings for us? Do you fear being unable to love so many or others' reactions?"

Jasirey leaned back on the couch. Her head hurt.

"Perhaps," said Favian, heart in his throat, "we should return to the island and relieve you of these decisions. Your pregnancy takes priority."

Though not looking at the men, Jasirey listened attentively.

Chen's eyes closed briefly in pain and opened with resolve.

They would leave if asked, make her life easier, but . . . "I can't do that to you."

Yusef covered her hand. "You can. We can return after the birth if you wish. Think only of what's best for you." He kissed the frown lines between her beautiful eyes and then bowed along with the others. "We'll wait for your decision."

The men quietly walked out. Jasirey sat, numbed into immobility without the emotional wherewithal even to pray. She had no idea how long she drifted.

A knock broke her daze. Everett brought in a tray and paused as he drew near. "Poor little mite, you look utterly lost."

Setting down the tray, he sat beside her and gathered her cold hands in his. He chafed at them gently. "They expect too much of you."

Jasirey blinked at him in surprise.

"Ian has informed us of your pregnancy so we may watch over you. I understand five are expected this time."

Averting her gaze, she nodded.

"And I assume, as your prophecy predicted, your husbands are not the fathers."

Her eyes closed, and Everett again berated himself for his first reaction to her marriage to four men.

Jasirey's eyes flew open, and her hand lifted to gently stroke his face.

Everett took it and kissed the palm. "These new fathers—security personnel?"

"And Mtombe," she mumbled.

"Really? Hmm. Well, he'll need to come round more, won't he? And the others?"

"Andwar, Yusef, Chen, Sajan, and Favian."

He nodded. "They seem fine young men." His gaze became more stern. "They best do their part in seeing you through this. It goes without saying the rest of us are here for you."

With a literal physical lifting of the anxiety, heavy as a boulder, that had been lying on her heart, Jasirey hugged him close. "Thank you, Everett. Thank you so much."

Still painfully guilty that any of her disquiet should have stemmed from his reaction to her marriage, he held her tight and hoped the matter had finally been laid to rest.

The boys usually visited their mother after the homeschool teacher ended the day's classes held in the common room between Christopher and Michael's bedrooms. The boys would arrive shortly. Everett scanned the tray once more to ensure he had included sufficient teen food, cupped Jasirey's face, kissed each cheek, and rose to leave. "I love you, my dear."

"I know." Her smile warmed him. "I love you."

He went out, and a little dumbstruck, Jasirey sank back until acute physical distress sent her dashing for the bathroom.

Christopher and Michael heard their mother as they entered the craft room and sat to wait. When she came out, her face drawn and blanched, Christopher jumped up, took her arm, and led her to the sofa.

"Thank you, honey," she told him. "You're getting so grown up. How are my young men today?"

"Better than you." Michael eyed her speculatively. "Security's buzzing. You're pregnant with the quintuplets like prophecy said?"

Her mouth opened and shut abruptly. She was beginning to feel like a fly catcher.

Michael grinned. "Can't keep secrets around here."

"So," Christopher said, "Mtombe and the guys who rescued you are the fathers?"

Struck dumb yet again, she nodded.

"You don't want to marry them?"

Jasirey managed a negative shake of the head.

"But they'll help take care of you, right?" He dreaded a replay of her pain and illness from the last pregnancy.

"You think . . . " She floundered. "We discussed maybe having them return to the island."

Michael stiffened. "Why? You love Mtombe. Don't you like the others?"

Jasirey stared at them in confusion.

"Mom," Christopher said, "what are you afraid of? Everyone here knows who you are, what you're about. You need them."

"That's it? Simple as that? The idea of other fathers, other . . . " She just couldn't bring herself to say it.

"Way back when Master Kai told us about you, he said the average number of husbands was fifteen, and some Jasireys had as many as forty-five." Christopher blushed. "I'm glad you don't have that many, but maybe it would've helped if you'd had more the last pregnancy."

Michael rolled his eyes. "Mom, you should see those guys mooning around. Can't you love them, even a little? Isn't that kind of like your job?"

Jasirey started to laugh. *Holy jumping cow.*

Christopher's elbow nudged her. "We believe your legend, in your destiny. In you."

Jasirey hugged him. "My Christopher." She held her arms out to Michael. "Thank you, honey. You've both been a big help."

"Well, sons can kind of be Protectors, can't they? Like Kimika?"

"Definitely." She wiped away her tears and joined her magnificent sons in the snack Everett had provided. "Just out of curiosity," she said, "how did you know I love Mtombe?"

Michael shrugged. "You look at him the same way you look at Ian, Lee, Liu, and Fael."

"Huh."

Christopher decided it was as good a time as any to broach another difficult subject. "I've been thinking of going to the island after high school to train in security and missions."

“Not me,” Michael said, oblivious to his mother’s shock. “I’m going to be a writer.”

That distracted Jasirey. “Really? What kind?”

“Stories for games maybe. Don’t know exactly.”

Jasirey carefully considered her response to Christopher. “Why do you want to go on missions? Any idea what you hope to accomplish on them?”

“They keep saying you’re supposed to set the stage for us. I think, in my case, it’s the other way around. Everyone knows you’re different from past Jasireys. I’m not sure what that means to the world yet, but I’ve got a really strong feeling you’ll be important and I’m supposed to help you somehow. So, I need to be prepared.”

Jasirey hugged her eldest close. “While not my first choice for you, I understand the importance of figuring out your own path.”

“Good. That’s settled,” Michael said. “You won’t send the new babies’ fathers away?”

“No, I won’t.”

“Great. I think you should tell them. Come on, Christopher. Let’s go get them.”

“Now?” Her voice squeaked.

Christopher grinned. “Never put off till tomorrow . . . ”

After hugging her good-bye, they bounded out. Jasirey had no time to formulate a plan before her Protectors bounded in with hopeful expectation radiating from them.

Jasirey suppressed a grimace. “My sons tell me I need you and shouldn’t let you leave.”

Yusef pounced, dragged her up into his arms, and grinned at her startled yelp. “To love as well as protect?” His black eyes drilled into hers.

Jasirey failed at masking the sorrow in her voice. “Please give me more time on that. I don’t want you to feel like drone bees, but I don’t need more sexual partners. And something you don’t seem to have considered. Not all of you will become fathers. Six of you, five babies, and the possibility that more than one child can be fathered by the same man.”

Yusef drew her down to the sofa. The rest sat on the floor at her feet. “Liu was thorough in explaining the possibilities. As far as we’re concerned, we were all there at the conception, and we will all take whatever responsibility for the children granted to us." He ran a gentle fingertip down her neck, caused a shiver, and followed with a whisper-light swish of lips.

Jasirey's pulse tripped. Satisfied when her lovely eyes darkened in response, Yusef nestled her into strong arms rather than press his advantage.

"Our love and physical presence shall become necessary to you," Sajan said. "Perhaps that disconcerts you more than the pregnancy itself. Since we shall stay here, I hope your acceptance will grow with time."

Favian knelt before her, cradled her face, and savaged her mouth with grazing teeth, nibbling lips, and a slinking tongue. Dazed, his treasured one panted.

Chen was of no mind to let Jasirey catch her breath or equilibrium and pulled her up to knead her finely rounded rear end and add highly combustible fuel in a searing kiss. His adored one's body began slowly to melt into his.

Sajan poked Chen aside and lowered the temperature with small kisses over her face and neck before handing her to Andwar, who cuddled their lady until her breathing eased and then gently set her aside, bowed, and followed by the others, departed.

Jasirey could only stare after them. Then she smiled. Destiny rolled on or over whoever got in its way. She refused to let it flatten her.

❦ ❦ ❦

After family prayers and tucking the toddlers in for the night, Lee gathered his wife onto his lap in their bedroom sitting area. "How are you, my little one? The situation with your Protectors has worked out to your mutual satisfaction?"

Jasirey's mouth pursed at his twinkling eyes. "Well, we talked about them returning to the island, but they're staying with us." And as Ian had predicted, Yusef, Chen, Favian, Sajan, and Andwar had started a campaign of seduction to win her heart. She quashed a kernel of resentment at feeling unable to talk to her husbands about her Protectors' hopes of a relationship with her because of Ian's aversion to the idea.

She described Everett and her sons' advice. The men were greatly impressed by Michael and Christopher's mature insight and compassion. It gave them a fine inkling of how their own youngsters might turn out.

Fael returned to the main topic. "And your Protectors' role in your life?"

Jasirey rested her chin on drawn-up knees. "I told them, I don't need more lovers. Truthfully, I think it's more that they need or at least want me, but pregnant again, I have to consider more than myself. Colin, Jaimie, Safia, and Sunny need their daddies. You guys won't be able to devote yourselves solely to me this time."

The husbands didn't argue. Jasirey's prophecy suggested the second pregnancy would be less harrowing—because of extra caregivers couldn't be discounted.

"Guys, I'd really like to take a long weekend soon and visit my parents before I get too ill or big to travel. We promised to visit again soon. What's it been, half a year?"

"All right," Ian said. "I'll make arrangements with work and for accommodations. What exactly did you have in mind?"

"Friday through Monday. I'm okay leaving the babies that long, though I'd rather at least two of their daddies stay home with them."

"As your husband of record, Ian must go," Liu said. "I am your healer and prefer to stay with you as well."

"Let's Fael and me off the hook." Lee's dimples flashed at her. "I'll set up security with Yusef. He's taking over for Kimika until he returns. You'll take Christopher and Michael?"

"Yes, they need to see their grandparents." She became pensive. "We should set up a date for your family to come visit. Call them—maybe for the babies' birthday?"

"Good idea." He hugged her. "Thank you."

"You do know you can invite them whenever, your entire family, a reunion if you want."

"It takes an organized wife to remember such things."

"Men," she scoffed and nipped at his bottom lip, even fuller than her own.

The twinkle in his hazel eyes deepened into a gleam. "We're easily distracted."

"Yes, you are. Liu, your parents won't come here?"

"I have suggested it. The paperwork alone overwhelms them. I offered to help, but they declined. I must respect their wishes."

"Will you go visit them?"

"Perhaps for the New Year. We shall see, precious one."

"Ian," Fael said, "perhaps you and Liu can set up individual dates while away." Ian's misgivings about other men in their wife's life, though seldom expressed, had recently begun to seep through Fael's blocks. He feared they might fester. Ian and Jasirey needed to talk about it.

"Charleston is a wonderful city for dinner and dancing," Ian said. "You might wear that very erotic one-piece corset.

She raised her eyebrows.

"Providing you can still get into it, of course, what with pregnancy body changes," he hastily added.

The others laughed. Her breasts had already begun to enlarge, one symptom the men didn't mind in the least. Tender, they responded wonderfully to the lightest touches.

When her men put those tender touches to good use, Jasirey let go her argument against tight corsets while pregnant. She knew Liu would explain the potential danger to the others.

❦ ❦ ❦

Yusef chose Favian, Chen, and two women to accompany the family to South Carolina. After landing, Favian drove Jasirey, Ian, and the boys directly to Jasirey's parents, Anne and Richard, in a rented van. Security permanently assigned to Anne and Richard had been informed of the family's arrival.

Liu, Chen, and the women followed in another vehicle.

Jasirey had left the timing of their visit vague in the hope of preventing her mother's compulsion to go overboard cooking. Anne was adept at anticipating and had prepared a huge lasagna and apple pie with cranberries.

At dinner, Ian praised Anne. "I see where my wife gets her culinary skills."

"She spoiled us," Jasirey said. "Store-bought, even restaurant pies can't compare."

Anne glowed happily. She had been informed that they had plans for Saturday evening and would visit in the early afternoon. Ian insisted on bringing them out to dinner Sunday night.

Richard readily agreed before his wife objected. He enjoyed eating out and did not enjoy his wife's snappish temper when stressed from taking on too much, cooking for so many. Nor did he particularly care for the role of chef's helper.

Fighting nausea, Jasirey woke early on Saturday morning. Liu had the vitamin-enriched protein drink ready that during her first pregnancy stayed down better than food.

They'd been testing her blood sugar regularly with, until then, no precipitous drops. Liu recommended she rest for the day if she wished to go on the planned evening's date with Ian.

"No, baby," Ian said. "You've come to see your parents. We can have a date any time."

Christopher suggested a solution. "Why doesn't Ian take Michael and me to sleep over at Grandma and Grandpa's house? You can pick us up tomorrow, Mom. Grandma will be happy."

Jasirey hugged him and pushed aside the regret that her parents would never know their other grandchildren. "Thank you, sweetie. That's a great idea."

She called her mother. She hadn't informed her parents of her first pregnancy of multiples. Neither would she say anything about her current pregnancy.

Anne commiserated that her daughter felt unwell but was ecstatic at having her grandsons overnight. They loved to eat, and she knew their favorites.

Liu went out for fresh herbs for Jasirey's drink. The two women who would stay as extra security accompanied Ian and the teens to Anne and Richard's.

Jasirey's parents had been told on the family's previous visit that, as a high-profile corporate leader dealing with sensitive products, Ian and his family required security.

Jasirey rested on the sofa in their suite while Favian and Chen played cards. Unable to get comfortable, she tossed and turned. Her legs felt cramped—not the ants from the previous pregnancy—perhaps from too much sitting.

She gave up. "Can we go to the pool for a bit?" she asked. "My muscles aren't cooperating."

Favian frowned. "Liu wanted you to rest. Has the nausea abated?"

"Hanging around the edges."

"Let's try something less active," Chen said. "Come to the bedroom. Favian and I can massage your muscles. You should be able to sleep afterward."

"Okay." She didn't have the energy to swim anyway and led them into the bedroom.

Favian lifted the hem of her sweater.

Jasirey instinctively tightened her arms about her body and turned pink.

He smiled kindly. "We have seen you naked. Massage works better skin to skin. Trust us." He kissed her temple. "No stimulation, just relaxation."

"Let me do it." Jasirey sat on the bed and pulled off her sweater.

Both men removed their shirts so as not to distract their lady with the rougher texture of clothing. Chen crouched to remove her shoes and pulled off her slacks as she lifted her lower body. She lay on her stomach still wearing her bra and underwear.

Chen gently patted her rear end. "Try to relax, adored one." He parted her legs slightly and ran firm, broad strokes from the back of her thigh to her instep.

Favian applied equally broad strokes from her neck to her buttocks.

Jasirey breathed and felt slightly foolish for having difficulty letting go under their unfamiliar touch. They only acted for her benefit.

Chen worked on her other leg as Favian concentrated on her knotted lower back.

She was half asleep when they turned her onto her back.

Well-versed in reflexology, Chen manipulated pressure points in her feet and pulled her deeper toward the twilight.

When she slept, Favian and Chen settled down on either side of her. Asleep, she cuddled into Favian's shoulder as Chen spooned her back.

The men drifted off.

* * *

Anne chattered nonstop as she hustled her grandsons into the kitchen. They hadn't had a sleepover since she and Richard moved to South

Carolina five years before. Unfortunately, she thought of the teenagers as five years younger and planned craft and cooking projects that no longer interested the boys. She described her itinerary in delighted detail.

Michael mostly managed to restrain his eye rolls. Christopher shrugged philosophically. Grandma was Grandma. They could put up with it for one day. Besides, one of the projects included his favorite peanut butter chocolate chip cookies.

Ian felt superfluous with Anne's plans, made his getaway, and headed for the hotel in high spirits. *Why not up the date schedule?*

Ian bought his wife a lovely bouquet of mostly purple flowers from the hotel gift shop. He strode through the hotel sitting room, wondered where security was, and tiptoed into the bedroom.

Favian woke, which woke Chen. Favian saw Ian and placed a finger to his lips.

Stance rigid, Ian stared. Jasirey curled between the men, her leg under the sheet draped over Favian's, her head on his shoulder. Chen's arm curled up over her hip, and his long fingers rested under her breast.

Jasirey groggily opened her eyes and struggled up, hampered by Favian and Chen's arms tightening about her as Ian's cold stare triggered their protective instinct.

"Ian," Jasirey said. "Is something wrong?"

Ian carefully set the flowers down on a table by the door. He hadn't approached the bed. "I thought to start our date early, but I see you're occupied."

He turned and softly closed the door on his way out.

"Ian." Jasirey pushed at her Protectors' arms.

"Let us speak to him," Favian said. He jumped out of the bed and retrieved his shirt.

"Hand me my sweater, please." She shivered from the jagged ball of ice rapidly forming in her gut. The hastily pulled on sweater covered the essentials. "Stay here."

Chen stepped in front of his lady.

"He's my husband." The men flinched and bowed their acquiescence. She swiftly hugged them for—she didn't know what exactly—and rushed after Ian.

He gazed out the large windows of the sitting room.

Jasirey approached and tongue-tied, stood quietly, not sure whether to defend her innocence or berate Ian for failing in his promise to support her choices and decisions. Her conflicted feelings made it hard to read his, and she wondered if he felt as confused as she did.

Ian sighed and placed his arm about her tense shoulders. "I'm sorry, baby. Seeing the three of you just caught me by surprise."

"I didn't expect you back so early." Excuse or apology—she hated the idea of either, hated the guilt eking into her voice.

"Yes, rather the point, isn't it?"

She had no idea how to respond to that.

"Shannon would've been waiting here just for me."

What? Way too late—way too late. Just who the hell had taken them to the island of the Devoted in the first place? Outrage muted Jasirey's speech, and quick on its heels, a sharp, rending pain. She drew an audible breath. *Ian*, her heart cried.

He let his arm drop and turned from the window as Liu entered and halted as his eyes swept from Ian's closed face to Jasirey's ravaged eyes. He quickly set down his packages. "What is wrong?"

Favian and Chen walked out of the master bedroom, and Liu thought he got the gist of events. He sent a warning glance at the men and led Jasirey to the sofa.

She clung to him.

"It will be all right, darling. Shh." He rocked her while stroking her hair.

The Protectors glowered at Ian and then, concern etched on their faces, sat on the floor by Liu and Jasirey. Leaving a foot of space between them, Ian joined Jasirey on the couch.

"Ian." Liu willed him to make it right with their wife. *Did he not see what his foolishness was doing to her? How could he still not have dealt with his self-preoccupation?*

Ian's cell rang. "I'm sorry, it's—I have to take this." He returned to the window.

It gave Jasirey time to calm her heart rate. She eyed him warily as he turned, his expression blank.

"Sheng Qian, the Chinese CEO I was negotiating with online when we went to New York City, is in town on other business."

“No. He’s here to see you,” Jasirey said.

Ian stopped himself from gaping at her. “Okay. Well, I’ve arranged a meeting with him in the restaurant lounge where we have reservations. Might I ask you to meet me there for dinner?”

She struggled to speak past the lump threatening to strangle her. “Would you rather cancel?”

“No, of course not. I’m sorry. I do have to go. I’ll meet you there?”

She nodded, and Ian strode to the bedroom to change.

Liu kissed Jasirey’s cold cheek and gestured to Chen to replace him. Liu carefully closed the bedroom door and faced Ian.

“Not now, Liu. I really must go. I’ll have time to think in the car. Just give me time.”

“You have had nearly two years. Do not do this.”

“We’ll discuss it later.” Ian grabbed a garment bag and his briefcase and yanked the door open.

Jasirey stood alone by the windows.

Ian breathed deeply, went to her, and kissed the top of her head. “I’ll see you later. We’ll talk.”

Her eyes closed.

Sheng Qian

Deep in conversation with Sheng Qian, Ian realized he no longer had the man's attention. With graying temples and several years older than Ian, Sheng Qian stared at the staircase. As did many others, Ian noted and let his gaze follow. His mouth went dry.

She stood at the top of the stairs leading down to the lounge. Jasirey—a gamine with hair sparkling in chandelier light, wisps fluttering enchantingly about a small face with stunning eyes the color of a blue spruce, and a lusciously full mouth that invited nibbles and . . .

Ian collected himself. "Excuse me." He rose and wound his way through the throng of tables. Every patron felt the intense current between the arresting lady and the black-clad man as he advanced on her with predatory grace.

Jasirey watched her eagle swoop in and accepted the offered hand that engulfed hers as he guided her back through the diners to his table.

Fascinated by his associate's warring expressions, Sheng Qian stood. The usually unflappable Ian exhibited pride, a surprisingly needful lust, and something darker, perhaps painful. The woman maintained a pleasant expression that gave absolutely nothing away. Sheng Qian itched to dig beneath both facades.

Ian released Jasirey's hand. "Shannon, this is a business colleague of mine. Sheng Qian, my wife, Shannon."

The woman glowed in the flattering candlelight. Her breasts peeked enticingly above the modest neckline of a black cocktail dress with sweeps of bold purple, emerald, and sapphire in the skirt.

"A pleasure." Sheng Qian bowed slightly over her proffered hand, crooked his thumb about hers so his fingertips splayed gently over her inner wrist, and lifted her small hand to his lips while peering steadily into her eyes. They widened at the unexpected touch. He let a bit of heat enter his own as he trailed his fingers past her palm and broke contact.

She answered his blatant proposition with a playful smile meant to divert him as she sat in the chair Ian yanked out for her.

The waiter arrived to take Jasirey's drink order. His eyes constantly strayed to her bountiful cleavage until she smiled. He stared into sparkling eyes and needed her to repeat her order twice—iced tea.

People seldom acted other than Sheng Qian expected. Excitement built at the possibility that Ian's wife might embody the unexpected. "It would be my pleasure to have you both as my guests for dinner this evening," he said, eyes on the woman.

"That's very kind," she said, "but excuse us. We seldom have time for a date night."

Ian seemed disappointed by her polite refusal. Sheng Qian found it interesting that Ian appeared to have no wish to be alone with his wife. *Something he had done and must answer to her for or the other way around?*

Sheng Qian bid them a gracious good night and planned to begin a search on the couple when back in his room. First, however, he would watch their dynamics over dinner and perhaps find an opportunity to cut in on a dance.

In the dining room, Jasirey ordered broiled cod and vegetables. Her stomach hadn't yet settled down. She studied Ian as he placed his order. It hurt to see him so conflicted. She'd done nothing wrong but nevertheless felt compelled to ease his discomfort.

Fingers clasped near his chin, he leaned on the table. "You look stunning."

Tears pricked Jasirey's eyes, but her expression remained shuttered.

"I don't want to hurt you, Jasirey. I know the problem lies with me."

"And that doesn't help or change anything."

Ian briefly closed his eyes, gathered his courage, and set out to break his girl's heart. He spoke in a monotone. "I'd like some time to figure things out. Long before today, I've been toying with the idea of going to China for business. With Sheng Qian here, now is the perfect time to accompany him when he returns to Beijing."

The waiter interrupted Jasirey's response to serve their dinners. "For how long?"

"I'm not sure. At least a month, possibly as long as two. It's not pique. It's business, an important business matter."

Jasirey forced her chest to rise and fall, just rise and fall on each slow breath. "Seems it's settled. When?"

"Tomorrow on Sheng Qian's private jet."

Jasirey stilled, breath stopped. She rose slowly. She would not be ill. "We should go. You must have details to see to." She turned and headed for the exit, for air.

Sheng Qian moved in as she neared the dance floor. "Leaving so soon? Surely not without a dance." He curled his arm about her waist and gave her little choice other than to follow. He pulled her close and clasped her hand.

Jasirey wondered when the music had started. A crowded floor prevented much movement. Sheng Qian's hand sat uncomfortably warm on her bare back. He aimed slow breaths at her neck. He didn't stand as tall as Ian, and her gaze skimmed over his shoulder.

"Forgive my presumption, Shannon. You seem unhappy. Perhaps a lover's quarrel?" She swung her face around and met his eyes, a ferocious gleam edging over her polished politeness that almost caused Sheng Qian to release her.

"If so, that's something to discuss with my husband. I'm sure you can respect that."

His arm tightened about her. He could not remember when a woman had last reproached him. Irritation and lust flared in his black eyes. Her eyes darkened leaving him unable to decipher if from anger, fear, or attraction.

Jasirey knew here was a man to be wary of, yet he appealed to her on some primal level. Relieved when the dance ended, she saw Ian waiting on the periphery of the dance floor. Sheng Qian bowed as he handed Jasirey to her husband.

"I see you've made another conquest," Ian said.

Jasirey's eyes flew to Ian's face, but his eyes remained riveted on Sheng Qian.

"I've discussed it with my wife and decided to take you up on your offer."

A frisson of triumph ran through Sheng Qian. "And will you join your husband?" he asked Jasirey.

Ian answered. "She's unable to get away at this time."

"A shame. Negotiations will be a drawn-out process." Sheng Qian handed Jasirey a card. "My personal number, should you wish to change your mind. I would be happy to make arrangements for you."

For the first time in his experience, the driver witnessed discord between their most precious lady and Ian. They sat apart, not one word spoken. Jasirey got out without waiting as usual for Ian to come around and open the door.

Liu, Chen, and Favian waited in the suite living room. Severe disappointment etched their faces as they recognized that the pair hadn't worked through their difficulty.

The men jumped up when Jasirey dove for the hall bathroom. Liu followed her as Ian strode straight to the master bedroom and left Favian and Chen to fume at their impotence.

Liu came out intending to ask one of the Protectors to fetch a nightshirt for Jasirey. One look, and he deemed it best to do it himself. He headed to the bedroom, where Ian shoved clothes into a suitcase. "It's business, Liu. I'm going to China for a month or so. It's necessary."

"Necessary—to place our wife's well-being in jeopardy? Miss our children's first birthday?" Outrage overwhelmed his fear and sorrow.

Liu yanked open several drawers before finding one of Jasirey's nightshirts and returned to provide what damage control he could for their grief-stricken wife.

In the bathroom, Jasirey removed her dress, put on the nightshirt, and joined Ian in the bedroom.

He sat on the bed. His packed bag sat between them. "I assume you won't be returning for the babies' birthday," she said calmly. "I think it best, for the health of the babies I'm carrying now, that you go tonight. We'd appreciate a call to inform us of your safe arrival."

She walked out and left him gaping.

On the following evening, Liu posed as security, and more security people stood vigil outside the restaurant where Jasirey brought her parents and sons.

Christopher and Michael quickly picked up on their mother's chaotic emotional state.

Liu mouthed, "Later."

It impressed Anne to have a son-in-law called all the way to China for business. "Whatever the Chinese lack in scruples," she said, "no one can say they lack business sense."

Jasirey stoically bore a few minutes of her mother and father's harangue on inferior cultures and managed to get a few points in. "The Chinese invented printing and the porcelain china you like so much, Mom." She didn't add gun powder as, in her admittedly biased opinion, she considered it more curse than boon.

Anne suddenly honed in on her daughter. "What's wrong with you? You're acting like you did when you lost that stupid stuffed cat."

Jasirey had to smile at the memory. "A white cat with a pink ballerina tutu and slippers," she said to the boys. She kissed her mother's cheek. "Not lost, loved to death, and you cleaned it, refilled it with stuffing, and sewed all the ragged places." Her brow puckered. "I have no idea what happened to it after that."

"You outgrew it and left it behind, as you should."

Jasirey wished she could bury her face in her mother's shoulder.

❦ ❦ ❦

On the plane the next morning, Jasirey gave in to her poorly coping body and slept most of the trip back to the compound. The men moved to the tail end to talk. The boys refused to be left out, and the men didn't argue. Everyone was reeling from recent events, but they knew they must deal with the consequences to Jasirey and the family. They began in prayer—heartfelt pleas for guidance and Jasirey's well-being.

"I do not understand," Favian said. "Ian vowed to protect and cherish Jasirey."

"He did not train as a Protector," Liu said. "His destiny lay in heading his corporation, which has become an important outlet for Devoted businesses and interests. He struggled at the notion of Jasirey consorting with men not her husbands, though I believed he had come to terms with her destiny."

Favian scoffed. "I still don't see how he can love her and hurt her so."

Christopher and Michael exchanged glances. Michael nodded at his older brother, and Christopher said, "Did you guys ever notice that Ian says 'my girl' or 'my love'? We didn't think much about it until we kept hearing the Protectors say that they belonged to Mom."

"Maybe he believes Mom belongs to him," Michael added, "or should anyway. But she doesn't, does she. It can't work that way—her destiny, I mean."

Chen bowed to the teenagers. "You're growing up into thoughtful, insightful men. I am proud to serve you."

Jasirey heard her sons. For the moment, gratitude for their growth and the men who influenced it overlaid her panic over the one man who had most influenced hers.

⁂

Lee and Fael met the party at the airport in their western Massachusetts hometown. Jasirey held their hands on the drive to the compound and, once there, headed for the playroom.

Holding on to furniture or people, Jaimie toddled. Colin had taken his first steps. Sunny and Safia scooted on hands and knees or padded bottoms—much quicker than the precarious upright position.

Dharum and Everett wheeled in two snack carts.

Everett's heart ached for Jasirey and burned at Ian for what he perceived as the injustice he did her. As he said to Lee, Liu, and Fael, "Did he not make the decision to bring her to the island? Second thoughts are pointless at this late date. The man certainly never lacks for attention, affection, or downright adoration from Jasirey. High time he came to terms with her prophecy."

Heightened emotions swirling in the room made Jasirey's head throb. She welcomed it as distraction from the hole in her heart and vaguely wondered if one could survive with that organ pierced. Ian—her first love, her safe place—had left her adrift and unfocused. Aware the rest of her men offered a safe harbor, she nevertheless felt numb and incapable of reaching out.

Liu, Fael, and Lee had learned the bitter lesson the previous year of leaving their wife unmoored and planned a strategy. As they could not be disassociated in Jasirey's mind from Ian, the husbands asked her Protectors to intercede and break through the wall she had erected to insulate herself from pain.

The younger men undertook the solemn responsibility with no little trepidation. The possibility of failure and Jasirey's temper equally daunted them. They decided to confront her in the pool room and left it to the husbands to get her there.

The following afternoon, the husbands advised their wife to use the pool to help ease the depression weighing on her. Favian, Chen, Sajan, Andwar, and Yusef joined Jasirey as she swam laps with a single-minded fervor the men at first admired. After half an hour, they became concerned. She displayed no inclination to slow down, let alone stop.

Yusef grabbed hold and manhandled her to the side of the pool. She gulped air too frantically to protest vocally, so she fought him instead. Training had made it harder to subdue her. None of the Protectors realized that, had she not been intent on beating someone—anyone—to a pulp, her mental prowess would have gotten her past them and out of the pool in seconds.

Jasirey's dam of sorrow and pain cracked with a cry that reverberated from wall to wall and ended in broken sobs.

As she quieted, the men recognized the essential need to connect emotionally before she resurrected her wall against them.

Yusef sat on the pool stairs and pulled Jasirey onto his lap. "I love you," he said and cradled her face to kiss her with tender devotion.

Chen gently set his adored one on a towel folded over the pool edge. Holding her gaze, he said, "You are love, goodness, wisdom. You are life to me."

Sajan nodded as he clasped her hand. "You have provided me with the life of my dreams, sweet lady. I shall be ever grateful."

Favian said not a word. Jasirey felt his words of love in her head as, a gift, he fully opened his complex mind to her.

Andwar asked, "All right, my heart?" Perhaps more than anything else, his need for reassurance did the trick.

She smiled, a pale version of the smile beloved by all of them, but a start.

Chen applied his expert fingers to her feet, found the correct reflex point, and soon put their overwhelmed lady to sleep.

Bundling her in a robe, they transported Jasirey to her bedroom. She looked tiny on the huge bed. They removed the damp robe and bathing suit, then covered her. Yusef reported her condition to Liu.

The three husbands let their wife sleep past dinner and then, unsure what her mood might be, caressed her awake. Lee gathered her into his arms.

Jasirey clung to him and began to build a container around the weeping hole lodged deeply within. "My men, my loves, what are we going to do?"

Liu kissed her forehead. "My darling, precious one, Ian will come to his senses. He has no choice. How long can he be separated from his heart?"

"We informed Master Kai," Fael said. "He plans to be here for the babies' birthday."

Jasirey unconsciously released more of her tension. Master Kai gave her such comfort. She worried about him, however. "You never really notice his age, he's so vital, but I wouldn't want him to take on more than his health can handle."

Liu doubted Jasirey realized just how old Master Kai truly was. "He is a venerated leader. No one asks more of him than seems safe. We cannot nor do we wish to control him." Liu's eyes sparkled. "We trust his wisdom. He is not quite as stubborn as our most precious lady."

The hearts of the three men lightened when she flicked her tongue out at them.

* * *

Colin, Jaimie, Safia, and Sunny enjoyed a huge birthday bash, though not in the traditional sense. The family banned presents. The babies already had more than they could use. Rather than clowns or magicians, the people juggled, performed acrobatics, and sang soft lullabies when the over-stimulated toddlers fussed and then conked out.

Master Kai, Mtombe, Jesse, Lill, Charlotte, and Lizzie joined the throng of people, all uncomfortably aware of the missing family member and frustrated at their lack of power to alleviate the inexpressible pain in Jasirey's eyes.

Lee's parents, Paul and Alva, and sister Beryl's family had come for the week, all in awe of the magnificent house and grounds within the compound and solidly in love with their rambunctious grandchildren, nieces, and nephews.

Jasirey strove to be hospitable, and running interference, Lee attributed her absences to pregnancy when, overwhelmed at several junctures, she fled to her craft room.

Mtombe had no tolerance for what he considered Ian's betrayal. *The man had been aware of the prophecy from the beginning.* Apparently, vague prophecies were easier to stomach than reality, though Ian had shown no objection to Mtombe's relationship with Jasirey. Partly at the request of Lee, Liu, and Fael, he planned an extended visit to support her through the storm.

Lizzie privately sided with Ian. A staunch proponent of true love and the sanctity of marriage, for her that meant two people—period. She couldn't imagine why Ian hadn't put a stop at the beginning to four husbands. And yet, Lizzie couldn't imagine Colin, Jaimie, Safia, or Sunny not having been born. That she saw no solution to the mess frightened her.

Michael and Christopher wanted to despise Ian for their mother's acute suffering, but talking together discovered they mostly felt sorry for him. He loved their mother and must be suffering, too. He'd let them know via a displeased Everett of his safe arrival in China several weeks before. Nothing since, though, not even a call for their brothers and sisters' birthday. That did piss them off.

Charlotte, Ian's administrative assistant, brought stuffed jungle animals chosen by Ian for the babies. While she doubted that Jasirey would take petty revenge on the messenger, she found herself profoundly relieved when Jasirey hugged her warmly in greeting.

Jasirey took Charlotte's hands. "You must keep in touch with Ian for work. How is he?"

Charlotte's head wagged. "His behavior doesn't make sense. I'd never have believed he'd do this. His personality, his life—everything opened up when he met you. I'm afraid he's hurting himself more than anyone else."

Jasirey rubbed a hand over her heart. "Is he?"

* * *

Jasirey spent the next day in bed fighting nausea and headaches that continued to pop up regardless of Liu's acupuncture. Jesse, Lill, and Lizzie had returned home.

The fathers brought the babies to play with their dads and mom on the master bedroom's big bed before lunch. The babies insisted on crawling over Jasirey to rest their heads on her chest and pat at her as she caressed them. Usually rambunctious, they sensed their mother's needs.

The fathers marveled at their little ones.

The three fathers brought the babies to the dining room for lunch with Lee's family while Mtombe took his with Jasirey.

Grateful he stayed for her and unable to face his departure, she didn't ask the intended length of his visit. Lunch settled like a rock, and Mtombe lay beside her rubbing her back. That relaxation served as the key to keeping the essential nutrients down.

For good measure, Mtombe added some gentle nuzzling to the back of her neck. Surprised to suddenly find a shapely ass snugged at his crotch, he reflexively grasped her hip and ground his rapidly awakening sex into her soft cheeks.

"Loveling, do you truly wish this?" He chewed delicately on her ear.

"Do you, my Mtombe? Do you truly understand the emotional consequences of our becoming lovers? Wanting to be with each other, in body and mind, will stop being a choice and become a persistent need."

He pulled Jasirey beneath him and crushed his mouth down on hers, his tongue demanding entrance, plunging and stroking.

Mtombe thanked all the deities that Jasirey met his ardor equally, twirling her tongue about his, sucking and nibbling. He cupped the side of her head and called on all his reserves to lean back and grit out a strangled word—"Loveling"—the only warning he could give her.

She refused to stop. He could not. Their clothing fell wherever.

He took one second to look into her fevered eyes, pulled her hips into his, pushed her legs widely apart, and dove into her scorching heat.

Jasirey detonated around him. Her tight, pulsing muscles set off his own explosion. Sometime later, he considered regretting their hasty coupling, but since Jasirey already slept, Mtombe—as he always would—followed his beloved.

❦ ❦ ❦

Kai joined Jasirey in the playroom before the babies' afternoon nap. He'd been there several days and ate with the people.

She'd seen little of him and had begun to worry he deliberately avoided her. Satoko and Mashita discreetly left them alone. For adults, a sofa sat against one wall. Low climbing toys, blocks, toy musical instruments, and four rocking horses made by the people filled most of the room.

Jasirey sat on the floor before the horses.

Master Kai dropped a pillow beside her and agilely sank down. "Your aspect appears lighter today," he said. "I assume your relationship with your Protectors fares more smoothly."

Jasirey zeroed in on his fathomless eyes. Defiance shimmered in hers. Done feeling guilty over her growing feelings for her Protectors, she refused to be embarrassed or apologetic.

"Excellent," Master Kai said cheerfully, his tone at odds with the humorless gaze teeming with power he pinned on her.

A visceral shock wave rolled through Jasirey. Confusion and hurt clouded her mind. Did he intend to cow her?

Unrelenting black eyes scorched her battered psyche.

Panic swamped her—fight or flight. Jasirey gathered the little left of her reserves and forced her jittering nerves into submission. Her eyes cleared and stared back impassively.

Not the result Master Kai sought. His eyes kindled, pushed harder.

The babies quieted and with interest watched the adults.

Jasirey didn't understand why the man goaded her. She fought the incredibly strong urge to yield to the mentor she adored. Her eyes filled with sheer, focused will. No one had the right to intimidate her. Not even Master Kai.

Master Kai reared back. His lips parted as the force of her determination slammed into him. He rejoiced. Their lady had fully assumed the mantle of Jasirey. His eyes warmed with love and pride. He opened his arms. "Dearest one."

Still confused, Jasirey hesitated but surrendered to the glow of love in his eyes and relaxed in body and spirit as he held her securely.

Master Kai chuckled as the babies interrupted, clamoring for their share of attention. He gently set his dearest love back to attend to her children.

Safia reached for him, which pleased him tremendously.

He turned out to be a great hand at putting little ones to bed. After cozily settling them in the nursery, he linked fingers with Jasirey and drew her back to the playroom and the sofa. With her emotions still raw, she warily met his eyes.

"Do you not yet perceive the purpose of my demonstration?" Master Kai asked as her brow furrowed. "I am considered a powerful person. You are far superior. No one can stand for long against your will. You have trained in techniques for harvesting and channeling that energy toward whatever course your wisdom directs you. As well as for the babies' birthday, I have come to ensure that you recognize and accept the full extent of your power."

Master Kai gathered her hands. "Every activity of the Devoted—missions, businesses, relief organizations—revolves around you. Dearest one, you are the center, the whole, and our light to the world. We have a mission we require you to handle."

Jasirey almost laughed. "What can I possibly do on a mission our teams can't?"

"Sheng Qian has been a person of interest to us for over a decade. He is positioned to effect change in his country. To date, in the few contacts made, he seems a man of no social conscience. His appetite for profit, power, female conquests, and anything that represents those things, such as opulent living, are renowned worldwide. Officially, the state considers his morals questionable. Unofficially, he is an important cog in the wheel of national prosperity, his excesses tolerated."

"I read that the state is cracking down on such people."

"True, but primarily those who have opposed the state's governance. Sheng Qian has thus far strategically weathered policy changes. He mouths Confucian beliefs of duty and responsibility to family and country but believes himself above any manmade restrictions, thus entitled to whatever his brains and guile can procure, himself invulnerable and answerable to no person or higher power. This makes him ruthlessly dangerous.

"Ian's corporation is a coveted conduit to furthering his already numerous holdings in your country. Should Ian prove unreceptive to his overtures, he may perceive you as an easier target. Sheng Qian has little respect nor use for women other than as vessels to satisfy his sexual appetites and as political or business pawns.

"He has a solid education, including a strong bent toward psychology. He will recognize Ian's deep feelings for you despite your difficulties at present and find it quite amusing to enlist your sympathies to incline your husband toward his agenda."

Pain sliced at Jasirey's heart. "This Sheng Qian doesn't sound like a man who might assume anything. He has no assurance of even meeting me again. Does he know about Jasirey?"

"It is not impossible. He would not place much credence in our belief that you are the vessel—or conduit, if you will—for achieving balance in the world, but he might find Jasirey an interesting mystery to unravel or preferably, disprove. He would take delight in doing so.

"This mission is not about Ian," Master Kai continued, "however much his negotiations with China work to our advantage. He has been there nearly a month with little forward momentum, so orders were sent for Ian to return to America. Ian lacks resources in China to deal with a man of Sheng Qian's connections. He knows your gifts counterbalance his lack and is willing to wait to return to China when you can begin the mission.

"We ask that you take the time while pregnant to learn the intricacies of Sheng Qian's world, perhaps a bit of the language. Then, after the quintuplets' birth, Ian shall return to China. Then you shall follow him, ostensibly to rein in an errant husband while in truth pitting your will against a most dangerous foe."

Jasirey recognized that pregnancy, birth, recovery, and weaning—with training and tutoring piled on top and the black hole in her heart continually siphoning her energy—would push her to her limits.

"I've been studying Mandarin," she said, "since we decided to teach the babies the languages of their fathers. I'm becoming proficient at forming written symbols for the language, and I'm not too bad at reading it. The spoken language presents difficulties, since one word can have four different meanings depending on the inflection you give it."

Jasirey said nothing at Master Kai's obvious surprise. "I've also read about cultural differences in how one is expected to treat others socially and conduct business," she told him.

⁂

Discussing strategies, Sheng Qian, and Chinese cultural norms—or perhaps simply being with Jasirey—lulled Master Kai. He knew instantly when his guard slipped, and a chill seeped deep down to his bones. He rose and shakily headed for the hallway door but collapsed onto a floor cushion. He thought he sat upright as Jasirey slowly advanced on him. A dark violet aura, danger shimmered about her.

Master Kai summoned his mental defenses.

She batted them aside with no more effort than batting at dust motes.

"The Imperiat's plan—you orchestrated it, ordered Ian to act out leaving me. The separation—like my clashes with Marcus, the deaths of Robin, Mirai, and Nikolai—served as means to trigger a growth spurt in my abilities, in my control. But you had a personal agenda as well, yes?"

"Dearest one—"

Relentless, Jasirey spoke over him. "I have Lee, Liu, and Fael to turn to, but my first truly safe place—Ian—would cause a hole large enough to need more, to need you for solace." Her lips lifted in a smile full of gleaming teeth. "Yes, your blocks slipped, but what you said before that started my suspicions. You ordered Ian home to the States, not to the compound. Just how long did you intend for him to keep up his ruse?"

A raptor assessing its prey, she cocked her head. "Tell me. Did you anticipate the pain—such a tepid word—Ian's absence would inflict? Would you like to?"

Master Kai held up a trembling hand. Whether to ward her off or beseech for mercy, Jasirey didn't care, and that lack of caring allowed her nonproductive, energy-sapping fury to drain away.

"I assume you figured out that your plan backfired," she said. "Ian's conflicted feelings, there from day one, have congealed. When he returns, he plans to stay in Boston. You aren't needed here. Return to the island."

Master Kai's entire essence shriveled along with his remaining strength.

Jasirey touched his hand briefly, impersonally.

Warmth and strength—neither kind nor gentle, simply practical—infused his body. He had no concept of how long he sat there.

Lee, Liu, and Fael found him and helped him up. He straightened his spine and followed the men to the breakfast nook in the master bedroom.

Liu placed a mug of tea in front of the old master. "I should like to examine you."

"No need. Jasirey saw to my welfare."

"She has asked us to escort you to the airport," Fael said. "May I ask what happened?"

Master Kai managed a semblance of a smile. "A rift of my own making." He switched the topic to the mission the Imperiat wished Jasirey to undertake in China.

Liu fought to relax his rigid body and looked to Fael. "Surely we could not have the legalities in place before Jasirey's pregnancy makes it dangerous for her to travel."

Master Kai interrupted. "The mission shall not start until after the birth of the quintuplets. Through intensive meditation and vision quests, the Imperiat determined that Jasirey alone has the capability to meet Sheng Qian as an equal and neutralize the threat he poses to the world. We cannot, however, ascertain the length of the mission, though we suspect events shall begin in China and end in the United States. In the coming months, prepare her as you would with your team for a mortally dangerous mission. Jasirey's destiny is at hand."

Silently, Master Kai prayed for all the powers that be to save her and the world from the disaster his selfishness may have just loosed upon them.

Acknowledgments

Thank you

—to Phillis Scott, copy editor and editorial consultant, for her continuing support and expertise

—to Elizabeth Lindgren, cover artist, for her creativity and artistic sense of what fits

—to Marcia Gagliardi, my publisher and editor—and more, friend—who keeps me on track and makes sure the book makes sense

Bonnie Arnot

About the Author

Bonnie Arnot loves stories about female heroes conquering new worlds as well as narratives about historical places and people who can seem just as fantastical to the modern world. She lives in western Massachusetts with her husband, two sons, and two cats.

Colophon

Text for *Strength of Jasirey* is set in Baskerville, a serif typeface designed in 1757 by John Baskerville in Birmingham, England, and cut into metal by punchcutter John Handy. Baskerville is a transitional typeface intended as a refinement of old-style typefaces of the period, especially those of his most eminent contemporary, William Caslon.

Compared to earlier designs popular in Britain, Baskerville increased contrast between thick and thin strokes, making serifs sharper and more tapered. He also shifted the axis of rounded letters to a more vertical position. Curved strokes are more circular in shape and the characters more regular, creating a greater consistency in size and form influenced by the calligraphy Baskerville had learned and taught as a young man.

Baskerville's typefaces remain popular in book design.

Titles for *Strength of Jasirey* are set in Brioso Pro, a new typeface family designed in the calligraphic tradition of the Latin alphabet. Brioso displays the look of a finely penned roman and italic script, retaining the immediacy of hand lettering while having the scope and functionality of a contemporary composition family. Brioso blends the humanity of written forms with the clarity of digital design, allowing designers to set pages of refined elegance. Designed by Robert Slimbach, this energetic type family is modeled on his formal roman and italic script. In the modern calligrapher's repertoire of lettering styles, roman script is the hand that most closely mirrors the oldstyle types that we commonly use today; it is also among the most challenging styles to master. Named after the Italian word for lively, Brioso moves rhythmically across the page with an energy that is tempered by an ordered structure and lucidity of form.

www.ingramcontent.com/pod-product-compliance
Lightning Source LLC
LaVergne TN
LVHW052345100826
845147LV00012B/755

* 9 7 8 1 9 5 6 0 5 5 4 5 0 *